THE PROMISES SHE KEEPS

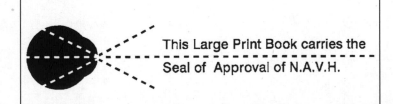

This Large Print Book carries the
Seal of Approval of N.A.V.H.

THE PROMISES SHE KEEPS

ERIN HEALY

THORNDIKE PRESS

A part of Gale, Cengage Learning

GALE
CENGAGE Learning·

Detroit • New York • San Francisco • New Haven, Conn • Waterville, Maine • London

© 2010 by Erin Healy.
Unless otherwise noted, Scripture quotations are taken from the King James Version of the Holy Bible: New International Version®, NIV®. Copyright © 1973, 1978, 1984 by Biblica, Inc.™ Used by permission of Zondervan. All rights reserved worldwide.
Thorndike Press, a part of Gale, Cengage Learning.

LIBRARY OF CONGRESS CATALOGING-IN-PUBLICATION DATA

Healy, Erin M.
  The promises she keeps / by Erin Healy.
    p. cm. — (Thorndike Press large print Christian fiction)
  ISBN-13: 978-1-4104-3816-4 (hardcover)
  ISBN-10: 1-4104-3816-3 (hardcover)
  1. Women singers—Fiction. 2. Terminally ill—Fiction. 3. Mysticism—Fiction. 4. Large type books. I. Title.
PS3608.E245P76 2011b
813'.6—dc22
                                        2011014794

Published in 2011 by arrangement with Thomas Nelson, Inc.

Printed in Mexico
1 2 3 4 5 6 7 15 14 13 12 11

For my parents
the artist and the framer.
All your works are beautiful.

1

In the silence of night, sounds of life have a greater chance of being heard.

One of these sounds woke Chase Ellis from deep sleep at a heavy predawn hour. His rousing was sudden and full, so that without any bleary transition he found himself aware of his own thoughts. He lay on his back under a rhythmic ceiling fan. The blades made their circuit and caused the fan's light chain to tink against a glass globe. This familiar noise usually rocked his mind into rest. Something else had disrupted him.

The shadows of his father's room possessed all their usual shapes, though Chase evaluated them as being darker than usual by twelve to fifteen percent. The saturated dimness was due to the time, a full three hours before his intuitive rising with the sun. He needed no clock to know this.

A vivid scene unfolded in Chase's mind:

On the other side of the world, where his father had slept and awakened for the past ten years, the sun blazed over a desert afternoon. There were no trees in that dry land, only people, who moved slowly like Tolkien's Ents. The hot light shone on his father, whom Chase envisioned as one of the world's most enduring trees. *Pinus longaeva* had been dated to thousands of years, and in some cases a tree stayed firmly upright long after its death.

Chelsea said their father was certainly dead by now, but in Chase's thoughts the man was green and bursting with seedy cones, and so Chase could not agree with her.

He heard the noise again. He lifted the corner of the blanket and peeled it off his body, then did the same with the sheet. He sat up, then pivoted so his feet swung together over the edge of the bed. The stiff fibers of the carpet brushed his toes.

By the timing of the overhead chain, which hit the globe precisely on each second, Chase counted one minute and seven seconds of waiting before the sound came a third time: the rattling of sticks in a tin can. It came from the room across the hall, which had been Chase's as a child before his father was deployed, before Chase's drawings took over that space and Chase took over his father's room.

Chase walked through shadows without turning on the light, because he did not need it and was not afraid. He knew the width of every passage and the protrusion of every sharp corner, the location of every shoe and book on the floor. He walked out of the room and through the hall, past the closed door of the bathroom. The rattling ceased.

His entrance into his old bedroom moved just enough air to lift the edge of a drawing tacked to the wall. The movement created a mild papery rustling among his other sketches — like leaves in a spring breeze — before sighing back to rest. This was his welcome.

Chase crossed the room and turned on the desk lamp, which leaned over a spiral-bound book of black drawing paper. The light bounced off his white T-shirt. The red fabric of his basketball shorts turned shiny and felt weightless against his skin. He did not play basketball, but he liked the texture of the pants. The brilliant bulb transformed the uncovered window behind the desk into a sheet of black glass, as black as the paper Chase used for his drawings.

On either side of the wide obsidian,

built-in shelving reached all the way up to the ceiling and all the way out to the adjoining walls, and each shelf was lined with cans and tin cases. These contained stumps and brushes and sticks and tools and pencils. White pencils. White was the only color Chase used.

But not only pencils. The cans and tins were filled with many white substances suitable for drawing: water-soluble ink pencils, oil paint sticks, oil pastels, white-charcoal pencils and sticks, pastels and pastel pencils, colored pencils, woodless aqua pencils, Conté crayons in which graphite had been mixed with clay, white-tinted graphite pencils, and china markers. He had a tailor's marker, blackboard chalk, a few paperless white Crayolas, stage makeup, cornstarch and talc (which could be liquefied and applied with the nub of a quill pen), and also bars of soap.

Chase listened to the shelves. He owned 210 containers, 105 on each side of the window, fifteen items on each of the seven tiers. He knew the contents of each. He waited for the one that had awakened him.

On the right side of the window, third shelf from the top, the sixth canister from the left began to hum. The former Progresso soup can, stripped of its blue label, contained a broken stick of quarter-inch General's white charcoal, one General's pencil, two Derwent Graphitint pencils, and a rubber blending stump. The hum increased to a rattling in earnest, a vibration that shifted the can toward the brink. Chase watched it fall.

The contents scattered across the carpet at his feet, and the broken stick of charcoal chipped on the lip of the can. The utensils begged for him to draw. Chase bent to collect each item and returned everything to the can.

As he stooped, a rustling of paper called out to him. Holding the can, he straightened, then pivoted to scan each wall in the room. He thought the sound came from there, from one of the hundreds of drawings tacked up in overlapping rows.

These were pictures he had made of trees. White, ghostly trees on dark sheets. For starters, Chase had drawn every species known to the Pacific Northwest: the cascara buckthorn, with its wavy-edged leaves and pronounced veins; the Pacific dogwood, covered like snow in the white bracts that framed its tiny flowers; the towering black cottonwood, its seeds hanging from strings like pearls on a woman's necklace; quaking aspen, the heart-shaped leaves fluttering.

11

When he'd exhausted the region he'd moved on to other species of the country, the continent, the world.

None of his art appeared out of order. He rotated until his toes pointed once again at the desk. Chase lowered the soup can to place it on the surface, but stopped. The black drawing pad that had been closed now lay open, a fresh slate.

This was highly unusual. Still holding the can, he pulled out his chair and sat. The Mi-Teintes pastel book was bound with wire at the top and contained sixteen sheets of 9 × 12 black textured paper. Each of these was separated by a translucent sheet of glassine. Chase stared at the exposed page. He heard the rhythm of the fan chain in the other bedroom.

At the top of the page a letter appeared, an *A,* as in the beginning of the alphabet, as in *A is for alder* or *acacia* or *abele.* The letter did not appear all at once, but as a tilting line that rose to the right, then fell down to the right, then was crossed in the middle, written by an invisible hand with an invisible pen.

Not a pen. A soft white wax. A china marker. Chase lifted his eyes to his shelves, seeking a flat Hershey's collector's tin with a hinged lid on the left side of the window.

Bottom level, third from the left. He retrieved it and flipped open the top with one thumb. All nine of his markers were inside, in Sharpie, Dixon, Berol, and Sanford brands. What instrument was making these marks, and how?

On the paper, a new letter had appeared after the *A,* following a space. An *l,* lowercase, and then an *o.* Bold strokes, firm and authoritative. *N.* Chase sank back into his chair, candy tin in one hand and soup can in the other, mesmerized. *G.* The letters formed words and the words formed a phrase.

A longing fulfilled is

Familiarity came over Chase like sunshine, a comforting assurance that everything about to happen was good.

Chase set the containers next to the sketchbook, then lifted the page to see whether the words were being applied from the backside or through the desk. Nothing. On the front, the script continued to flow. He lowered the page and ran his fingers over the fresh words, which had taken on the texture of the paper. The silky wax and dry pulp were braille to Chase. His fingertips tingled.

A longing fulfilled is a tree of life.

At his bidding, an image from his mind

became lifelike in the room. It was helpful for him to put the contents of his head out in front of him. And so he was able to see the figure of a Great Basin bristlecone pine tree — far too large for the room, impossibly large, and bent by the confining ceiling — leaning over the page, writing with one of its branches.

Chase did not evaluate why he had envisioned *Pinus longaeva,* because the words on the page demanded his attention. They were an adage he knew well, a passage from the Bible's book of Proverbs in the thirteenth chapter.

He picked up the broken white charcoal stick and made several broad strokes along the margin of the page. The strokes formed a shape: a complex trunk, wide and twisted like flame, a branch. He set the charcoal in the soup can and wiped his fingers on his red shorts and reached for the Graphitint pencil, which would give him finer detail than the charcoal. With this he created a cluster of needles. Many, many spiny needles in tight brush formations.

Trees lived and breathed and should not be made motionless on paper, and this had always presented some challenge to Chase. He lifted the notebook and let the page dangle. He shook it firmly one time, causing the sheet to buckle. The branches moved. The needles stayed erect. Chase was very pleased. He returned the book to the desk, then held the pencil above the proverb.

The majestic tree of life he intended to finish drawing vanished from his mind.

A longing fulfilled is a tree of life. Draw the longing, for time is short. Fill the heart, for days are full.

All he could see were words, and then the meaning of the words disappeared and all he could see were strokes. He saw the movements of a man's hand gripping a grease pencil and forming each symbol, the sweeping and swooping of lines, the tight angles, the free-flowing tails.

This was his father's handwriting.

Chase felt happy to see it. He turned the page over and waited for the bristlecone to reappear, waited for his father to write more.

2

The bluffs above the ocean were the winds' playground. Brisk breezes dashed in all directions and teased the twisted cypress trees. Tarnished clouds advanced low over the Oregonian coastline, bringing rain to challenge the late-morning sun. Where storm and sunlight met, shades of blue and gray shimmered.

While she waited for the artist who'd hired her, Promise leaned out over the weather-worn split-rail barrier separating her from the sharp drop to a narrow strip of sandy beach some forty feet below. The wood complained, and she retreated.

If she were the suicidal type, this would be a poetic time and place for dying. But she wasn't. Her life was going to end prematurely, there was no doubt about that in the mind of anyone who knew anything about her, but it would end only against her will, and only at the height of her fame.

Which was on its way. Soon. Very, very soon. She pleaded with whatever unseen force governed the world that this would be true, because her days were winding down with every turn of the earth.

For two weeks Promise had ignored the familiar heaviness creeping into her lungs, the declining pulse-ox numbers, the less productive chest-therapy sessions, the fatigue that hit her earlier in the day than usual. She knew as well as she knew her name that she was sick and wouldn't be able to avoid the hospital many more days. This didn't bode well for her plans. Auditions for the fall musical production — which two agents had just this morning promised to attend — were next week. It would take every antibiotic and home remedy known to man to keep her on her feet until then.

There were at least a dozen advantages to dying young, enough that Promise generally ignored the fate that shadowed her like a pesky black puppy. Feeding the needy animal was a waste of resources and didn't do a thing to solve the problem that most frightened her: dying before anyone really knew who she was. It wasn't that Promise wanted fame, exactly, but that she didn't want to be forgotten. Fame was a practical means to that end.

She coughed several times to loosen up her lungs and then lightly slapped her thigh in a perky beat and hummed to ward off the anxiety that crept up on her.

The teasing atmosphere of the sky turned mean. Her long hair snapped at her eyes and caught at the corners of her mouth. She pulled her woolly wrap tighter across her chest and thought about leaving, asking Zack Eddy to reschedule. On the bright side, he would have to work quickly, and she wasn't being paid by the hour. But her health deserved a hasty retreat. She'd give him five minutes.

Which was precisely when he arrived. The sound of a car door slamming turned her head. Behind her, in the lot at the end of a meandering downhill path, Zack had parked his economical Honda next to her flashy BMW Roadster, the only other vehicle at the park. His dyed black hair, gelled flat to his head like a slick beanie, didn't budge under the huffing sky.

He bowed into the trunk of his car, retrieved a bag on a long strap, and slung it over his shoulder, then locked up and hoofed it to the trail. He wore skinny jeans tucked into socks, skateboard shoes, and layers of T-shirts. No jacket, like a local. Truly, it was more blustery than chilly, though a reversal probably wouldn't have mattered to him. Zack's trademark trench coat was missing, and she thought, smiling, that she'd only seen him wear it indoors.

She shouted at him and waved. Her toes lifted her heels off the ground in a sort-of jump. Real, take-to-the-air jumping was something she avoided for energy-conservation reasons.

Zack responded with a slight hike of his chin.

She modeled in Zack's life-drawing class at the university for spending money to call her own, even though her wealthy parents gave her everything she asked for and even more that she didn't. But independence wasn't something they could buy on her behalf. Her tiny paycheck gave her the mental strength she needed to keep up with her career plans, short-lived though they might be.

Zack was the last student there she had come to know, but not because she hadn't made the same attempts to befriend him that she'd made with nearly everyone else.

She pegged him early on as intelligent but morose, willfully depressed because the concept of tortured genius was perennially trendy. The trench coat he usually wore had a suspicious, illicit smell. She imagined he wrote dark poetry in the bleakest hours of the night, after finishing shadowy and sinister charcoal drawings.

His first words to her, which he spoke after three months of silence, were a question: *Will you pose for a painting I've got to finish?* Finding his question sweet and boyish rather than spooky, she'd made him promise not to draw her bodily form in the context of anything like a coffin or a Goth castle or a medieval torture chamber. He answered this request with the most beautiful, genuine, happy laugh, giving her hope that his black moodiness was only a front.

"Been here long?" he said when he crested the hill, not even breathless. The climb had taken her fifteen slow minutes.

"Awhile. You don't happen to keep your long coat in your car, do you?"

"No, why?" He kept moving toward the wood fence. Looked out, looked down. Test-kicked the post for no apparent reason. A light shower of powdery dirt rained off the rail.

"Thought I might borrow it."

"If I had it, you could. That's what I call a drop."

"The higher the bluff, the better the vertigo."

There was no laugh to reward her joke

this time. Zack withdrew an expensive-looking camera from his bag. He attached a lens that was probably capable of photographing Mars, then repeated the looking out, the looking down, this time through the digital display. Not what she had expected.

"This lighting is killer," he said.

"Where's your sketchbook?"

"With the trench coat." He directed the camera at her, took a step backward. "I liked what you were doing when I was coming up. Holding that shawl thing tight, chin back over your shoulder."

"Look, I'm sorry if I wasn't clear about this when we scheduled, Zack, but I don't do cameras."

Zack moved around her like an orbiting moon. "What do you mean, you don't do cameras? No, no. Keep your back to me."

Promise faced him in full. "No pictures."

"What?" The shutter clicked.

"Zack, I mean it."

His eyes rose above the massive lens. "Why? What did you think I'd be doing up here?"

"Drawing. Sketching."

"In this weather?"

"You called it," she said.

"I'm a painter."

"Painters make thumbnails. For reference."

"I take pictures for reference."

"I guess we both made some assumptions, then. Sorry about that."

Zack exhaled between thin lips and studied the morphing horizon. "What's your thing about pictures?"

"I can't control them."

"What?" He came closer and leaned in as if he was having trouble hearing. She smelled the alcohol in his hair gel.

"I can't control what you'll do with pictures of me."

"You don't have the same objection to those videos of you singing. I've seen them all over the web." An uncontrollable twitch at the corner of his mouth was almost a smile.

"That's not the same. I own the rights to those."

"Who cares about rights anymore?"

Promise didn't like to argue. It was her policy to make friends, not enemies. "Some people do. Did you see the one I posted last week?"

"Maybe."

"What did you maybe think of it?"

He took a picture of her. She crossed her arms but tried to keep a playful expression.

If he persisted with this and posted photos of her online, against her will, ugly ones would get the most attention. No point in helping that to happen.

"Do you think I have a chance?" she asked.

"I don't know anything about music."

She raised her eyebrows.

"I think you've got a nice voice. But your stuff is a bit perky for my tastes."

"Three different agents e-mailed about it."

He lowered the camera. "No kidding."

"And a record label. But a small one. I really want an agent."

"Is all that stuff you claim on your website true?"

"You mean did I write all the lyrics? Did I make the musical arrangements?"

"No. I mean, do you have cystic fibrosis? You cough a lot in class. Are you really going to die before you're, like, twenty-one?"

Promise was open about her disease — this broad disclosure was part of her strategy — and most people thought she was seven notes short of an octave to pick a career that was dependent on a healthy set of lungs. But they didn't have the guts to say so, as if her feelings might be as fragile as her health.

"Actually, I'm twenty-two already. The life expectancy of people with CF keeps going up, you know."

"I didn't."

"It's somewhere in the midthirties now."

"So do people feel sorry for you? Say you have a nice voice just to make you feel good?"

She'd wondered now and then. "Some. I guess."

"I'll bet the agents who wrote to you might like your story more than your voice. It'll sell albums, you know, especially when you die."

Promise blanched.

Zack shrugged, and his shutter clicked away. "But I don't have any reason to lie to you. You sing good enough."

"I hope you're not studying to be a doctor or minister or something, where it'd be your job to make people feel better."

He finally gave her the laugh she was looking for, though it had cost her more than she'd wanted to spend.

"No worries about that. Can we get to work now?" he asked, still smiling.

"What are we going to do about my photo issues?"

"Hate to break it to you, but you actually have less control over how people paint you

24

in class."

She shook her head. "A drawing is only an interpretation of me, and artists take more care to protect their intellectual property than they do a snapshot. It's not the same. Class paintings of me aren't going to show up all over the Internet or be sold on stock photo sites or to tabloids or wherever."

His thin eyebrows, dyed to match his hair, disagreed with her. "Are you calling my photography *snapshots?*"

"I've never seen your stuff. I wouldn't know what to call it. But why do you think Dawson doesn't allow cameras in class?"

"I've never met a model who —"

"I'm an artist's model, not the runway type."

"Still, it's strange."

"Strange looks good on celebrity," she said.

He sighed, maybe thinking, maybe annoyed. "It doesn't seem like a good plan for someone who isn't a celebrity yet."

"I've wasted your time," she said. "That's my fault. I know someone else who —"

"No. I wanted you. I mean . . ." He gestured to the waters. "I've got minutes to make this work, then the moment's gone. We're here. You're perfect, this is perfect.

25

Can't we work something out?"

"Like what?"

Zack's fingers fiddled with his camera's dials. He was clean-shaven, baby-face smooth but grown-man angular in the cheek and narrow jaw, every limb and feature long and slim. He'd be an interesting subject for drawing himself.

"Like what if I give you my memory card when we're done here? You make the prints for me, erase the card. No electronic files anywhere."

"You could scan the prints."

His expression was definitely annoyance this time. "I respect your . . . issues, I really do. But I'm in a bind here." He started shooting at the ocean-scape without her in the frame. "I've got less than two weeks to get this piece done. If it doesn't happen today, it's not going to happen at all. And I mean really, never. When I'm done with this, I'm done with painting. This is it. And like you, I'd like to go out with a really good work under my belt."

Promise wavered. She wasn't principled for the sake of making life difficult for others, and she thought he was trustworthy. Weird, in a brainy-artsy kind of way, but in the absence of contradictory proof, trustworthy.

"I won't scan your pictures," he said. "Okay? I don't know how to prove that to you. I can only give you my word. I promise not to scan your pictures." He smirked. "I promise, Promise."

She relented, stepping between his camera and the sky, her back to him as requested. His camera shutter was fast and rhythmic. She wondered how many prints she'd be developing for him.

"So what are you going for?" she asked, removing the wrap from her shoulders. She had to cough a few times.

"Leave that on," he instructed.

"This?" It was a favorite burnt-orange wool that she'd worn for comfort and warmth.

"It's a good color. Besides, the wind will blow right through you without it."

"Most people don't like orange."

"Earthy rust, stormy blue. Lucky me that you're strange. It's a study in contrasts."

"A fine cliché."

"Not for me. I prefer shades of black, see?" He pointed to his T-shirt-and-jeans ensemble.

"So if I hadn't worn orange, what would you be going for?" She struck a pose that matched the weather's glum mood.

"Not that." He frowned.

"The more you tell me the better I can do."

"Don't think about it as 'doing,' okay? Just be."

" 'Just be.' What does that mean?"

"Whatever it means when you pose in the classroom."

"There are no cameras there. I'm sorry, but honestly, you might have picked the wrong model."

"I didn't."

"Well, I guess that settles it then."

"Seriously, be yourself. Relax. It's you against the world out here. That's all I'm after. It's simple. You've got nothing to worry about."

"I should levy a surcharge on you for breaking my policy," she said. She returned to the position she'd been in while waiting for him to show up.

"How'd you get a name like Promise?" he asked.

"You talk a lot for an artist."

"You have a narrow stereotype of us."

"My name's a long story. How long is this going to take?"

"As long as the light lasts. Try turning around here. That's good. If we run out of time, maybe you can finish your story over coffee."

"Why don't we keep your information gathering to imagery for now?" Her words came out more curtly than she intended.

"Message received." Zack's voice was level, but he hid his face behind the camera, which might have meant something or might have meant nothing, and uncertainty only made Promise more stiff and un-natural. As a classroom model she was used to stillness, to holding poses for a half hour or more.

Still, the dancing air begged her to move with it, and when Zack didn't say more she responded with subtle shifts in her weight, in her posture, in the line of her neck. She hid her ugly fingers, misshapen at the tips by her disease, in the folds of her wrap. She ignored her hair entirely. She felt a drop of rain tap the bridge of her nose.

Bowing her head away from the sounds of the working camera, she turned her shoulder and felt her hip brush the split-rail fence post. A splinter snagged the wool shawl, and she paused to release it.

"I'm a little jealous that you're going to see these prints before I will," Zack said, continuing to shoot as if this mundane task of splinter-removal was worth recording.

When she finished, Promise leaned into the wooden support and lifted her face to the sky's spare drops.

"I like that. You're good."

Zack was a camera head on a human body. The sunlight was nearly swallowed by the clouds now.

"Why are you going to stop painting?" she asked.

"Asked you first."

"Asked me what?"

"How you got your name. Turn your chin this way."

"My father named me Promise, over Mom's objections. She wanted to call me Trinity, but Dad thought that was pretentious, maybe even sacrilegious." She propped her foot on the low rail of the fence and pushed herself up to sit on the top beam. She had worn her sheepskin boots today, as she did nearly every day, since Zack hadn't given her other instructions.

"Does this mean you're going to have coffee with me?"

"No."

"Can you go sideways and balance one foot on the top?"

Promise complied, and the rail groaned under her slim form. "Be quick."

"Look away." And seconds later, "Now back at me over your other shoulder."

"I'm a pretzel already, Zack."

30

"Trust me."

She nearly lost her balance. Of all the foolish positions to allow herself to be put in. After two or three camera clicks, she announced, "I'm coming down now."

"Got it."

The fence creaked when she dismounted. "Actually, the real reason my dad wanted to name me Promise was because I was born the day after he was deployed to the Gulf War."

"What can you do with that shawl?"

She opened it like wings, and the wind snapped it.

"Let the air have it," Zack said.

"Do I have a choice?"

"Try just one hand."

Exposed now in her lightweight turtleneck, Promise shivered. Her eyes followed the updraft of the wool that buckled like a flame.

"I don't think this is working," she said.

"Sometimes it seems that way, but you never know."

"My dad said I'd be Mom's Promise from him, no matter what happened."

"What if we try draping it over the post without you?" Zack suggested.

She saw there was little point in her telling the story so long as coffee wasn't involved, which disappointed her a little. On a professional job like this one, though, personal tales probably weren't appropriate. She was always messing that up, especially with peers. Her expectations of life and theirs rarely aligned, it seemed. She needed intimacy swiftly; they weren't conscious of time the way she was, though maybe everyone should be so aware. This was something she would definitely have to work out before —

The selfish wind yanked the wrap right out of her fingers.

"Oh, drat."

The fiery sheet hovered briefly before dropping to the scruffy ground, then escaped the toe of Zack's skateboard shoe when he tried to pin it down. It rolled once, evasive, then returned to the air on a puppet string and streaked for the water.

Promise kept her eye on the fringe and made three long strides, quick and agile, then lunged for it.

Her body went through the decaying wood rail as if it wasn't even there, as if it had chosen that precise moment to disintegrate into a pile of termite dust. She would have expected a splintering or clattering or some audible protest from the wood, but there were only Zack's distressed shouts and a fluttering of weighty fabric and the skidding of her body slipping over loose rocks as the ground released her to the air.

Not now, not now. This is not the right time.

And then the silence of the fall.

3

After devoting more than six decades of her life to mastering the magical arts, Porta Cerreto didn't need a spell or an incense or a ritual in order to have a vision. She liked being in control of things, though, so she preferred these methods to spontaneous revelations. Still, sometimes the spirits of truth sought her out first. When they did, she tried to take their attention as a compliment.

Today, however, they caught her flat-footed.

She was standing on the historic-downtown sidewalk of a charming city. This seaside district was known to locals as "the Shore," though the beach-front was techni-cally a few blocks away. She faced her new gallery, which she had quite cleverly named ART(i)FACTS. A potbellied contractor was installing the front door, a beautiful glass entry with beveled edges, an oak frame, and matching sidelights. Under the name frosted into the glass, a stylized chisel and mallet chipped away at the motto: UNEARTH YOUR TRUTH.

The morning storms had passed on, yielding to a stunning domed-sky day. Porta breathed deeply. The air approved of her plan to open in this town, at this time of year. Oxygen seasoned with ocean salt promised her efforts would be nourishing, appealing, and enduring. These were good omens, and she expressed her gratefulness with sighs of relief. At seventy-two she had little time for efforts that would not be profitable.

Beauty had long since failed to satisfy her. True enough: the people who entered her art gallery through that gorgeous glass door wouldn't exit in the same state, not if their spirits were receptive to their true callings. At one time, the prospect of enhancing others' lives had been noble enough. But now, as her own wheel of life came full circle, she wanted more.

Porta heard a delivery truck brake at the back of the gallery. More artwork for tomorrow's grand opening would be aboard, and she hoped for one piece in particular. The carpet had been laid, the furniture arranged, and now her designers were hanging canvases and frames on the walls.

She entered the neighboring "Irish" pub, an Americanized hangout that didn't come close to being authentic, and nodded to the old owner, who had kindly suggested she use his store as a pass-through while her front entry was blocked. He waved and placed a foamy beer in front of an early bird at the bar. The man had been in business here forty-two years, he'd said, and Porta believed the fisherman sweater he wore daily was certainly the same age.

At the rear of the pub, she emerged onto a wide alley and spotted her delivery. The driver dropped a clipboard onto the back of his open freight truck, then jumped in. He slipped a hand-operated pallet jack under a wooden shipping box, roughly four feet by three feet, then dragged the crate onto the truck's lift, which whined and whirred and lowered its load to the ground.

She looked at the labels on the crate and clapped her hands together once. "Ah, the one I've been waiting for."

"If you say so, ma'am."

She accepted the necessary shipping receipts but declined to sign them. Instead, she directed the man to the ramp at her small receiving dock. "Let's have a look first, shall we?"

Thirty years ago, at a more golden time in her life, she had commissioned a sculpture from a promising young Iranian artist living in Jordan. The object was carved from a solid piece of jade Porta had acquired from a Zoroastrian mobed. The priest had been fond of her, having traded the large stone for a small collection of sardonyx jewelry and a few more personal, sensual favors.

She had taken the priceless green rock to the Iranian and asked the young sculptor to find the beautiful woman within it. The figure that emerged would be her Ameretat, the Zoroastrians' divine feminine ideal of immortality. Ameretat was not a goddess, per se, though Porta found it helpful to think of her as such. Her verdant form had become a sort of divining rod to Porta, for the sculpture that she also called *Ameretat* held a jade pot of rich, real soil. This soil would, according to the mobed who blessed it, give birth to a blooming vine when in the presence of life that could outwit death.

This was one piece of art that would never be for sale.

Its size, however, required that Porta be separated from it whenever she was uprooted and transplanted. She had not laid eyes on the *Ameretat* since leaving it in New York six weeks earlier with twenty pages' worth of other insured inventory and shipping instructions.

Inside the gallery's storeroom she instructed the driver to put the crate in the center of the floor, then fetched a flat-head screwdriver and hammer from under a workbench.

"Do you mind?" she asked, holding them out to him.

Within seconds the metal brackets holding the five-ply birch together at the sides were moaning and creaking, giving birth. Porta lifted the lid and took off the top layer of cushioning foam. A golden-colored head appeared.

Gold, not green. Metal, not gemstone.

"This isn't right."

Inside the box, the metal sculpture was held steady by plywood braces. The driver helped her to remove these, then placed his hand on the figure's head and tilted the entire piece forward until he could grasp the heavy base. He set it in front of her on the concrete floor.

Porta crouched in her black business suit and frowned.

This was no goddess of immortality. Instead, a young boy walked with his cheerful face turned up to the sky, eyes shut beneath the implied sun, hair uncombed, shoes untied. The sculpture wasn't bronze, but some less reflective metal alloy that she couldn't name right away.

"This crate has been mislabeled."

The driver consulted the shipping container and then examined his clipboard. He allowed her to look over his shoulder at what he had: copies of the airway bill, the pro forma invoice, the shipper's invoice.

"It all appears to be in order, but this isn't the piece," Porta said. "I can show you photographs. There's been a terrible mistake. The one that should have come was jade. A jade woman with wings like an angel's."

The driver shook his head but didn't argue, and she imagined that this happened all the time, though none of it was his fault.

"Let me make a call," he said and returned to his truck.

Porta stared at the little boy. The smell of fresh paint coming from the gallery mingled with her disappointment. This was practically disastrous.

It wasn't a poorly made piece, but the boy was too sweet and too innocent and far too commercial for her liking. It was a wonder there wasn't a bird on his shoulder and a dog at his heels! The concept was amateur. Common. Uninspired. She flicked the child's head and heard a hollow hum.

She groaned. Where was her *Ameretat?*

The hum persisted and rose over the sounds of hammering and low voices from the front room. What material was this? Porta raised her aging but pretty hand — she cared deeply about the appearance of her hands — and placed it on top of the upturned forehead to put an end to the vibrations. She did not expect the warmth of a fever. Even more unexpectedly, her fingers sank into the boy's scruffy hair as if it were soft wax; it surrounded her knuckles. In a second it hardened and gripped her tight.

The bones within her fingers began to tingle.

If she had not been seventy-two and on intimate terms with the spiritual elements of the earth for most of her life, she might have shrieked, or cried out for assistance. But she recognized the unexplainable for what it was: not a physical event, as trapped as her hand really felt, but a perception of reality. A vision. The announcement of a message, prepared for her and delivered into her own hand. Quite specifically.

She relaxed, preparing herself to receive. The hum transposed into a buzz, and then a ringing in her ears.

"Your moon is waning, crone." It was the child speaking to her.

"As it does for us all," she said.

"Porta Cerreto ought to believe what she says. And yet she doesn't think death will come to her."

This announcement was mildly troubling. Death was a subject — and a state of being — she aimed to avoid.

"I have devoted my life to the search for immortality, that is true."

"Her search is vain."

"Why?"

"Because she has put her faith in gods that have no power over death."

Who was this rude and sassy little boy that found her unworthy of direct speech? Until she identified him, she would have to summon her self-control or risk offending a deity who might be greater than he appeared.

"Who has this power, if they don't?"

"There is but one who knows the way."

"Who? I'd like to meet her. Or him, if that's the case."

"Porta Cerreto walks away. She leads many down the trail to death with a torch high above her head."

She attempted to withdraw her hand from the trap of the child's wild hair but couldn't.

"That's a lie! Don't disrespect me any

longer — speak to me! Tell me who has the power you speak of."

The sculptured child opened its eyelids, and the spaces behind them were vacant. Porta stilled.

The child spoke. "Behold, I have come out to withstand thee, because thy way is perverse before me. No man or woman hath ascended up to heaven, but he that came down from heaven, even the Son of man which is in heaven. She that believeth on him is not condemned: but she that believeth not is condemned already."

This vision was an underling, escaped from the pit of hell to tease her as if she were a novice!

"What is your name, demon?"

"*I* am your life! Neither is there salvation in any other: for there is none other name under heaven given among the people."

"What is your *name?*"

"It is by the name of Jesus Christ of Naz —"

Now Porta shrieked, a cry of fury. She spat on the metallic hair that seized her and kicked at the child's pedestal and uttered a curse: *"Avaana! Avaana ahmega, no stolia eudah avaana . . ."*

Her hand came free. The sculpture toppled, and she crouched over it, agile

42

because she had held on to her youth in a way this . . . thing would never acknowledge. The vision skewed. Her fingers took the child by the throat as she ranted, commanding the abomination back to its underworldly hole. The eyelids closed.

The lips kept moving.

"In five weeks of five days, Porta Cerreto will breathe her last."

She raised her voice to drown out the monster's words but heard them anyway.

"How long wilt thou go about, O thou backsliding daughter? Yea, I have loved thee with an everlasting love: therefore with lovingkindness have I drawn thee. Porta, Porta, I call to you."

She turned the sculpture onto its face and slammed it into the ground one, two, three times.

The hum that had speared her ears faded away. She finished her curse, breathing heavily.

She stood. She smoothed her pant legs with the palms of her quivering hands. It had been a long time since anything like this had happened to her. In fact, she couldn't recall any incident in her long history that was quite so upsetting. She'd consult the Raven, find out what he knew of this shenanigan. What trickster would have imitated the poser god who insisted he stood above every other deity in the universe?

Porta had long ago rejected the One who rejected all humanity, and all deity associated with him, be they spirits or sons. *The man has now become like one of us, knowing good and evil. He must not be allowed to reach out his hand and take also from the tree of life and eat, and live forever.*

It would not be beneath her own son to mock her with such a joke. A housewarming gift of sorts.

As she stood over the still, cheap form and her shock faded, the stunt finally struck her as funny. She chuckled and bent to right the figure. Poor little boy, abused in such a manner.

Five weeks of five days. Did that mean five business weeks? Or twenty-five days in a row, counting weekends? Or something more cryptic? Whatever it meant, it didn't seem to be a long time; it might take however long it was to track down the *Ameretat,* which was to have taken center stage in her front window, where the figure could evaluate everyone who came through the doors. This, after all, was Porta's aim in drawing lovers of art to her: only beauty was immortal, and only beauty would draw the life-giver she sought. The *Ameretat* had not yet identified the one, not once in three decades. But Porta had faith that it would. In its own time, it would.

She imagined this child sculpture in her front window and weighed whether she had the nerve to put it there. It might draw a broader crowd than the goddess would have, which was important to a new gallery in establishing itself.

But the real reason she wanted to put it there was to thumb her nose at the devil who'd tried to scare her. If her son saw it there on his first visit, the reward of his expression would be worth her display of such schmaltz. And if she couldn't sell this overly cute thing in five weeks, maybe she deserved to die. Ha!

Porta walked lightly to her dock door and leaned out in search of the deliveryman. He sat on the driver's seat of his cab, ear pinching a phone to his shoulder.

"Never mind!" she called out. "I'll keep this one, sort out the rest later."

He lifted his sunglasses as if he hadn't heard.

"Just bring me the papers. I'll sign right now."

Porta went back into her storeroom and examined the little guy. He was durable if nothing else. The piece was light enough to lift onto her workbench. She touched his face, avoiding the hair on his crown, and found it solid as ever. She ran her fingers down his tender arms. The boy was an odd choice of messenger for whoever dreamed it up.

She glanced at a calendar hanging over the table. Today was Friday, August 10. Her grand opening was tomorrow. She counted weeks. Five would take her into the middle of September, around the fourteenth or fifteenth. Nothing significant about those dates came to mind. The fall solstice would fall a week or so afterward. She counted squares. Twenty-five days from today landed her finger on September third. Her seventy-third birthday.

An involuntary shiver passed between Porta's shoulders as she stared at the date. The significance of it changed nothing, but she was filled with a knowing that she resisted. The spirits of the fates and not some prankster had come to her this time, in all their veiled mystery. The truth was, her immortality was not secure, and though she felt closer to it than ever, it remained outside of her grasp.

No, no. Some truths were not truth at all, but a choice to be made, a pessimism to be rejected. She rejected this one. The fullness of life would come to her. It would hear her call and walk through those front doors of her gallery to reward all her years of faithful searching. When it arrived, she'd seize it and never let go.

Porta crossed her arms and scowled. She considered what special induction she needed to bestow on this particular piece of art. Considering the circumstances of its arrival, the usual spell she placed on her works ran the risk of being insufficient.

She lifted the child off the bench and carried it out through the gallery into the private viewing room that occupied one corner. The space was a misshapen pentagon, because its door stood at an angle between the walls that protruded into the main store. Porta liked this detail, because the unequal sides would have irritated her sisters back east to no end. The area was lit by three recessed lights. One of these fixtures formed a cone-shaped spotlight at the center of the room.

This is where potential clients would interact with artwork alone, undistracted, aided by the room's charms and the scents coming off the heated rocks of her incense bowl. Her former family would have been rankled by this sales technique too, but

Porta failed to see the problem with helping a customer's brain along, showing it how to see what it was trying to see anyway.

Porta placed the sculpture in one corner near an unlit candle. She bent to lift the edge of the area rug that covered most of the unfinished concrete floor, then she rolled it away to the wall. That done, she moved the little boy onto a black dot she'd painted on the slab, precisely in the center of the room.

There was a wall switch hidden behind the candle where she'd placed the statue. She flipped it on, and the dim recessed lights were extinguished and replaced by florescent blue beams from a projector installed in the ceiling. Thanks to technology, she no longer had to waste time casting her ceremonial circles with chalks or salts or silky cords or dry pine needles. The computer-generated image of a perfect three-dimensional circle — a snake biting its tail — floated over the floor like a hologram. The snake's head was positioned to the north and also provided the circle's door; Porta didn't care that the snake didn't face east, as tradition requested. With the aid of a tiny remote control, she could cut the door and also close the circle without being distracted from the more important details of her spells.

The sculptured boy stood in the middle of all this, and she appreciated how the snake held him captive.

She scolded the child. "You've had your fun. Now you're in my house, and you'll play by my rules. I'll be right back."

Porta closed the door and returned to sign the paperwork. Then she would drive all tricks from that hunk of metal forever.

4

Promise didn't die.

Not only did she not die, she did not lose consciousness. She did not break any bones. She felt her back hit first, then her hips and heels, every angle of her body digging and grinding into the coarse cushion of earth. The wind left her, and her eyes widened in an effort to do what her open mouth could not. She rolled, and everything rushed back in, the hardest and most painful breath of her dying lungs' life. She inhaled sand.

This was followed by coughing that seemed as though it would never end, and a sticky, hacking mess of grit and mucous. When her body gave up its efforts, she returned to her back, breathless and spent but whole.

The heels of her hands were abraded during the slide, and the tip of her chin was bruised by a jutting tree root, but this was not enough to convince medics of what had happened in spite of the splintered fence and the frantic 9-1-1 call from Zack's cell phone.

She thought the fall should have killed her. Instead, by the time the EMTs arrived she had found her feet, brushed herself off, and retrieved her wool wrap, which had snagged on a barnacle-ridden rock in the shallow ocean water. Emergency crews fetched her with a complicated rope-and-pulley contraption, then gave her a cursory examination and a lecture on what idiot stunts like rock climbing without proper gear cost the county annually in taxes. They didn't believe she had fallen through the fence. She would have been a lot worse off than she was, a medic said. A police officer on the scene made her take a Breathalyzer test and glared when she asked if it measured caffeine.

There was simply no way for her to avoid the gravity of the incident, no matter how anyone looked at it.

Zack vanished without speaking to her around the time the cops demanded to know who had claimed she fell. They sent her home with a stern warning and little sympathy. She called her friend Jenny, who had filmed and directed the videos that so successfully showcased Promise's talents.

Jenny came over to Promise's high-end apartment with ice packs and Epsom salts and a healthy dose of skepticism for how far Promise had actually fallen. But Promise accepted her comforts and the distraction of Jenny's gossip, which quickly turned to a strategy of brainstorming how to follow up with another, more popular production for the online masses.

Jenny was going to be a film producer, if Promise couldn't talk her into becoming her manager. Jenny was a social-networking genius. She had stuffed Promise's link into the virtual mailboxes of thousands of people who loved a solid ballad and an inspirational spin: *Sick girl who shouldn't be able to sing does it anyway — and* does *she!*

When Promise's chest therapist, Sue, arrived for a routine home-PT visit, Jenny left them to what she called their "rhythm and blues" routine. Sue had the rhythm and Promise had the blues. The one time Jenny had stayed to watch Sue pound thick mucus out of Promise's tiny body, she'd objected to the severity of the hits to such a degree that Sue threatened to pound *her,* and Promise had to ask Jenny to leave.

Promise shared her large three-bedroom apartment with Michelle, her lifelong friend who also had cystic fibrosis. The third room had been converted into a home-therapy area. It contained an adjustable slant-board table to help Promise and Michelle with postural drainage, an inflatable vibrating vest that shook one's whole body, a nebulizer for delivering medications by mist, a mechanical percussor that they rarely used anymore because both women favored the vest, and a PEP mask, all of which conspired twice a day to spook deadly mucous out of their chests. A spare oxygen tank stood in the corner, but this was only for emergency reserves. Each woman had a portable oxygen concentrator in her bedroom for use at night.

The therapy room also contained a flat-screen TV monitor with satellite and Internet connections, a dock for MP3 players, and a fully stocked entertainment center to keep the friends occupied during their forty-minute treatment sessions. The state-of-the-art room — like the rent for the apartment and tuition at the university and payments on the Roadster — had been provided by Promise's parents, who loved her with warmth and with money and supported her independent living.

In the therapy room, Promise positioned herself facedown on the reclining board to start, and Sue got to work. After only a few minutes in which nothing came up, a per-plexed Sue — a veteran therapist — said Promise's lungs were clearer than they'd been in the last six months. More clear than she'd ever seen in any patient of hers who had cystic fibrosis, in fact. As Sue clapped the backside of Promise's rib cage again and again, she asked what her patient had been doing differently.

Nothing except cliff diving. When Promise stuck to her story, Sue said, "If falling off a rock is what it takes to get you looking this good, we'll have to start prescribing it. Extreme percussion. You young people seem to like the dramatic stuff."

"Maybe skydiving without a chute would be even more effective. Maybe we should conduct a study," Promise joked.

"I hope you didn't think I was being seri-ous."

"If you won't share the stage with me in our comedy routine, I'm going to find me a new therapist," Promise said. The prevailing assumption that the dying didn't have a sense of humor seriously needed to die.

But terror, delayed though it was, caught up with Promise that evening.

After a dinner of whole-grain salad and enzyme supplements that aided the work of her digestive tract — cystic fibrosis wasn't only a disease of the lungs — Promise climbed into her Roadster and drove across the city to the hospital to visit Michelle.

Promise lived in this city and attended the university rather than a superior fine arts school because proximity to this particular facility was critical to her mental and physical health. She figured she'd spent nearly a quarter of her life in this hospital's beds, fending off bacterial infections and evaluating her overall well-being and participating hopefully in experimental studies.

It was her home away from home. The nursing staff were her surrogate parents. Her best friends convened here all the time — a hangout for the chronically ill.

Michelle, Promise's partner in outlandish dreams of the future, had been here for the last three weeks. Her body was rejecting the new lungs she'd received nine months earlier, the lungs that were to have taken her to Paris for a week at the Louvre.

Promise punched the elevator button out of habit, then decided to test Sue's observation by taking the stairs. She ascended easily and arrived on top of the world, deciding to embrace the rush of energy rather than analyze how she'd come to have it. She entered Michelle's room humming.

Michelle turned her head toward Promise,

her face swollen from the high dose of steroids given to her for rejection therapy. Oxygen tubing draped over her ears like fashion accessories. She lifted her hand toward a laptop that was asleep on the rolling table by her bed. "I saw the views of your video are up to, like, twenty thousand or something."

"That's because you keep watching it!"

"Can't help it. I'm your biggest fan."

"Well, I'm happy for you to drive up the numbers. They're getting attention. A couple agents said they'll come to the audition next week."

"Sweet." Michelle closed her eyes, tired already. "You'll knock 'em dead."

Promise placed her purse on a chair and started fishing in it. "Sue says get better and come home. I bore her and she'd rather talk to you."

Michelle smiled.

"Mom sent Regina Spektor's new CD, because you love her."

"I do."

"The day I sing like her will be the day I've died and gone to heaven."

"You're equally good, Promise. Just for different reasons."

Promise pulled the music out and placed it on the bedside table, then sat. "And Zack

Eddy finally said more than a sentence to me today. It turns out he's a photographer too. I've got his phone number and decided you should ask him out."

"Does he like hospital food?"

"He likes black clothes and hair gel. I'm pretty sure that after an afternoon of your company and some Jell-O, he'll loosen up. You're the one for him, my dear."

"Sounds downright dreamy."

"Really, he's quirky but sweet. Think about it."

Michelle sighed, shallow and shaky. "Too late. Summer term's almost over."

"We're all here for fall, Micky."

Her friend's eyes turned glassy. "I'm going to miss the start of classes."

"We've done this drill before. So you'll get in a little late. Everyone understands. I can get your books and —"

"My lung function is down to 78 or 77 or something."

Not good numbers, and they kept moving in the wrong direction.

"You should put up a notice about my room, Promise. Get someone to move in with you."

Promise leaned forward and put her hand over Michelle's. "Don't talk like that."

"You shouldn't be alone." Michelle

glanced down at Promise's touch when she said this. Her shifting eyes gave Promise the weird impression that Michelle wanted her to say the same thing. But it wasn't like her friend to be so needy.

"I'm hardly alone," Promise said. "I'm practically famous already! And everyone's coming back for fall term soon."

"I don't think I'm going to make it home this time."

"That kind of thinking will keep you here for sure."

"It's got nothing to do with my brain."

Promise stroked her friend's fingers, clubbed at the ends like her own with abnormally wide tips and convex fingernails, a reminder that they walked the same path.

"The biopsies show chronic rejection. We knew it could happen. We've seen it, haven't we? I'm about to become a statistic."

"Not in my book."

"I haven't accomplished anything."

"You've read *War and Peace.*"

"I swear if you make me laugh right now I'll boot you out."

"You've given teddy bears to every patient ever admitted to this floor."

"Not true — this time they're bringing me presents."

Sagging flowers bent over the window

seat. "Teddy bears lead extremely long, exciting lives. Think of how many have you to credit for their journeys."

Michelle's laugh was little more than a broken sigh. "This wasn't what I wanted, Promise."

"I know."

"There's never enough time for what we want."

"It seems that way, doesn't it?"

"No one gets it. Except maybe Mom and Dad."

"They didn't want this either."

"But it's different for them."

Promise squeezed her hand, knowing there was nothing worth saying just then.

"I wish I could be at your audition next week," Michelle said after a long silence.

"I'll ask Jenny to tape it for you."

"You need to go get what you want, quit hanging around places like this. It's a waste of time." There was irony in Michelle's voice, though, a wishfulness that Promise noticed but didn't know how to tend.

"Your time maybe." The joke seemed all wrong.

"Sing something for me? Something from the musical? Or whatever."

Promise felt unprepared, startled by the strange request. Broadway didn't belong in a hospital room, and her mind was void of everything else in her full repertoire. "Oh, I don't know. I'm not warmed up."

"Tell me all about it, then," Michelle said, gracefully allowing the awkward moment to float away.

"Will do."

"You know you can always waste as much of my time as you want. I like your voice better than Regina Spektor's."

That night, alone in her apartment, Promise lay in bed, separated from sleep by the sensation of falling that repeatedly jarred her awake. The third time this happened, she sat up, surprised to find her hands shaking so badly that they fumbled the oxygen tubing when she attempted to remove it from her nose. Really, it seemed like too much air. The gentle, invisible flow of oxygen on her skin was like the rushing wind of a screaming plummet.

Promise had decided a long time ago, with the help of her parents and trusted psychologist, not to have a lung transplant. Shari was the first person Promise had known to die after getting new lungs, when Promise was just ten, and then James, and then Rael. Eight more of her friends had died of CF without the transplant, five in

the last two years, some of them on a waiting list that simply didn't move them to the
top in time. The trick was to get on the list
while still healthy enough to survive the
high-risk surgery, which came with no timeline or guarantees.

She chose to let the lungs God gave her
wear out on their own, in their own time.
On days like today, it seemed like a good
decision. In the future, when she lay where
Michelle was because she'd missed the opportunity, she'd probably second-guess it.

How much time did she have, really? How
many more years or months before she lay
between hospital sheets and turned to dust,
and her name vanished from the face of the
earth like those indentations of her body in
the sand, erased by the rising tide?

She had to work quickly.

5

Every Saturday Chelsea Ellis and her twin brother walked the same figure-eight-shaped route through the streets of the Shore. Bleak or beautiful, cold or warm, winter or summer, Chelsea and Chase would leave their historic downtown home at 2310 Morris Street at precisely 2:15 p.m., order an ice cream at Marlene's Sweet Shop at 2:35, eat it while examining the Reed's Menswear window fashions at the bottom of the route for exactly six minutes, then toss out their soggy napkins and return to their front door by 3:00.

The routine persisted comfortably for ten years, during which Chelsea sampled each flavor in the ice cream shop at least ten times, and as exuberantly as possible. Chase ate only chocolate-chocolate chip but always expected her to give a full review of her flavor of the day. With so much practice, she developed descriptions worthy of a wine critic. Chase would quote her for days after.

"A piquant blend of bright minty aromas, balanced by nutty cocoa notes. Nutty notes, nutty notes."

With the exception of Chelsea's ice cream choice, each forty-five-minute outing was the same as all the others — no surprises, no disappointments — until one sunny Saturday in August when Chase descended the stairs of their home at 2:13 with a zippered black portfolio clutched under one arm and a fistful of seven white pencils in his opposite hand.

Chase had never walked with any of his artwork. It had been restricted to the protected confines of the house since his seventh Christmas, when their father gave Chase his first set of paper and charcoal pencils. The wind, the dirt, and, most of all, the prying eyes of strangers distressed Chase to the degree that he decided, with Chelsea's encouragement, to shelter his art from all these elements.

So when she saw the portfolio, Chelsea worried about this new development on many levels, the greatest being that Chase probably wouldn't explain the reason for the change, which meant she wouldn't be able to foresee his needs.

"Did you want to draw something while

we're out?" Chelsea tugged a baseball cap over his forehead to shade his fair cheeks.

"I have already drawn." But he didn't move to open the portfolio.

"Is it okay for the art to go outside?" she asked, seeking clues more than answers.

He nodded and nodded, a long bobbing agreement that made Chelsea think of a dashboard doll. Chase didn't meet her eyes. He never looked at her directly.

"Dad said it was okay," Chase said, and Chelsea didn't know what he meant, so she nodded in return. "I drew the longing," he said.

"Okay," she said.

They left the house as always, down the front steps abreast, then along the slab sidewalk toward town, Chelsea on the inside and Chase on the outside, the protective position. Chase's posture of guarding Chelsea was sweet, she'd always thought, maybe even empowering to him. For this reason she encouraged it, though in reality she was the one who shielded him: from loss, from disruption, from need, and from unkind souls. People tended to misunderstand.

The likelihood that the twin of an autistic person would also have autism was less than 10 percent. Depending on the day, this statistic gave Chelsea great relief or great guilt.

Chase held his pencils with the tips pointed directly upward, as if they were a full glass of water. He walked with his face to the sky and often closed his eyes, the path so familiar to him that he knew the precise number of steps to each fixed obstacle, curb, and door. Chelsea believed he could see reality more accurately than the average person. His mind was like a photographic reference guide, a satellite GPS, a swatch book of colors and textures. She kept an eye out for new hazards, like rocks that might turn his ankles, or toys left unattended.

"Would you like me to hold your portfolio while you eat your ice cream?" she asked when they reached Marlene's. She reached out and pulled the door open, grinning at him. "Or do you plan to use chocolate in your sketches today?"

"No," he said, and he walked past the gaping entry, face still turned toward the sun, eyes shut.

Chelsea continued to hold the door open, shocked by this unannounced change.

From her position behind the counter, Riley, who scooped their ice cream most of the time, lifted her eyebrows as she watched

Chase move past the front windows. She turned her questioning glance on Chelsea, who finally let the door swing shut and bounded after her brother.

"Where are we going today?" she asked.

"To the longing," Chase said to the sky.

"Café chair," Chelsea warned.

He avoided it with catlike grace.

Five shops down from Marlene's, Chase stopped, opened his eyes, and turned to face a storefront head-on. It was one of the smaller downtown venues, a narrow place with a one-panel door and sidelights abutting a large plateglass window. A cheery yellow canopy spanned the width of the store, and a silver GRAND OPENING banner dangled from the scalloped edge. In the center of the door, a frosted logo announced the name. ART(i)FACTS: UNEARTH YOUR TRUTH.

Behind the front window, on a display stage, a sky-blue backdrop like a photographer's sheet fell behind a sculpture on a pedestal. A child of four or five, eyes closed, had been captured walking, his face turned up to the outdoor canopy as if it were the warming sun.

Chelsea did a double take. Had Chase seen this before today? To the best of her recollection, this gallery hadn't been open a week ago, the last time they walked from the ice cream parlor to the men's shop. Even if Chase had seen the boy's stance, her brother's posture while walking was years old. He wouldn't be mimicking this. In fact, the figure seemed to be a copy of Chase as a boy.

"What's this?" she asked Chase, staring at the child. It was familiar to her in a way she couldn't describe, a way that had nothing to do with her brother or the child's form. She wasn't sure what materials the artist had used to make it. Two or three metals of different textures and colors, as best she could see.

Chase was already inside.

In spite of her twin's remarkable knack for drawing, he hadn't expressed any prior interest in galleries or shows, and Chelsea, whose passions lay primarily in financial markets and marathons, had little appreciation for much of what was considered art. She found it random and impenetrable and entirely in the eye of the beholder. Even so, she'd taken a few classes in college, mostly to gain entry into Chase's private world. She'd been to a few exhibitions. Chelsea stepped over the threshold.

None of the galleries she'd ever entered had looked like this.

Sunlight filled the long room as if the building had no ceiling, and the first place Chelsea looked was up. Bubbling domes of skylights floated above. The walls themselves were difficult to see. Every square inch, floor to ceiling and front to back, was covered with eclectic two-dimensional art. Framed drawings and unframed canvases. Matted photographs and mixed-media collages. Watercolor and oil and acrylic and pastel and charcoal. Abstract and literal. Traditional and contemporary and all manner of styles and periods that she couldn't begin to name.

There were sculptures and vases and screens throughout the room, arranged around soft, wide-seated chairs that suggested one would need to sit and stay awhile in order to view everything properly — if it were possible to focus on anything. Several patrons were seated, studiously quiet. Two others stood at the rear wall, necks craned toward the upper tiers.

The exterior walls of a small private room were also covered with art, all but the door, and in front of this space, a narrow table offered up appetizers and toothpicks and delicate flutes of champagne. The little black dress and heels Chelsea reserved for her fund-raisers and high-powered cocktail meetings would have been appropriate.

Between these people and a desk in the corner stood a slight woman elegantly dressed in a tailored red jacket and pencil skirt. Chelsea put her in her seventies. She was likely the proprietor, or maybe a docent. Her spiky blond hair was extremely short and strangely youthful. Her suit and jewelry, though attractive, were the wrong color red for her complexion.

The woman's eyes were on Chase. Chelsea instantly felt unwelcome, though her gut was conflicted over whether this was because their Bermuda shorts and running shoes should have stayed outside or because she saw prejudice in the woman's gaze.

Chelsea hoped Chase didn't plan to stay long.

It seemed he hadn't noticed the crazy collection of artwork. He'd found an ottoman in front of an occupied love seat and placed himself directly in front of the man and woman sitting there, portfolio clutched to his chest and pencils erect in his fist. He was staring at the woman's shoes, stylish high-heeled sandals that showed off neat red toenails.

"Excuse me," the man said. His brows met over his nose, disapproving.

"Yes," Chase said.

The woman smiled a little, but her eyes frowned.

Chelsea approached quickly and squatted next to her brother. These were the encounters she hated, the run-ins that fed stereotypes and brought all her conflicting feelings of defensiveness and apology to the surface. She saw in the man's crouched brow the uninformed decision that Chase was rude and backward; she saw pity in the woman's silent expression, and maybe even fear.

After thirty years, this never got easier.

"Chase." Chelsea kept her voice low and firm. "This is not a good place to sit. Come with me now. We'll go to a better seat."

He laid the pencils in an even row on the floor next to his sneakered feet. The couple's eyes were on her, evaluating her competence, weighing how much time to give her before they became more vocal or moved themselves.

"You're blocking the view, Chase."

"She is the view," Chase said, and he unzipped his portfolio. "A longing fulfilled is a tree of life."

"Let's move," the man said, but the woman made no motion. She was staring at Chase's book.

Several loose sheets of heavyweight black

paper lay inside the folder. Chase preferred a particular brand, which his aide, Wes, ordered and Chelsea paid for, at four dollars per sheet plus a surcharge to have them cut in quarters to form 17 × 15-inch pieces. Stonehenge Rising, 100 percent cotton, archival-quality paper. The surface had almost no texture at all, which allowed Chase the greatest control over detail.

The woman saw the drawing on the top of Chase's pile and lifted her fine-boned hand to her lips. The image was a sprawling oak with low-slung branches that nearly touched the ground, a knot at the center of its thick trunk.

Then Chelsea saw with the kind of pleasant discovery that accompanies second glances that it wasn't a tree at all, but a woman's head. Wild, windy hair formed the tree's waving boughs. The trunk was a straining throat. Full, parted lips and a delicate nose appeared in the minutely detailed leaves under eyes that were closed. The high forehead was tilted upward toward heaven, like the child in the gallery window, like Chase on his walk. It was dramatic and impressive.

Chase bent to pick up the hardest white pencil, the colored graphite, and Chelsea thought a light remark might help put the couple at ease. "You're full of surprises," she said to Chase while looking at them. "I didn't know we'd be showing your work today."

Her brother froze, his outstretched hand hovering over the pencil, his bent form covering the page. "No," he said. "Definitely no."

"Right. Of course, you're right. I misunderstood. You don't have to show anyone. But maybe we could sit over there while you work."

Chase's posture relaxed, and Chelsea exhaled. He made no motion to relocate.

The woman on the sofa was still staring at the drawing, and now she put her fingers to her throat. The man's expression had softened too, from judgment to question. Chase picked up the pencil and applied it to the tree trunk, and Chelsea noticed a gnarled line that was thicker than the others running alongside of the knot.

Her mind made a connection between unconscious observations, and she lifted her eyes to the woman's fingertips. They trembled near a long scar that ran vertically along her windpipe. Did she think the line was connected to her scar? It was impossible. Chase had never met this woman. And yet the untamed mane of hair, the full mouth, the high cheeks, the mark . . . There was a symbolic resemblance. Chase's pencil made a scritching sound on the paper.

Within the knot of the tree he hastily drew the crosshatched lines of a grassy mass that gave the space a new appearance of being hollow. In the grass pile — a nest — he placed a bird, throat extended to the heavens just like the tree's branches, just like her peaceful face. The little beak was parted.

The woman on the sofa gripped her companion's hand.

The process took Chase no more than one minute to complete. Then he returned the pencil to the floor, removed the drawing from the portfolio, closed the folder, and placed the image on top. He bent and collected his pencils in his fist, stood, laid the tree-woman image on the ottoman where he had been sitting.

"I love you," he said, and Chelsea wasn't sure if he was talking to the woman or his drawing. He left the gallery.

"I'm sorry for interrupting you," she said to the couple, backing away toward the door.

They didn't reply. They ignored her entirely. The man had picked up the paper, and the woman's fingertips were reaching out for it.

The other woman, the one in red, had not moved, and she was frowning at Chelsea.

6

Promise went into her audition believing it was the most important one of her life. Though fall classes didn't officially start for another week, screenings for the university's stage shows were traditionally held pre-term. It was understood that these tryouts were scheduled early for the benefit of the most serious performing arts students — the ones who took classes year-round because opportunity doesn't know summer from any other season, and snoozers lose.

Also unspoken was the harsh truth that Promise had already lost too much momentum for someone serious about a career as a recording artist. She'd missed innumerable auditions because she'd been strapped to oxygen tanks and nebulizers in a hospital. She should have been a junior by now but had yet to complete a term with a full load of units. Technically, she was still a sophomore.

Today, however, Promise believed she finally stood a serious chance of taking the lead role. Her goal: the character of Elphaba, the misunderstood witch of *Wicked,* the satirical adaptation of the "true" story behind *The Wizard of Oz.*

Promise's confidence in her star qualities was invincible today, and at the back of her mind she connected this faith to her tumble through the ocean air. Her lungs, pounded clear by that superhuman clap, were at their greatest capacity since the day she'd come screaming from her mother's womb. Her prospects glittered with gold: a leading role, interested agents, optimistic buzz. This was her time, and no one could say how long it would last.

She would stretch it out like a string of whole notes. *Listen up! I'm going to die young, but no one will ever forget me.*

Her mother made the three-hour trek from her island home on Puget Sound to support Promise. They met in the campus theater's parking lot.

"Promise! You look ready to own the stage!" They embraced.

"I'm so ready for this."

"You're going to do great." Promise's mother always spoke positively, though the fine lines in her forehead worried day in and day out. "Which agent should I flirt with?"

"Don't you dare even *look* at them!"

"Your dad sends kisses."

Promise's mother called daily and visited weekly for lunch or a shopping trip or a movie. Or a big audition. Whenever Promise required hospitalization, Mom took up residence in Promise's apartment and stayed close by until she was discharged.

By some accidental grace, Promise was able to recognize her extravagant childhood as a sign of her parents' fear. The possibility that she might die having never been to Disneyland or the national parks or Europe gave them goals within their control, manageable tasks that propelled them toward happiness and optimism during periods of good health. It was critical that Promise be educated, if only for education's sake; it was unthinkable that she would have to wait until Christmas or her birthday for the latest gadget or technological wonder; it was of the essence that she learn to ski and play the piano and host carte blanche parties for her friends. Every illness and hospitalization was saturated with the anticipation of future experiences that would make the uncontrollable reality of her life pale in comparison.

This was their coping mechanism, and Promise embraced their love without complaint, even though no amount of money or generosity could chase away the monsters that made the most noise under her bed at night: that she might never know the reason why she was born; that she might die and then fade away.

What if she'd died on that beach?

Why hadn't she?

Promise shook off the possibilities.

Mother and daughter parted in the fluorescent white hallway outside the audition room. Promise prepared for her turn, pacing, continuing the light warm-ups she'd been doing for hours. She sang a stanza of her song at a quarter of the volume she'd belt from the stage. She breathed the sweetest, fullest breaths.

The door opened, and the emotionless Dr. Anderson summoned her by waving his clipboard. She smiled brightly and rushed in. He returned to his seat.

The audition room was a neglected dance studio on the west side of the building, with mirrors on three walls. At three in the afternoon on this hot August weekday, the drawn curtains on the fourth wall were no more use against the penetrating sun than sheets of tissue paper. Promise felt small on the expansive floor, which was large enough for a fully cast rehearsal of *The Nutcracker.*

Today, however, her voice would compensate for her size.

She consulted with Steve, the soundboard tech who'd visited her at the hospital once when an illness had forced her to drop out of a spring term. "No Good Deed" would start loud with a cry of protest as Elphaba's lover was dragged away to be punished for saving her. Promise would audition without a mic. They checked the volume of the accompaniment.

When Promise was satisfied, she took her place in front of the small audience, five instructors who would direct various elements of the production, and went through the formality of introducing herself and her number. Two men she assumed to be the agents sat on opposite sides of the room. One fanned himself with a sheet of paper. The other was texting. Her mother dutifully sat in the front row without glancing toward either one of them.

Jenny and three more of Promise's friends burst in through the rear door, waving, and scrambled for a seat. She acknowledged them with a quick grin and her toes-only "jump." The presence of people who loved her would give wings to her voice.

Sweat glossed her forehead and caused her blouse to chafe at the armpits. She nodded at Steve and closed her eyes, lifted her face to the fluorescent lights. Two short bars of bursting trumpets and rushing violins was her only intro, and then came the drawn-out shout of desperation: her lover's name pouring from her lungs as a twelve-beat syllable. She finished it with air to spare and then, like a seagull diving for an ocean fish, dropped her volume to a controlled, articulate plea. She began the murmur of Elphaba's chant, a frantic effort to summon the powers that could save the one person who hadn't turned against her.

It wasn't required that she dance, but it was impossible for her not to move through Elphaba's frantic emotions. Desperation for her lover's safety spun Promise in circles. The agony over all the suffering Elphaba had endured, over the backward results of every good thing she'd ever tried to do, would bring her to her knees and then to defiance by the end of the song. Because her goodness was rejected, she would never seek to do good again.

Perfection ran through the center of every note, like hope through Promise's blood. If there was any problem with this audition, it might be that she'd never be able to sing the number so well again.

She hoped Jenny was recording it.

7

Porta had not yet locked up the gallery when she carried a pitcher of cool water into her private viewing room. She poured it over the rocks that warmed the incense in the bowls, extinguishing the heat. At the end of each day, the air was thick and in motion, looking for a window but finding lungs instead. This special concoction of scents, which could not be found in stores or potion guides but only in the back corners of her mind, took the edge off one's need to come and go quickly. It relaxed the body and the senses. It built bridges between reality and perception in everyone but her, after years of exposure.

The water hit the rocks and hissed. Steam rose from the bowl, and the damp masked the bittersweet scent.

"What's that?" someone demanded.

Water slopped out of the pitcher.

"Zachary. I didn't hear you come in."

He crossed the room and stood by her side. "What's that you just snuffed out?"

"Oh, a little of this, a little of that."

"Smells like rat puke. You keep rat puke around for incantations and stuff?"

"You know what rodent vomit smells like?" she taunted.

"No, really, what is it?" he insisted.

"Why, you think you can get a good price for it on the street?"

"Can I? It smells like something I tried down in Guadalajara once."

"Might be." Porta left him bending over the bowl, sniffing the remnants. He would never guess what it was.

She went out into the main room, which was dim at this hour, its primary source of lighting being the skylights. She would turn on the security spotlights before she left.

It was not without strategy that Porta had moved to this coastal college town. This boy here, her only child, born to her as a single woman of old age, was the primary reason she had come, but not the sole reason. She hadn't been careless about it. The per capita income even in this tourist trap of Pacific Northwestern romanticism was high enough to support the arts. Years ago Zack's constant need to be free of her was a scab yanked off her heart again and again. But when the tough, nerveless scar felt nothing, she came back.

It was the least she could do to deflect any blame he'd try to place on her for the failures of his life. Besides, this was one location where she hadn't yet searched for the deity who would grant her highest desire. Her plan was to charm two birds with one spell: to finally find her living, breathing Ameretat and to be near her worthless, ungrateful son.

She had no reason to believe that the person who would lead her to immortality was more likely to be found here than anywhere else. Still, she hadn't regretted choosing this location. Not even when that golden-haired boy in her front window had numbered her days.

Nor had she second-guessed herself when Zachary proposed she commission him to do a painting for the studio. Zack was conniving and had weaseled out of her an agreement for a monolithic sum of money, money he would likely spend on destroying his brain cells. But she agreed. She was a blameless mother, nurturing her child's natural gifts and helping him to make a living. It wasn't of her concern what he did with money he'd earned.

Porta paused at the desk. A small shaded

light on a bronze base cast a weak beam over a handful of snapshots Zachary had thrown down, fanned out across the blotter like poker cards.

He stormed out of the viewing room. "Do you have that going in there twenty-four-seven?" he demanded.

Porta picked one up. A girl. A cliff. A stormy sky. An orange scarf. Very nice composition.

"Are your clients breathing that junk?"

"It's harmless, Zachary."

"It's illegal. You think cops don't buy art from galleries like this?"

"Most of them can't afford it. Besides, the last thing any of my clients are thinking about when they go in that room is what it smells like. And if they are, most people like it."

"Of course they like it! When someone finds out what you've got going in there, they'll sue your a —"

"Do you think I don't know how to protect myself? I've been doing this for longer than you've been alive."

"You don't have any right to mess with people."

"The product is completely natural," she said. "Harmless. It clears the mind and

84

helps people to see what they're meant to see."

"Oh yeah. That's been my experience with natural stuff."

"Watch your tone. Do you know how hard it is to find clarity in this world?"

Zack gawked at her, and she felt exasperated.

"I provide people with a gift, son. I give them beauty and the insight to see themselves in it. Hope. That's all a person wants from this life. It's what spurs us on."

"You're so full of yourself."

Porta picked up another photo. "People come in here looking for —"

"Something to hang on their living room walls."

"At first. But they come in, and I invite them to look past the obvious. They see something they like, I urge them to consider listening to it as well. I give them an opportunity to shut out the noise of the world and ponder their experience with a piece. Everyone's soul can hear art speak. I just . . . turn up the volume a little bit."

"Nothing like the power of suggestion."

"You're too naive to understand. Every gallery I've opened has been a raging success."

"Then why close them?"

"When the needs are met, my services are no longer needed. I move on."

"All hail Queen Porta, saving the world one Rockwell at a time."

"You're a little self-righteous for a boy who spends most of his allowance on whatever it takes to drown out life. Or at least his own mother."

"Why would I waste my money on anything to do with you?"

"Precisely what I was wondering. What'd it cost you to steal my *Ameretat* and pay someone to hex that cute little sculpture?" She motioned toward the front window.

Zack shook his head. "What? Did you get into an argument with your coven again? Someone having a little fun with you?"

She lifted her chin slightly. Porta wasn't offended by his barb. She was merely more doubtful that her blood ties to her son were strong enough to anchor her here for as long as she had first thought. After all, her aim of this lifelong exercise was to end her loneliness, to secure true friends, to attain the kind of power that guaranteed she would never be rejected again. She'd had to discard so many people who couldn't rise to her standards. It was a sad state of affairs that she could find so few honorable people with whom she could share her objectives.

Not one, in fact.

"Prophecies aren't something for a novice to mess with," she warned.

"Better not go uttering any then." He headed back out to the front. "Just let me know which one of those you want me to paint."

"Which one of what?"

Porta's attention returned to the images in her hands. He was going to paint directly from a photograph? She sighed. So, she would be paying *ten* times what it was worth. At least!

She spread the images across the surface of the desk so she could see them all clearly. The girl was stunning, as pretty as Porta herself had been half a century ago, except her skin was fairer and her hair darker. She was tiny, this one, barely a hundred pounds. Those hands, though! Monstrous. Porta adjusted her glasses and held one of the pictures a few inches farther off. Graceless, knobby hands and stumpy fingers.

Porta set aside the images where the hands weren't covered up by the scarf.

Except for details like this, the photographs were each so similar to each other that she wondered why he hadn't just decided for himself. Why had he even brought more than one?

In the short foreground of each, dime-sized purple flowers formed a scattered audience for the young woman. An old split-rail fence was the only prop. Storm clouds stacked up behind her in lumpy rows, and the wind played with her hair and the fringe of her wrap.

Pretty, yes, but ho-hum. Nothing here that Porta could identify as powerful enough to grab anyone. But that wasn't how this worked, was it? The art was about what others could see in it, not what she wished they could see.

She stacked the snapshots together and then cast them off one at a time quickly, looking for The Thing she might have missed. If she couldn't find it, she'd throw them down like lots and let the Fates pick one.

At the bottom of the pile, the very last image came between her thumb and forefinger thicker than the rest. She examined it and found explanation simply enough: two photographs stuck together, apparently because the one on the bottom had been wet at some point. The glossy paper tore slightly as she peeled the sheets apart.

Now here was something worth looking at.

The dry rot of the collapsed fence was

golden and fragile, and strangely detailed. She could see splinters in the wood the size of split ends. Behind this, a pair of upended sheepskin boots fell out of a titanium sky, chased by that billowing fringed scarf the color of the setting sun. Tiny clods of dirt hung in zero gravity where they'd been kicked into orbit.

A high-def slice of life and death, a thousandth of a second wide.

Porta carried this small photograph to the workbench in her storeroom, where she turned on her magnifying lamp and swiveled it over the image. The resolution was clear and sharp. Zack had a fine camera.

Years of experience as an art buyer told her right off that clients would be drawn to the mystery of the victim and her wrap, or in some cases, to the astonishing energy of the free fall contained in the frozen moment. That alone was worth some money — more, if Zack would put any effort at all into making a name for himself.

Her eye, though, was drawn to a detail that she suspected would go unnoticed by everyone so long as she didn't point it out. She positioned the light over the clunky boot soles, which cut the horizon at the same point where rain clouds had gathered to make their stormy challenge.

They spread out to the right and left of center like a parade crowd making way for the main attraction. They were nimbus clouds: thick, hearty, and ragged, except for the one dead center. This one was more gold than gray, a filtered spotlight created by the obscured sun. Moreover, the cloud formed a nearly perfect circle that framed the booted feet.

A nimbus of an entirely different kind.

In art — in paintings, sculptures, stained-glass windows — the nimbus appeared as a halo behind the heads and bodies of divinity, be they saints, gods, or devils. In children's stories, the nimbus was reduced to the status of a broomstick. In classical mythology, as in Porta's personal philosophy, the nimbus was an aura — a mist, a cloud — that surrounded gods and goddesses who walked the earth.

A gold nimbus was reserved for deity.

If the fall had killed this girl, Porta would cancel Zack's commission and disown him for showing such disrespect for the dead. The image should be destroyed.

If she lived, Zack would introduce her to his mother. The possibility of meeting the subject of this photo took the sting out of losing her *Ameretat*. It could be that the jade figure was about to be usurped by flesh and blood.

8

The lady in the red suit who had watched Chase give away his oak tree picture caused his palms to sweat. In his mind, when he looked for her tree he discovered an alien species, a noxious weed that did not belong in the Shore with the people he loved. She was *Ailanthus altissima,* unfortunately named the "tree of heaven" by people who did not understand it. The common name that he preferred for the growth was stinking sumac.

He sat in a wide wood-slat patio chair on the rear porch, his portfolio balanced on his flat knees. The lawn at the bottom of the steps was bright green and small and surrounded by a variety of evergreen trees standing in close quarters. They guarded the old house and in the past had given him much to draw. But today he didn't even look at them. His shoulders hunched over his smooth black Stonehenge paper. Without needing a reference, Chase drew a short trunk, then filled in the towering plant with years' and years' worth of impenetrable foliage. At full maturity, such an unstoppable tree as the stinking sumac could grow to eighty feet.

The plant was attractive, but dangerous. It had compound symmetrical leaves plus a single teardrop-shaped leaf at the tip of each branch, which was wrapped in pale gray bark. Close to the trunk, dense yellow flowers and pretty reddish-pink fruit sat on top of the branches. These attractive details were, as its more fitting name suggested, odoriferous, like the stench coming out of that room inside the ART(i)FACTS gallery. It had a root system that was nearly impossible to kill and from which arose shoot after shoot that overran native plant life.

It generated toxins that prevented healthy plants from growing in its presence.

It produced seeds as swiftly as mice produced offspring. The female trees especially. Unlike mice, however, the weed could reproduce itself either sexually or asexually.

It was not deterred by poor soil, polluted environments, or any amount of hacking at its trunk.

Once the stinking sumac took root, very little could stop it from overtaking the earth. In two hundred years, *Ailanthus altissima* had done a better job of conquering North America than any European colonist. Stamping it out had become a global concern.

Chase worked quickly. This was not a drawing he wanted to spend much time on. Placing it on a two-dimensional surface would free up space in his mind for more important demands on his concentration, though, and this is why he gave it any time at all. Over the past week, the Great Basin bristlecone had appeared to him nightly, writing stories with the grease pencil on the pastel paper: stories that Chase turned into images, stories about people Chase knew and didn't know, stories about longing and truth and beauty.

Or stinking sumacs that needed to be contained.

Chase sensed Wes come and sit beside him. Wes was Chase's friend and helper who came to the house most weekdays while Chelsea was away. Wes was a good presence, an emergent rainforest tree with sprawling buttress roots that rested on the top of the soil. Such roots were wide rather than deep. On top of the earth, they could stabilize the tree against battering winds, and they could get the most nutrients from the poor-quality rainforest soil.

Wes held flash cards in his fist. These flash cards had black drawings on white paper and were faces made to help Chase learn what people meant when they looked at him a certain way. Chase was not interested in those drawings today.

"Which tree is that?" Wes asked.

"The stinking sumac."

"I suppose it's good that you can't draw the smell."

"It smells like rancid peanuts."

"What prompted you to draw such a reeking plant?"

"He looked up and said, 'I see people; they look like trees walking around.' " Chase said this without looking up.

"Who said that?"

"A blind man."

Wes nodded once, and his short beard touched his chest. His gray-streaked hair was held back in a band at the nape of his neck. "They are like people, aren't they? That's a metaphor."

"That is a simile, a comparison using *like* or *as*. People are trees. That is a metaphor."

Wes cleared his throat, and one corner of his mouth lifted. "That's new for you."

"What is new?"

"Thinking metaphorically is unusual for . . . you."

Chase frowned. He wasn't sure how anyone could think metaphorically. "I have been drawing trees for twenty-five years. That is not new."

"Are all your pictures of trees about people?"

"No."

A gnat landed on Chase's drawing. He lifted the page to his lips and blew the bug off.

"Chelsea told me about the picture you gave away Saturday."

Because Chelsea had told Wes already, Chase had nothing to add. He began working on the roots of the stinking sumac, which were deep and long.

"And who is this tree like?" Wes said.

"The woman in red, with the stinking room."

"Is she a bad nut?"

Chase shifted on his seat. From the corner of his darting eye he could see that Wes was smiling like he had made a joke. He did this sometimes, but Chase understood that Wes was his friend, and friends did not make fun of him.

"A bad nut is a metaphor for someone who does no good," Wes said.

Chase was not sure what he meant, but

the real problem was that Wes was not listening.

"People are trees, not nuts."

"What kind of tree am I?" Wes asked.

"Aglaia affinis."

"Is that a good tree?"

"It is a strong tree with good roots."

Wes flexed his arm and touched his soft bicep. "I think I'm a little squishy."

Chase did not see what that had to do with trees.

"But thank you. Are you planning to give this drawing to the stinky woman?"

"Yes." Chase drew an ax embedded in the trunk.

"Why did you start giving your drawings away?"

"Dad said I should do this."

Wes shuffled the flash cards. "When did he say that?"

"When he drew in my book. He said I should draw the longing, because time is short."

"What's the longing?"

"It's the truth."

"The truth about a person?"

"Yes."

"How do you know what that is?"

"I see it in my head."

"Like you see your father?"

"Yes. He is not dead."

"Maybe he isn't." Wes pointed to the stinking sumac. "What will you say when you give that to her?"

"I love you."

Wes's face became a little bit like the one in the flash card where the eyebrows made a mountain point over the eyes.

"Everyone should know the truth," Chase said.

Wes said, "She might not like it."

Wes was usually a better listener. A person's like or dislike of something had nothing to do with whether it was true.

"Everyone should know the truth," Chase repeated. He finished the stinking sumac and placed it under the pile of blank pages.

9

When Zack called Promise Friday night, leading into the conversation with broken thoughts and unfinished sentences, she couldn't identify him right away over the music and the laughing and the loud talk swirling around her home. The artist who'd witnessed her fall off a cliff had not crossed her mind for several days.

But then she pieced together that he was asking if she was okay — it took her several seconds to determine he was referring to her physical self — and that he was embarrassed about not having called sooner. He said something about needing to see her.

"It sounds like you're busy," he said.

"What?"

"Is this a bad time to come over?"

"Not at all! We're just celebrating. If you want to be a stagehand this year, come on over."

"A what?"

"Say again?"

"Uh, do you mind if I bring someone with me?"

"Not if you'll help to eat all this food!"

It wasn't until afterward that Promise thought Zack might be coming over to apologize for running off on her, in which case the timing wouldn't be great. It was impossible to tell if he was feeling down or if that was his usual tone or if the party had just drowned him out.

Well, she'd prove to him that she was better than fine, that she didn't blame him for her thoughtless dive. No matter the case, she'd cheer him up. She'd made him laugh before.

Tonight, laughter was required. Cast announcements had been posted, and as the new Elphaba, Promise had declared herself hostess of a kickoff celebration.

Jenny arrived with a DVD she'd burned for Michelle of Promise's audition. Susan, who'd play Elphaba's counterpart Galinda/Glinda, helped her with an eleventh-hour catering plan, and Steve brought a keg of beer. Dr. Anderson arrived with scripts, which cast members began to use for impromptu spoof skits, and stayed just long enough to accept the presentation of a canvas director's chair and megaphone, both of which had been spray-painted gold and labeled *The Wizard of Us.*

Zack and his friend didn't show up until after Dr. Anderson departed and Promise's neighbors were starting to call for quiet. She did her best to mellow the roaring by changing up the music to something more low-key.

She actually heard the doorbell with her own ears, and knew it had to be Zack, because everyone else was coming and going without notice.

On her stoop, Zack clutched a slim manila envelope. He stood behind a woman who met Promise's eyes with daring curiosity that verged on being rude. Promise thought of her as an aging pixie, an uninhibited sprite who might be full of magic or mischief depending on her mood. Tonight it seemed to be on the delighted side: happy-spiky platinum hair, surprised caramel eyes almost too large for her face, graceful arms and legs draped in an expensive black pantsuit that might have fit Promise.

The woman wore a considerable amount of makeup, expensive makeup that made her years hard to judge. Deep lines at the sides of her mouth made Promise think she was older than she otherwise appeared. Sixtyish. Maybe seventy.

"Zack was right about you," the woman said before Promise found her voice. She reached for Promise's hand and took it in both of hers. In contrast to her high style was a cheap bracelet braided from some worn black threads. "Oh yes!" The woman looked at Zack. "This is incredible for us. Just incredible."

"Promise, this is Porta Cerreto. Promise . . . uh . . ."

"Dayton. Hello." Promise felt usurped by this strong personality. She tried to match it, bright, smiling. "It's nice of you to come by. Can I get you something to drink?"

"A brandy would be nice," Porta said, stepping into the house and looking around. Jenny and Steve were quizzing a crowd on the sofa about lines from Andrew Lloyd Webber musicals. Zack shook his head at Promise's offer.

"I've, uh, got some beer. Or water, coffee. Sodas in that cooler."

"Never mind then," Porta said, examining a large batik print of an African village hanging by itself on one wall. "This is a beautiful place, sweetie, but it's not at all you. You didn't do the decorating, did you." It was a declaration, not a question. "The leather and Craftsman have all the wrong energy!"

"My mother picked these out," Promise said, then felt obligated to add, "I think she's got great taste."

"Of course she does," Porta said, somehow managing not to contradict herself.

Zack frowned at Porta. "So you're feeling all right?" he asked Promise.

"Better than ever!"

"Which can hardly be all right," Porta said, examining the leaves of a droopy fern.

Zack cringed. "Porta, please."

"You told me she's dying, Zack. How can she feel all right?"

"We're all dying," Promise said lightly.

"Not today, it seems."

"Next time, you don't get to come," Zack said to Porta.

Promise held her smile in place. "I hope you haven't been worried about . . . anything." She directed this at Zack.

"Is there somewhere we could talk?" He glanced at the lingering partiers, who'd taken no notice of him.

"Sure." Promise led her guests to the end of the hall and into Michelle's empty bedroom, because it was tidier than hers and less prone to generating unwanted questions than the therapy room. Porta seated herself on Michelle's bed and crossed her legs.

Zack turned to Promise. "I hardly know

you, and I didn't mean for this visit to get weird. But here's the thing: I'm not sure exactly what happened on that cliff, but I know what I saw, and my camera isn't arguing with me."

"If it hadn't happened to me, I might not believe it either."

"How can you not be hurt?"

"I can't explain it," Promise said. "But really, everything's absolutely fine."

Zack nodded. "Well, Porta's here because she thinks she knows why that fall didn't kill you."

"Really."

"Yes," Porta said. "I deal with these things all the time."

"Porta just opened a gallery out at the Shore," Zack said. "ART(i)FACTS."

Promise clutched her hands in her lap, wondering why Porta didn't explain what she meant. "I've heard of it. Someone at school told me a new place was about to open."

"She asked me to paint something for her gallery. The scene I was having you model for."

"Right. I remember."

No one picked up the conversation immediately. Porta stared at Promise. Promise glanced to Zack. Zack fiddled with the brad on his envelope.

"Zack tells me you model," Porta said.

"For drawing classes at the university."

"Naturally."

"What?"

"Promise, art saves lives. Don't you realize that this is why you chose modeling? You are dying, and your life can be preserved in art. You might be the next *Mona Lisa,* a *Venus de Milo,* a Madonna —"

"Actually, I'm a singer."

The announcement cut off Porta's rambling like a guillotine.

"She's good," Zack offered. "Her voice."

"A girl with lungs like yours. Singing."

Porta was far more pleased by the strangeness of this truth than Promise thought anyone should be. She expected it to turn heads, of course, but Porta's interest was somehow invasive. The woman clapped her hands together and laughed loudly enough to override the party in the front room. "Then the part about Madonna fits, no?"

Promise's neck felt hot. Zack was watching her, his face unreadable. How much had he said to this woman?

"You were going to tell me why I didn't die when I fell."

"Yes, well, I'm afraid the answer isn't what you think," Porta said, taking a deep breath,

105

beaming. "It's nothing but a happy co-incidence that's really about my gallery. You fell off a cliff and Zack's camera caught you and the reason you didn't get killed was to alert me to the critical importance of this picture. I want the image, see, but Zack says you have a thing about photographs and he made you some silly promise. So here I am."

Zack withdrew an 8 × 10 print and handed it to Promise. She knew little about photography but could see the peculiar beauty of this image in which she fell from the sky.

"It doesn't look real," she said.

"Nor does your survival," Porta said. "That's the magic of it."

"I hardly believe it myself. Who else would? Everyone will say it's fake."

"It only matters to me that one person believes it's not."

Zack handed Promise a slip of paper. A check made out to her from ART(i)FACTS.

"What's this?" she asked.

"Your fee."

"This is much more than we —"

"This picture's worth a lot," Porta said. "You should be fairly compensated."

Promise felt confused over the mysterious subtext of this conversation, and irritated by the possibility that she was being paid

106

off by someone she'd never met for something of no clear value.

"I don't care about the money," she said.

"I didn't think so, but fairness is good for my conscience," said Porta.

"If I'd known this would be the outcome, I never would have done it," Promise said.

"Aren't you glad you did, dear? It's rewarding to be part of something so . . . spectacular." Her words were snakelike hisses.

It was absurd, this awe over a lucky photograph, this oversized payment.

"No." She held the print to her chest and thought about all she had accomplished this week and how important it was for her to protect it. "Look, I have to be so careful about things now, you know? An agent wants to sign me and I've got this big production to do and . . . and . . . no pictures. No pictures but the ones I get done myself, okay? Zack, if you want to do some studio stuff for me we can talk, but —"

"He's no good at that." Zack rolled his eyes. "He's no good at anything but accidental fortune."

Inexplicably, Promise felt as if the cruel words were directed at her. "If this image is as good as you think it is, that's totally untrue." Why didn't he defend himself? What was this woman's deal?

"We're here merely as a courtesy," Porta said, reaching for the photo. Promise didn't resist her taking it. "It's not actually a picture of you, see? We don't need your permission to show off the soles of those mass-produced shoes. But I'm so happy to learn that you're a woman of principle. That's really what I wanted to know, if we had that in common."

"You're a bully, Porta." Zack's voice lacked muscle to do anything about it.

Porta took the manila envelope from his hands as easily as she'd taken the picture back.

"Anyone who's been through what you've been through would be shaken," she said to Promise. "We didn't mean to upset you, but of course it was inevitable." She pressed a business card into Promise's palm. "I hope you'll come by the gallery sometime. I'd like to show you what I do, what it means for people like you." Her magic-fairy eyes were wide and bright. "People like us. When you're ready."

"Who's it for?" Promise asked.

"What? The gallery?"

Promise couldn't hide her irritation. "The picture. Did you have someone in mind?

That one person who'll believe it's real?"

"Wait, wait." Zack held up his hands to defend against her unintended implication that he'd put her life in the balance on purpose. "Porta asked for a painting, and this photo was pure luck. I *never* would have —"

"I didn't mean that, Zack. You didn't do anything wrong."

"It wasn't luck," Porta said. "It was destiny. No, Promise, I don't have buyers in mind, only artists, people interested in enduring themes. I never know who a particular piece is for, or precisely what it will say to them. The art decides who it will save, and not the other way around."

Nothing Porta said made any sense at all. By the way Zack shifted toward the door, Promise believed he shared her unease.

Porta seemed not to notice. "That photograph of you dying will save someone's life. And how it will happen will be as mysterious as how you survived." The woman moved her hand and placed it over Promise's heart. "I do wonder if you might save more than one person."

10

Zack hated himself for allowing his mother to drive him home. He hated himself for living even one day in the same state that she lived in. He hated himself for his pathetic will, and for his failure to protect Promise's one simple request.

Porta's headlights caressed a hillside as the car took a curve on the two-lane road that led back to the university and Zack's dorm.

"What was the point of all that?" Zack said. "You're tired of mocking me and have promoted yourself to innocent bystanders?"

"What on earth do you mean? There was no mocking. On the contrary, I am in awe of that girl."

"If you had any respect for her you'd let this go. Or just let me paint the stupid picture."

"You don't want to paint it."

"Oh, give it up."

Porta laughed. "You say *respect* so nobly, but all you're thinking about is the zipper on your pants."

Zack swore. Tonight, before he did anything else, he'd destroy that picture file.

"Do what you want," Porta said as if she'd read his mind. "It'll be more valuable if there's only one copy."

He stared straight ahead, trying to call up a scenario in which he could retrieve the sole surviving picture from the trunk of the car, where Porta had stowed it before driving off. There, too, was another reason to hate himself: he shouldn't have made the enlargement for her, but the original print had been damaged by his own weak tears. It was his fault that she'd fallen. He'd never meant for Porta to see that one.

"There's a check for you too," she said. "Did you think I'd given all your share to her? Is that why you're so upset?"

He couldn't dream up any heroic strategy for regaining that photo, short of stealing it off the walls of Porta's studio at a later date.

"I think you'll find it a generous payment," she purred.

"It's all about your conscience, isn't it?"

"Oh, not in this case. When it comes to you, I have no doubts about which of us is indebted to the other. It's a parent's duty, you know. But I have no regrets."

"It seems you never do."

"It seems you think that's a character flaw."

Porta reached across him and opened the glove box. The light inside shone on an empty space, save for a slim linen envelope.

"That's it," she said.

Zack returned his eyes to the road, didn't even shift in the seat.

Porta laughed. "Zachary! Really. What's all the show for? You're free to blame me for whatever it is you think you've suffered in this life except for your low standards. *Those* could only have come from your Y chromosome. So don't think for a minute that I believe some little girl with ugly hands has overhauled your personality in a week! For heaven's sake, take the money."

"*You* think she's more than a little girl with ugly hands." It became a conscious thought of Zack's only after he said it.

"It doesn't matter what I think of her."

"You would have rather had a daughter like her than a son like me." He hadn't meant it to come out like a whine.

"Poor baby. I'm obviously not the one to make you stop feeling sorry for yourself."

Disgust came over Zack like a landslide, and for once, it wasn't self-disgust. It was simple, elemental hate, thick and murky. And highly motivating. It was time his mother understood that he wasn't a child anymore.

He took the envelope out of the compartment and clapped the door shut. He knew that the check would pay for the high he needed to do what was on his mind. And when it was done, he'd have enough green left over to get out from under her thumb.

11

The week after Chase first deviated from their route, Chelsea waited for him at the foot of the stairs in their home's entryway, waiting to follow his lead. Very few of the days since the visit to the art gallery had transpired predictably. Chase maintained his rituals, his manner of brushing his teeth and folding his clothes and eating the raw foods their housekeeper Rena had prepared, of falling asleep at 11:01 p.m. and rising at 5:59 a.m. and reciting Scripture aloud while he tied his shoes. Everything else, he abandoned: his attention to tutoring and therapy sessions, his favorite TV show, his meticulous examination of the classified ads. In lieu of these activities, Chase drew.

At his request, Chelsea had agreed to an order for twice as many sheets of black Stonehenge Rising paper and a gross of white charcoal pencils. In addition to this freshly fueled obsession was an uncharacteristic secrecy. Her twin had begun denying her requests to see the pictures and was selective about what he did show off.

"It is not for you," he said so often that Chelsea stopped asking.

Her brother's personal assistant, Wes Bridges, had no explanation for the dramatic change of behavior and had agreed to go walking with them this Saturday. Now Wes stood by the sidelights of the siblings' front door, looking out, watching cars go by.

Chelsea looked at her watch. 2:17. Late. She paced.

"He's a grown man," Wes said in response to her restlessness.

"A grown man with special needs."

"Sometimes he's going to meet those needs in ways we don't understand."

"That doesn't mean I have to like it."

Wes nodded. He'd been a professional companion to Chase for the last three years and was perhaps the most patient, helpful, and unorthodox assistant to come through their doors. Chase had become more independent and easygoing under Wes's influence, so much so that Chelsea was of half a mind to blame Wes for this strange turn of events.

The man was ten years their senior, and subtly paternal toward Chase. Toward

Chelsea, though, he was friendly but not fatherly, which sometimes complicated things. He seemed more than politely curious about her interests: her training for the next marathon, her fund-raising efforts on behalf of autism awareness, her slow climb up the professional ladder at a cutting-edge brokerage firm.

He was graying and wore his beard short and his hair longish but tidy. He blamed his soft middle on his love for hanging out with friends over fried seafood. He'd invited Chelsea to join them on many occasions, and she had almost accepted, finding his unstrained movement through life peaceful. Even attractive. Desirable.

This same quality also held her at arm's length from him. She feared Wes was incapable of understanding her driving need to protect Chase, to provide for him financially and emotionally in the absence of their parents. The burden of life was on her fully, and her decision to bear it had cost her a great deal.

Wes came from a wealthy family that had never known want. The Bridges clan reminded Chelsea of the famous Kennedys, politically active and socially conscious. Wes cared little for the spotlight and seemed most at home in the unglamorous world of volunteerism. He'd been connected to Chase by a support network that provided in-home assistance to people with special needs at a significantly reduced rate. One Chelsea could afford.

Standing in the entryway of her home, Chelsea stared at the back of Wes's head with a confused mix of frustration and longing.

"There's got to be an explanation for this . . . this . . . *upheaval,*" she said.

"I'm sure there is. Chase could probably explain it himself if he wanted to."

"You know he couldn't."

"No, I don't." Wes turned his back to the window and leaned against the closed door, crossing his feet at the ankles. "All I know is he chooses not to."

"Chooses." She shook her head. "I don't think he *chose* autism."

Wes gave her a kind smile, a peace offering. They'd had this argument before. Wes never had said that Chase chose his circumstances, but he believed the world made more sense to Chase than Chase made sense to the world.

"You seem more upset by all this than Chase does," Wes said as Chase descended the stairs.

That was the hard truth.

"A vacation does wonders for stress," Wes said gently.

"No time."

"Just a day off."

"You know my schedule."

"Dinner then. You have to eat. Let me take you down to Rizzoli's. Good food, good people, good music."

Chase arrived on the landing.

"Bring a friend," he said. "Whatever puts you at ease."

"I'll think about it." Whom could she possibly ask to go with her? No one came to mind.

Wes held the door open for Chase, and her brother walked out of the house without stopping to let Chelsea put on his hat, without altering the measured beat of his steps. Chelsea weighed what to do with the baseball cap, then decided to take it with her and locked the door behind them.

"It is Saturday," she heard Chase say to Wes as she jogged to catch up.

"That's right," Wes said.

"You should walk over there," Chase said to him, pointing with his white pencils to the other side of Chelsea.

"I can do that," Wes said, flanking her other side. There was barely room for the three of them abreast, and Chelsea couldn't walk without rubbing Wes's arm.

Except for the close quarters, the trio walked downtown in pretty much the same manner as usual, Chase's eyes closed, chin to the hot summer sky, portfolio under his right arm, pencils erect in his left fist. Today, the air was full of ocean salt. Chelsea lagged slightly as they neared Marlene's Sweet Shop and waited to see what Chase would do.

He strode past it and turned the street corner without opening his eyes.

He proceeded directly to the ART(i)FACTS gallery, entered, and left Wes standing at the front display window, captivated by the sculptured child who seemed to be copycatting Chase's walk. Chelsea paused next to him.

"Huh," Wes said.

"That's not a very articulate critique."

"It reminds me of the piece in your living room," Wes said.

"You mean you're not thinking this is the spitting image of Chase?"

"That too, but the thing in your living room. It's a tree, isn't it?"

"A cedar tree, I guess. But I have to take Dad's word for it. I could never tell my trees apart."

"This one has a similar style, like it could

have been made by the same person."

Chelsea shook her head. "Dad made that tree, so it's impossible."

"Your dad's an artist?"

"My dad was a soldier. But he tinkered with metalwork, no formal training. Most of his sculptures rusted in the yard — all that ocean air. He gave them all away, just said 'here, take it' to anyone who complimented one. I think his art gene got passed on to Chase."

Wes stepped toward the entrance. "Speaking of . . ."

There were a few more patrons in the bright gallery this Saturday afternoon. Nearly all the chairs were occupied. In the far corner opposite the dainty desk, the stylish blond woman Chelsea had noticed during their last visit stood on a ladder that put her near the top of the high ceiling. She wore white gloves and removed a large piece of framed art from the wall, a pale and abstract watercolor that seemed even more washed-out under the bright skylights. She descended the ladder and took the painting into what seemed to be some type of viewing room. A patron followed her in. Through the open door, Chelsea watched her set the work on an easel, then exit the room, leaving client and art alone together.

"Huh," Wes said again.

"You're full of observations today," Chelsea murmured.

"Do the artists know this is how their stuff is displayed?"

"If they're starving, maybe it doesn't matter to them."

"How does she sell anything in a setup like this?"

Chelsea barely made out his words, and yet the woman looked their way as if she could hear their conversation and disapproved. Then, seeming to recognize Chelsea — or at least her too-casual look — the blonde scanned the rest of her guests and stopped when her eyes alighted on Chase.

"Business doesn't seem to be slow," Chelsea said before moving quickly to her brother's side.

Chase was standing in front of a studio-size photograph that had been dry-mounted on a foam board and left unframed. He stood too close to the picture, his nose a mere inch away from the surface.

The photograph was an unremarkable image at first glance, a familiar scene of a storm rolling in over an ocean bluff. A bright orange kite floating in the sky over Chase's head — no, a scarf or blanket maybe — caught her eye.

"Those are pretty colors," she said to Chase. "The orange and the blue."

Chase's grip on his pencils had turned his knuckles pale.

"If you take a step back you might be able to see it better," she suggested. Her brother didn't move, but he was breathing loudly through his nose, which worried her.

"Do you like this one?" Wes asked.

Chase turned around like a drum major in a parade. "No. No, I do not." He walked off toward the back of the gallery. His warm breath had lightly fogged the matte surface of the picture, and Chelsea could see the moisture evaporate. One, two seconds, then gone. The veil rose off an upended pair of sheepskin boots and denim jeans, maybe a man's, maybe a woman's. Someone was falling off the cliff behind earthy clods of dirt suspended in the air, protesting the disaster.

It had to be manipulated, a photograph altered by someone with a morbid sense of beauty. She found it distasteful and understood why Chase had reacted to it. She, too, turned away.

Because there were no unoccupied chairs, or for some other reason Chelsea wasn't privy to, Chase took up a new position with his back to a painting of a beach paradise, a cheap-looking thing that Chelsea thought she might have seen at a discount store. He aligned his pencils on the floor and then stood, hugging his portfolio to his chest, pressing his lips into the zippered edge at the top.

An aging man who had been interested in something on the wall near Chase asked him if he was okay. Chase came out of his trance. Then he opened his case and began to sort through the loose papers, slowly turning through sketches until he stopped at one. The man, watching all this, leaned toward it.

"Now that's a pretty good drawing there," he said. "You do that?"

"I did," Chase said. Chelsea glanced at Wes, who'd also noticed. Chase rarely spoke to strangers. He withdrew the picture from the portfolio.

"That'd be a sequoia tree," the man said. "I got a grove of 'em near my house."

"I know," Chase said.

"Do you, now?"

"You and your brother used to cut them down."

The old man scratched his head. "That we did. Mm-hmm. Have we met before?"

Chase made a sound like a buzz saw behind his teeth.

"Because my kids are always complaining that I tell the same stories and then forget I told 'em." He looked more closely at the drawing. "You're not supposed to cut those trees down anymore, you know. Back when we were doing it, it wasn't illegal like it is now."

Chase closed his binder and placed the image on top.

"Go figure," the man said. "You can't cut down an old tree under any circumstances, but when an old man starts to forget a few things, his kids got all kinds of ideas about what to do with his roots!"

His clear eyes turned shiny, and Chelsea felt an ache in her throat for him. She moved in their direction.

"This is yours." Chase held out the picture to him.

"Well, that's real nice of you, it is, but I got no business taking something this good off your hands. You should talk to that nice lady over there and see if she'll put it up for you here."

"This is yours." Chase jammed the heavy page into the man's chest.

"Chase, maybe he doesn't want it," Chelsea said. "He means well," she said to the man.

"It is *his*." Chase let go of the art and it

flopped toward the floor.

The man groped for it and caught the corner before it hit the ground. "Now I didn't mean to upset anyone." He held the image out in front of him at the distance required by aging eyes. "If you want me to have it that bad, I'll . . ."

The thought went unfinished as the man's sight focused on the details of Chase's picture, which Chelsea couldn't see from where she was standing. But she could see the gentleman's face: the lips closing slowly into a tight muscle of controlled emotion, the tears pooling behind the bifocals at the low end of his nose, the ever-so-slight nod of approval.

Chase reopened his collection and began to turn through them again methodically, paying no attention.

The man cleared his throat and adjusted his glasses. He swallowed but seemed to have trouble looking at Chase, who wouldn't have noticed, as he was not having eye contact with anyone.

"Well, now, that's the nicest thing anyone's done for me in quite some time. Very unexpected. But . . . nice." He studied the drawing again while saying, "Thank you, young man. Maybe you'll let me buy it." He stuck a hand in his pocket as if to fish for a wallet, but Chase left them, stepped over his pencils, and headed toward a seat a woman had just vacated.

Wes nodded to Chelsea, indicating that he'd stay close to Chase.

"He'd never accept your money," Chelsea said as the man stared after her brother. "But it's nice of you to offer."

"An odd fellow, is he?"

"He has his own ways."

"That he does. I like them." He looked back at the drawing. "I like them very much. I hope he understands that."

"He loves trees," Chelsea said. "He can probably tell you anything you want to know about them."

"That so? He's a genius of sorts? What's the word — a savant?"

"No. Not in the way you mean. He's just very focused on what he loves."

"They're misunderstood quite a bit, aren't they? Smart people."

Cheslea smiled at the gentleman. "Do you mind if I ask about the picture? What it is that you like about it?"

He withdrew a handkerchief from his pocket and swiped low over his forehead, discreetly catching the corners of his eyes on the pass.

"That's the question of the day, isn't it?

I'm not sure I know how to say." The man held out the image for Chelsea to see. A giant sequoia towered over a young man who sat at the base of the trunk, reading a book and eating an apple.

It was a pleasant drawing, but straightforward enough that Chelsea couldn't imagine how it had drawn out the old man's emotions. She cast around for something to say. "It's a good tree."

"Except I'm not so sure it's a tree," he murmured, and he pulled the sheet of white charcoal on black paper back to himself.

It was a strange half second in which Chelsea tried to look at the image again, but it was floating away from her eyes, and the movement of the tree's leaves, which she was startled to think she saw, might have been nothing but the bending of the paper.

"Yes, well, thank you," the man said, though Chelsea hadn't spoken. "I'm sure I won't be needing anything else here today."

"Bye then."

The man moved out of the gallery, nodding at the white-gloved woman as he passed. She assumed a pleasant expression for him, but her eyes registered the artwork in his hands.

When the door had closed on the gentleman, she glided across the floor toward

Chelsea.

"I'm going to have to ask you and your friend to leave," said the woman.

Chelsea stood guard over the white pencils that Chase had left on the floor. His ball cap was still wadded in her hand.

"Why?"

"I'm in the business of selling art, and it does me no good if patrons can come here and get it for free."

"Seriously, my brother is no threat to your business."

"That man just walked out of my gallery without buying a thing."

"I'd think that happens a lot, people walking out of a gallery without making a purchase."

"He wasn't empty-handed. Get those pencils off my carpet, please. This isn't a studio."

From the corner of her eye, Chelsea saw that two more people were distracted from this woman's collection by the sheets of black paper they held. How many drawings did Chase plan to hand out today? Wes was talking with him near the front window as he freed another sketch from his folder.

Chelsea risked disturbing the pencils in the hopes of buying her brother a few more minutes to finish here of his own accord.

"Chase has autism, and —"

"Yes, it's the most obvious thing I've seen in anyone."

"— and he loves art."

"And you love him and would defend him to the death, the loyal big sister. That's all very nice, and plain as day. Why else would you be the one I'm standing here talking to? It's certainly not going to convince me to turn this gallery into a show-and-tell art class for the handicapped."

"There's no need to be rude."

"I meet rudeness with rudeness, when necessary. So unless you're here to purchase a piece, it's time for you to go."

"How much do you want for the sculpture in your front window?"

"Oh?" Her demeanor changed like a theater backdrop, an unfurled canvas falling to the stage with a *smack.*

"Maybe I shouldn't bother asking, though. I can't imagine you'd sell anything so precious to a 'handicapped' person."

"But you have no defects, do you?"

Chelsea's speechless lips parted.

"How does that sculpture speak to you?"

"What?"

"What does it say about your life?"

"My life?"

The woman took a slow, yoga-worthy

breath and then exhaled on an equal count. The angles of her narrow face seemed to soften.

"We should begin again. When I'm emotional I forget that not everyone sees the way I do, and you and I haven't had a proper encounter."

"*Improper* isn't exactly the word for it either."

The woman held out a fine-boned hand. "I'm Porta Cerreto, owner."

Chelsea allowed her touch. "Chelsea Ellis."

12

Promise once read the story of a thirty-seven-year-old man with cystic fibrosis who ran the New York City marathon. After finishing the race, he decided that his next goal would be to run it again, faster. And she had figured if this disease could run 26.2 miles, then it most certainly could sing.

Her parents had bought her a karaoke machine for her thirteenth birthday and allowed her to go to an *American Idol* audition when she was sixteen. She made the initial cuts but had to withdraw when pneumonia took her out for a month. When she came home with an application to the university's performing arts program, her mother and father understood that she didn't intend to enroll in classical music studies.

Since then there had been seasons of illness when Promise wondered if they had allowed her to chart this course because they honestly believed in her or because they thought that in the end it wouldn't matter. Today it was easy for Promise to think they really, truly believed, as she did; she could do this. She wanted this.

A few miles from the school, down at the Shore, Promise sat at a wrought-iron table outside the Irish pub where she had just concluded a meeting with her agent. Her agent! The sun warmed her hair and her slim arms. It was too beautiful a day to sit under an umbrella. She sipped a tumbler full of ice and seltzer water.

The agent had filled her head with a vision for the future as intoxicating as any alcohol. They discussed the pros and cons of a theater versus pop career, and of course, he wanted to see her out in the faster, hipper world where he lived. But she was making a fine start of things. Her health would be their unknown quantity. They'd have to be strategic, stay a step ahead of it. Make hay while she could still hold the pitchfork. He instructed her to stay healthy, to put the university production on the Broadway map, and to make more videos with Jenny, create a fan base. Anything more than that, she should call him first. In the meantime, he'd be working his contacts.

He reviewed his representation agreement

with her and referred her to an attorney who would give her confidence in it, and then he left her. She basked in happiness and listened to the melting ice shift in her glass. She grinned at strangers and waved at a few passing students she recognized but didn't know.

They'd soon know her.

In a small park across the street, people were soaking up the end of summer in some kind of arts-and-crafts festival. A live band performed on the open-air stage.

She wanted to jump up on the table and sing something with them, something big and round that matched the size of her anticipation. Instead, she turned her face up to the sky and spread her arms wide and laughed aloud.

Promise held this position for several seconds and then sensed eyes on her. She straightened up.

Porta Cerreto was watching her. The woman stood in front of the store next to the pub, under a yellow awning and a GRAND OPENING sign. This must be the gallery she and Zack had mentioned. Promise had been too giddy to realize it before now.

When Porta saw that Promise noticed her, she turned away. Promise's excitement settled in her stomach like too much candy. She wondered what had happened to that photograph, and whether she'd been wrong to refuse her permission to sell it. She should have asked the agent.

Another woman, tall and athletic-lean, with her long blond hair pulled back into a ponytail, had come out onto the front sidewalk with Porta. Together they stood at the front window and started discussing whatever was behind the glass.

Promise decided to go see what all Porta Cerreto's fuss was about. But first, she'd call Michelle and tell her all about her career coup. She took another drink of the bubbly water and picked up her cell phone, then started stacking her agent's scattered paperwork into a neat pile while she waited for her friend to answer.

Zack had filled the trunk of his car with the few possessions that mattered to him before descending into oblivion. Once he started down that staircase, it would be impossible to know whether his favorite jeans were back at the dorm or on his own body. It was an unnecessary kind of distraction.

In his long career as a half-engaged student he'd made something of an art out of habitual behavior. Without being fully conscious, it was possible for him to stop drinking in time to prevent an unmanageable hangover or to take the exact number of depressants that would lose their edge before his earliest class started. If there were PhDs granted to those who could lose their minds while still putting one foot in front of the other, Zack would have earned his years ago.

And so he was able to spend Friday night passed out in the driver's seat of his car in an unsupervised parking lot, then wake shortly after lunch Saturday and, drowsy with the not-too-hot heat of the enclosed space, take only the number of pills he needed. Courage in a capsule. Just enough to drive his car into the plateglass window of his mother's self-aggrandizement and then drive out of it forever.

Well, he might have to walk if the Honda wasn't as loose as he was.

Zack turned the key in his ignition and drove in an almost straight line out of the lot.

Chelsea could feel the warmth of Porta's small body next to her as they looked in the window. "This gallery exists to match individuals with the art that will save their lives," Porta droned. "The very name reflects my goal — more important than the art is the lifesaving, life-changing truth it reveals to the person with whom it connects. Thus, ART(i)FACTS. The *I* being quite personal to each client."

"How does art save lives, exactly?"

"The answers to that are as unique and numerous as the individuals who walk into this showcase. I like to think I have something here for almost everyone, something that will shake a person out of her comatose manner of living and breathe fresh air to the deepest, most secret parts of her being."

"That's why your collection is so . . . random?"

"It may look unintentional to an untrained eye, but I have a perceptive ability like few others, and I use it to rescue people who want rescuing."

"Well, since I'm blind, it won't surprise you to hear me say this all sounds like a gimmick."

"It's not that you are blind, but that I can see truth more clearly than you. However, those who *want* to see shall, if they look hard enough."

"Ah."

"Yes, consider this observation: you are a capable young woman, fit and healthy, attractive, who has devoted your life to the care of someone you love."

"Generalizations like that are obvious and easy to make."

"You're pursuing a career in finance, are not dating anyone, have taken over the role of head of the family in the absence of a parent — parents? — yes? And you wonder when you wake up in the middle of the night and can't go back to sleep if this is to be the sum total of your life, this taking care of others while there is no one to take care of you."

The white pencils Chelsea had picked up felt slippery in her fist. "Do you always do that?"

"What? Get it right the first time?"

"No, serve up strangers' guts and feed it to them. It's small-minded."

Porta laughed. "On the contrary. Most people can't even name the things that poke their souls until they bleed. Identifying these pains is the first step toward healing. Living instead of dying. How'd I do with you?"

"I don't know you well enough to say."

"I'll intuit from your defensiveness that I hit a bull's-eye. I usually do. It's a gift."

Chelsea's discomfort grew. She believed her unease had little to do with her lack of education in this field or with Porta's eerie insightfulness. She glanced past the backdrop that framed the sculpted boy and saw Wes near Chase, who was taking yet another drawing out of his folder. She would endure this distraction on his behalf for only a few more minutes, then Chase would be finished, even if he thought he wasn't.

Chelsea lowered her voice. "Intuit whatever you want. Call it saving lives, though I think that's bogus. I can't see what any of this has to do with art."

Porta directed her to stand in front of the child, where the shade of the awning protected the glass from reflections.

"Tell me what you see," Porta instructed.

"A nice little boy."

"Beneath the surface of the boy. Tell me what made you take notice of the piece the first time you saw it."

Chelsea shrugged. "He looks like my brother."

"What else?"

"I really don't know. I've never had to articulate this kind of thing before, why I like something. I do or I don't."

"There's always a reason."

"Sure there is, but in my experience, if you start picking at it — especially the things you like — the enjoyment gets lost. Why dismantle a good thing?"

"Well, this isn't an art appreciation class. I

bring art in to find the people who are willing to hear it speak to them. You don't have to overanalyze anything, but it might do you good to listen. Unless it's beyond you."

Chelsea crossed her arms and cocked her head to one side. "Someone said it looks like something my dad might have made."

Porta made a sound in her throat that Chelsea interpreted as *Isn't that interesting?*

"He seems safe, content. Carefree." She recalled feeling that way as a child. "His parents are probably close by somewhere."

It seemed less urgent now that Chelsea go back inside to fetch her brother. The sweet little boy seemed to beg her to stay for just another minute.

"How much did you say you wanted for this?"

"Five thousand."

"Is that the going rate for saving a life these days?"

Porta placed her mouth close to Chelsea's ear. "It's a meager donation from the perspective of those who understand what this is all about, Ms. Ellis. If I'm wasting your time, please, you need only say the word."

Chelsea rolled her eyes. "Is the artist worth five grand?"

"Who knows? The better question is whether *you* are. What's your own life worth to you?"

Chelsea didn't even have to examine that question. Of course she wasn't worth a five-thousand-dollar hunk of metal. But then again, why not? This wasn't some designer dress, some flashy car or exotic vacation.

She wondered if this was the reason the sculpture had caught her off guard the first time she saw it. She had thought she was seeing Chase in the form, but maybe she was — as Porta suggested — seeing a reflection of something deep within herself. Something she needed to know. Something that would answer the questions rattling her heart.

The child no longer looked like her brother, but like herself. This didn't take too much of a mental leap, as they were twins, but Chelsea's decision to see it this way changed everything. She took a step closer to the window.

The child looked like her because it was *her* child, her parents' grandchild, her brother's niece or nephew — a person who might never come into existence because of the limitations placed on her by her present circumstances. Porta *had* seen: the doubts, the loneliness, the loss of family, the sacrifice Chelsea felt at being bound to her brother, though she loved him as much as she loved

140

her own life. The revelation manhandled Chelsea's mind.

In that moment she wanted to possess this sculpture more than she had ever wanted anything. She wanted the tips of her fingers to stroke the textures of the metals, she wanted to memorize every curve and soldered seam, she wanted to decode the meaning of the child's expression. If she could do this, if she could have this, she felt certain she could begin to find her way back to the confidence she once knew before her father was lost. She could possess the peaceful security of her child's existence, of —

Chelsea gasped. Chase was looking at her from around the child's backdrop. Blue eyes directly into hers, for the first time in thirty-one years.

Chase turned away. Chelsea thought she heard Porta swear under her breath. She looked back at the sculpture, confused.

The pull had released her. She turned around.

"I'll think about it," she said to Porta.

The dealer's gaze was strangely neutral, detached. "You're welcome to do that for as long as you need. Or until someone else thinks faster."

Porta turned back into her gallery, her purposeful stride sending a focused message: it was time for Chase to go. Chelsea quickly stepped through the door and around Porta. At least she could *move* faster. She caught Wes's eye.

"Chase," she said. "It's time."

Her brother had collected a few spectators while she was out. Two women and a man looked over his portfolio. Wes observed from a nearby chair, as if there was nothing out of the ordinary about any of this.

"There is one more," Chase said, withdrawing a page.

"If it can wait for another day, it should."

"It cannot."

"We have to go now."

Chase approached Porta.

"It is for you," he said.

Chelsea saw the elegant, bushy tree dotted with flowers and an ax embedded in the trunk. Porta silently refused to take it, though her customers watched.

"Outside are the dogs, those who practice magic arts, the sexually immoral, the murderers, the idolaters and everyone who loves and practices falsehood," he said. Chase let go of the paper and it dropped, heavy and graceless, to the carpet. "I love you."

Porta's mouth flattened into a smug line.

He closed his portfolio, tucked it under his right arm, and reached for the ball cap that Chelsea had been carrying. He placed it on his head himself, took the white pencils from his sister and held them upright, and returned to the photograph on the main wall.

For a moment Chelsea feared he was going to draw on the sheepskin boots of the person who was falling.

"Don't touch that," Porta said.

Instead he kissed the soles, a light brush of lips that barely alighted on the image, then he left the gallery in the same manner he had entered.

Michelle managed to talk for a few minutes before begging out of Promise's call for a nap. It wasn't a good day for her, colored by nausea and weakness and a painful abdominal obstruction that all conspired to bring Promise off her high. Promise made less of the meeting with the agent and let her friend cry. She committed to visiting Michelle that night.

Promise closed her phone on the sadness. Who could explain how their paths had parted after so many years traveling together? It could have been Promise in bed and Michelle in Paris. Or both of them living the dream.

Or both of them dead, as it was for all

people in the history of the world and would be for Promise and Michelle too, one of these days. Unless a cure showed up before their time, their lungs would eventually give out, lacking the strength to exchange oxygen for carbon dioxide, suffocating their blood, their hearts, their brains.

And yet even that might go differently for each of them.

Remember that great singer who had CF? The one with the cool name?

She was really amazing, wasn't she?

She steamrolled all life's obstacles.

Not to mention all those people who said it was impossible!

And then there would be Michelle, vanished, remembered only by loved ones who'd vanish soon afterward, as life required.

This was not worth thinking about.

Promise thought that the screaming from the festival had become unreasonably and suddenly loud. The shrieks . . .

Didn't come from the party. They shot out of a side street, from screeching tires, from loitering men and women jumping as if the pavement was scorching their feet, waving at her and pointing. At what?

A runaway car was on her and all she could do was close her eyes.

She felt metal and wind graze her face, a deadly quick bullet mere inches off target. A shadow passed over her. She smelled burning rubber and suntan lotion.

The wrought-iron table clattered away, crashing into the other furniture. Her chair tipped over and dumped her body out of it, her head hitting concrete, her mind knocked into a state of hyperawareness. A vise clamped down on her elbow and pinned her. She heard a bone crack in her right forearm. Glass and ice shattered.

The pages of her contract fell like snow.

Promise's lips were smacking for air. She couldn't move her arm, which was held to the ground by the bent metal railing that, when erect, had separated her table from the sidewalk and street. Now the rail was pinned by the rear tires of a scrappy blue car that had gone straight into the pub's window. The lower half of her body, unharmed, was under the carriage as if she were a mechanic who'd rolled out to answer someone's question.

The driver's door opened directly over her nose, and Zack stumbled out of the car, tripping over her body, reeking of something mind-bending. He saw Promise and their eyes met, each disbelieving the other. The palms of his hands went to his slick beanie-haired head, and drug-tainted remorse came out of him as a groan.

13

At five fifteen Saturday afternoon Porta received Zack's one phone call, which confirmed what she expected: that he was at the police station in need of some financial aid. She told him she'd be right down, hung up the phone, then made him wait until after the gallery closed at six (and then she had a bite to eat) before bailing him out.

Wisdom never moved too quickly, especially not where recalcitrant children were concerned. She had stood aside for the afternoon's drama, as there was no need for anyone to know her connection to the fool who'd crashed into her neighbor's establishment. Unless she was lucky, the media would unearth it soon enough.

She had been lucky of late, however. Her prayers to the Fates had not gone unheard. They saw her efforts to bless humanity with the gift of life, and her encounter with

Promise would be her reward. When Porta saw the child rise from the sidewalk with only a bloody arm for injury, she knew without needing the jade *Ameretat* to confirm it: Promise was the one.

Of course she would have to confirm it regardless. In the meantime, however, her task would be to earn the child's trust.

The child! As if Promise Dayton were a weakling. Porta would have to learn to think of this one as the goddess she was. The oddity of it was that Promise seemed unaware of her own state.

On her way out of the gallery, Porta locked the door and cast a wary eye on her metallic little boy. Would he have a revised prophecy to offer her now that the gods had given her Promise? She doubted it. Still, she couldn't explain why the demons had colluded to torment her, or with whom. In light of what she'd been learning about her son, it was plain that he had no gumption to pull off such a thing. She wished he had, because this unanswered question dogged her.

A week had passed since the statue first threatened her. It was difficult to ignore this.

Porta made a discreet stop at the hospital to assure herself that Promise hadn't sustained any serious injuries, then meandered to the police station to fetch her son. She made Zack return with her to the gallery. Having no car and a monstrous headache, it was inevitable that he let her have her way. Porta did this because her sixth sense told her that the girl, who had an obvious soft spot for the screwup, would come looking for Zack.

He refused to enter the gallery's private room. He sank into her desk chair and lowered his head between his knees.

"You've found the one," Porta said.

"What *one?*"

"Stupid boy. Your mind is a haze. The one I've been looking for. The one who is immortal."

Zack lifted his head and guffawed. "It was an accident. Don't read anything into it."

"There are no accidents, Zack. You know that."

"Don't tell me what to think, old crone."

"You show your mother more respect!"

Zack dropped his eyes.

"We've spent our lives looking for a girl like Promise."

"You," Zack spat. *"Your* life."

"That child has connections to the gods. She holds the keys and doesn't even know it. She wouldn't know what to do with them if she *did* know it."

"She's just a girl prone to accidents."

"That's not what you told me the first time you laid eyes on her."

Zack pouted. "I didn't know her then."

Porta walked in a slow circle around her boy, born so late to her that she believed even then he would play an important role in her ultimate achievements. He would be like the boy Isaac born to the old woman Sarah when she was past ninety — a hope, a goal. She laid a hand on his shoulder, wooing, always. This stubborn child needed so much of that even in adulthood.

"When are you going to learn to trust your own gifts?" she asked softly. "When are you going to understand that I'm not the only one in this family who can see?"

"Promise is dying of a terminal disease. She's a living waste. That's all I see."

"That's guilt speaking, son. You've done nothing wrong by her."

"Nothing right either."

"I see. You're not feeling guilt. It's regret. You like her."

"You don't know the first thing that I feel."

"You love her, then. Do you remember how you described her to me last spring when she modeled for your class the first time?"

Zack crossed his arms. His eyelids were

heavy drapes over his thoughts.

"You called her the most beautiful creature alive. Too beautiful to be limited by pencils and paper that could never do her justice. You should try your hand at poetry."

He lifted his eyes just enough to glare at her.

"What you saw in that woman was not only beauty, Zack, but life. I told you this when we were at her home, didn't I? 'You were right about her,' I said. Won't you accept that?"

"It doesn't matter."

"Why not?"

"Because you're going to outlive her."

"She has the Fates' favor. Perhaps both of us will live forever." She glanced at him. "All three of us maybe."

"Fat chance of that."

Porta fingered the bracelet on her left wrist. The braid of combed lamb's wool, died black, had never been touched by a pair of scissors. She wore this bracelet in defiance of Atropos, the Fate who cut the threads of life at will and often unfairly. The goddess had severed Porta's mother from the world a few hours after Porta was born. Aware of her condition and infuriated by the injustice, the woman had leveled a spitting insult at the Fate by naming her child

Porta, a shortened reversal of *Atropos.*

The event had forever informed Porta's spiritual journey.

"We have to show Promise the truth about her gift," Porta said.

"What gift are we talking about now?"

"She is immortal."

"No, she's not!"

Porta raised her eyebrows. "Unless she knows, she can't reach her full potential. She must know her own power or the Fates might try to steal it from her."

Zack shook his head. "You're one of the crazies."

Porta crossed her arms and leaned down to his eye level. Her black enameled bangles rattled.

"I'm clearer headed than you are, Zack, today and every day. You've fouled up your spiritual energy. I have years of wisdom on you, and you'd better be grateful for it, because today the crone has eyes to see that you've entered a period of soul searching and transformation. It doesn't have to end in death. The wheel of life spins in you, as it does in all of us."

Zack's laugh was bitter. "Yeah. That's why I tried to drive my car into your store. Funny how that doesn't concern you at all."

"She was *there.*" Porta took her son's face

in her fading hands. "The Fates took you to her though you had other plans."

"Shut up. My head is killing me."

Porta turned her back on her son. She could be patient. He was smarting with the shame of failing to kill himself. It was a curse of her heritage, this preoccupation with death. But Zack would be okay. His attraction to the girl whom death could not touch made Porta confident of this. He would live. He would live long and well, and perhaps forever.

It was the greatest wish a mother could have for her child, however unworthy he may be.

Porta said, "It's time I had myself a daughter."

Zack lifted his eyes to her now. Toxins lingering in his blood made them seem wider and whiter than normal. But she knew they couldn't prevent him from understanding her.

"It's your job to see to it that she becomes one of our family," Porta said, "one of us. And in time you'll come to see that there is no other possible explanation for why she continues to live."

"Shut up," he said. "Just shut up."

14

Chase spent the afternoon drawing boots instead of trees. The boots were falling off a cliff. The boots were peeking at him from under the car that had crashed outside the stinky gallery. The boots were walking and dancing and resting and running. They were the same boots, sheepskin coverings with rounded toes and furrowed treads and tufts of wool peeking over the tops. Dozens of pairs of boots jumped from black page to black page scattered across his floor.

When he had tried to touch the boots on the sidewalk today, Chelsea had yanked on his arm. The force hurt him. She turned him away, and Wes agreed they should go because crowds got in the way of people who could really help.

Chase hoped the woman whose feet went into those boots was not dead. He felt that if she was dead he would have to stop drawing — not just boots or trees but everything

— and the possibility of this caused his hands to quake like aspen leaves in wind. His lines were wobbly.

He knew the boots belonged to a woman without knowing how he knew, until the vision of the Great Basin bristlecone showed up in the bedroom that was his studio, as it had been doing for several days now. Its roots glided over the sheets of paper and nudged the swift images that Chase had created with the square end of a pastel stick.

Chase's hands stopped shaking.

"Listen," the bristlecone whispered. "I tell you a mystery: the perishable must clothe itself with the imperishable, and the mortal with immortality."

"First Corinthians 15," Chase said. "Those boots will not last forever."

"Nor will your pictures, or her songs," said the tree, who had the voice of his father and of the wind at the same time. "Nor will fame or accomplishment or the memory of anyone who walks the earth."

"Is she dead?"

"No one was made to die."

"For as in Adam all die, so in Christ all will be made alive," Chase said. "Verse twenty-two."

"Yes."

"But is she *dead?*"

"Not yet."

Chase looked at all the boots and saw dirt from a grave digger's shovel heaped over them, and the sight of it made his eyes burn. "I don't want her to die."

"Tonight, I'll show you her tree."

With his left arm Chase swept his desk clear of finished and half-finished drawings, and with his right he pulled a fresh sheet of black paper out of its designated drawer. He picked up the white pencil that would give him the soft lines of the tree, the general shape of it.

"Which tree is hers?"

"The tree of life."

"Arborvitae. Of the family *Cupressacaea* and the genus *Thuja.*"

"Not exactly."

"Which species?"

"It's not what you think."

Chase waited, and when the image filled the center of his mind, his room was emptied of the bristlecone. He swiftly copied the vision to the page and found he needed a pencil with a firmer tip to draw the required number of ultrafine lines. He exchanged the softer charcoal pencil for the white-tinted graphite.

The tree rose from a short thick trunk and split, then split again and again into hundreds of slender twigs. Its body was wide and sat low to the ground, reminding him of an oak, but this plant was dense with branches that bore no leaves.

A tree of life, with no leaves.

Also strange were the structures that arched over the tree like the St. Louis Gateway Arch, multiplied. Chase used chalk sticks and swept these onto the page last. He had seen something like this once in a travel book about Japan, in one of its public parks.

He thought it beautiful but strange, then and now.

Maybe the woman longed to go to Japan.

What was her name?

What was the name of this tree?

Chase rose from his desk and left the room and moved swiftly downstairs into the den where he and Wes studied together when rain made them go indoors. He walked to the bookcases and began removing books, looking for an image that would identify this tree.

His sister was standing at the front window, looking out.

"You looking for something?" Chelsea's words seemed far away.

"I need to find a tree." He started with the index of More and White's *Illustrated*

Encyclopedia of Trees, running his finger through the *T*s to *Thuja,* the scientific genus for arborvitae.

"I was thinking of Dad," she said.

"Dad is a Great Basin bristlecone pine." Chase memorized the page numbers and started turning to them. "*Pinus longaeva.* An evergreen of the *Pinaceae* family, one of the oldest trees on earth."

"Is that your way of saying you think he's still alive?"

"No. I would just say, 'I think he is still alive' because that is the way I always say it. I want to find a tree."

Chelsea bent over him where he crouched on the floor in the posture of a wise man pondering truth. "Which one?"

"I do not know yet."

"Good luck then." Chelsea touched him on the shoulder and then let him look in peace.

Chase did not eat supper with her that night. He stayed in the study, paging through his favorite botany books until after nine, when he returned upstairs.

Chelsea rinsed her dishes, then followed him to the upper level of their townhome. Chase had taken over the upstairs area of the house after their father was abducted in

Iraq while on a patrol chasing Saddam Hussein. Chase's bedroom and bathroom became an art studio, and he began sleeping in their father's room. He dusted it daily and washed the linens weekly. Everything else — the arrangement of the furniture, the pressed clothes hanging in the closet, the baseball caps dangling from the bedposts, the dress shoes under the box springs — remained as it had been the day their father was deployed. Nothing added, nothing taken away, ready for when their father returned.

Until today, Chelsea had surrendered her heart to the likelihood that their father had been murdered. She had suggested on more than one occasion that he would likely never return, but her brother either didn't understand this abstract idea or chose to reject it. Wes had urged her long ago to abandon the topic. For Chase, to say that his father was dead and not merely away on duty was no different from calling his father a liar. The man had said he'd see them again. So it would be.

She knocked on the door of Chase's studio.

"Enter," Chase said.

His room was slightly more chaotic than the last time she'd been in it. She had been surprised by this when the mess of artistic expression developed in Chase's teens. It seemed to run contrary to the orderly systems and habitual behaviors that most persons with autism developed. Wes assured her that this mess was indeed systematic, even if its order was only evident to Chase. Chelsea took his word for it.

There was a path of carpet from the door to the desk, and this avenue cut through a forest of black pages bearing images of boots. The boots he'd kissed in the photo at Porta's studio. These were spread across the floor, as there was no more wall space available for tacking them up. Trees of every species imaginable — for all she knew, some might have been wholly imagined — filled the room with more white than black.

Chase was seated at his desk, bent over a new page. His window was wide open and afforded him a view of the front walkway and of the lone chokecherry tree that the city had planted in the sidewalk. Its clusters of white blossoms had long faded. A streetlight shone down through the slim branches and oval leaves. Chase glanced up at the scene, then back at the book.

"Are you drawing the tree?"

"Which tree?" he asked.

"The chokecherry outside."

"No."

Chelsea knew he wouldn't elaborate.

"May I see what you're working on?"

"It is not for you."

"I know. I promise not to . . . intrude."

Chase continued to draw but turned his shoulders away from the image just enough for her to peek. It was a thick, leafless tree loaded with slim branches that must have taken him hours to put down. She took it to be a winter scene. Though not blooming, the tree flourished under a series of arches.

"What are those arches?"

"A Japanese garden."

"It's beautiful," she said. "Who's this one for?"

"I have a book for you, but that will be later." He worked swiftly, filling in more branches with tiny buds, and again looked outside.

"Are you waiting for someone?" she asked.

"Who?"

"You keep looking out the window."

"Yes."

"Why do you keep looking out the window?"

"The wind smells good."

Chelsea leaned against her brother's desk. There was a clear plastic cup holding an inch of water at his left, a small cardboard box of cornstarch, and a neat row of pencils. She watched him work. Though she knew little about the technical side of his passion, she admired the difficulty of this particular method. To draw white on black was to draw in a manner contrary to instinct and tradition. It was to draw backward, in a way, to create images with light rather than with shadow.

"So, you're making a book for me?"

"I am."

"What's it about?"

"You."

"Must be a short book."

Chase's eyebrows drew together as he continued working.

"I liked it when you looked at me today," she said.

"Thank you."

"I wish you would do that more often."

"I hope I will not have reason to," he said.

His tone wounded her. Why was the eye contact that she craved so repulsive to him? "What do you mean?"

"You should not be with Porta Cerreto."

"Oh, she's a little odd, but probably harmless."

"No, not harmless. She stinks."

Chelsea relented. There were worse criteria for assessing a person. "If you say so."

"It has nothing to do with what I say."

"I meant I'll trust your judgment of her."

"By oppression and judgment he was taken away."

After thirty-one years, communication with Chase had not become any less complicated. He was communicative and articulate, intelligent even, high-functioning by many diagnostic standards, but he often made connections that were difficult for Chelsea to follow. She had learned to navigate his emotional isolation and his tendency to interpret statements literally. Still, she never stopped hoping that somehow, someday, a door might open between them that allowed them both easier access to each other. His eye contact with her today was a creaking door. Now it boomed shut.

"You should stay away from that woman," Chase said.

"So long as you don't need to go back to the gallery, I'll avoid her."

"I am finished there."

This announcement surprised Chelsea. "Are you going to keep giving away your drawings?"

"If Dad keeps asking me to."

Chelsea drew a calming breath.

"Does this mean you aren't going to look

at me eye to eye again?"

The pencil Chase held, which appeared not to have any kind of wood casing on it, was dull. He dipped the tip in the cup of water and applied it to one of the arches. The white was transformed from wax into light.

She listened to the tool stroke the paper's surface.

"I love you," Chase said to her.

"I know you do, Chase. It's okay."

A car pulled to the curb on the opposite side of the street. Chase looked, and his pencil stilled.

"When did Dad tell you to give away your pictures?" Chelsea asked, turning her back on the window. She heard the car door close. Light footsteps crossed the road.

Chase didn't answer, his eyes fixed on the scene outside. Chelsea turned back around and followed his gaze. A young woman with sleek dark hair was coming up their walk. Her right wrist was in a cast. Sheepskin boots were on her feet, a ridiculous but common summer fashion statement among the female students in this college town. Chelsea immediately thought of Porta's photo.

"Chase —"

He was running down the stairs.

15

Late Saturday evening, with her arm casted between her fingertips and her elbow, Promise freed herself from the probing questions of a reporter for the university's student website. The peppy woman had hounded her from the moment the ER discharged Promise.

There were rumors going around that this was Promise's second near-death experience in a matter of days. Was it true? How did the rush of death compare to her daily struggle against cystic fibrosis? Had she and Zack been dating and recently broken up? Did Zack target her, or was it a freak accident? Had she seen Zack's photos of her posted online? What was the story behind those?

Promise's habit of being polite even to annoying people wore thin. She hardly knew Zack, which was exactly what she'd told police officers, who hadn't connected her to the cliff-diving incident yet. She claimed she had nothing to say *about* Zack, though the longer the interview went on, the more Promise wanted to say *to* him. Oddly, the sophomore journalist seemed happy to fill the silence. Promise started asking questions about Zack. Where did he live? What year was he? What was his major? The chatterbox was a fountain of information.

After a half hour of this, Promise managed to repeat her answers enough times that the student ran out of ways to reinvent her questions. They parted in the hospital parking lot.

The encounter with Zack's runaway Honda had bruised her ribs and broken her arm but preserved the good health of her lungs. Promise took deep breaths and felt a wonderful surge of energy. Only a week ago, this was the time of day when she would have been exhausted, wanting to dive into bed and hook herself up to an oxygen tank.

While she drove her Roadster through the campus in search of Zack's dorm, Promise let her mind search for theories that might explain the correlation between these freak accidents and her energized state. She found none.

But thanks to the reporter's loose tongue, she did find the room where Zack had been living through the summer and his room-mate, James. James leaned against the door frame and said Promise was prettier than her pictures and should have dinner with him. Right now. Promise played coy and asked what he meant by prettier than her pictures. He turned to his computer and booted up a social media site, then showed her the photos Zack had posted in an album titled "Broken Promises."

The ten images, all taken of her on the cliff before the rail broke, were strangely romantic and made her blush. She'd never seen herself looking so . . . beautiful. In these pictures, not even she could see the clubbed fingertips that had always embar-rassed her, the skinny legs that were more bone than flesh, or the back that hunched over every cough. The features made her an interesting model, she'd been told, though she quickly learned that students tended either to ignore or exaggerate these traits.

These cropped frames, though, were as honest as the image of her toppling from the heights. That photo was not here.

She stared at the screen for about a minute, then said she had plans for dinner with Zack. The roommate scoffed. "Enjoy the prison food," he said.

"Prison food?"

"Zack's in jail, pretty girl. From what I gather, he doesn't plan to move back in with me either."

"What do you mean?"

With the exaggerated gestures of a game-show model, James threw open the doors of a nearly empty closet, showed off the drawers of a nearly empty desk, and passed a trash can full of textbooks under her eyes.

Promise thanked him and left.

At the police department, she learned that Zack Eddy had been released on bail, and Porta Cerreto posted it. The discovery messed up Promise's thoughts. She had originally thought Zack had been aiming his car at Porta's gallery. There was tension between them the night of their visit, and she sensed he was as upset as she was about Porta's decision to sell the photograph.

He couldn't have been aiming at Promise, she thought. How could he have known she was at the pub? But if he was after Porta, why would the woman be posting his bail instead of hiring the city's best prosecutor?

Promise would find Zack and ask him herself.

Unreasonably energetic and hungry, she stopped at The Earth's Grocer for a micro-wave dinner whose ingredients wouldn't wreck her fragile digestive tract, then returned to her apartment. While the meal cooked, she rifled through a catchall basket on her kitchen counter for the business card Porta had given to her. She powered up her laptop and conducted a quick Internet search of Porta Cerreto that provided Promise with an address different from the gallery's, possibly a home. She found nothing useful about Zack Eddy besides the site James had already shown her.

Though she was breathing well, abiding fear of this roller coaster's downside commanded Promise to stick to her health routine. In her therapy room, she donned her chest-therapy vest and turned on the compression machine. This procedure was usually painless, but tonight she groaned when she felt the bruising on her ribs. The pain occupied her mind for nearly an hour.

When the agony was over, she programmed her GPS with both addresses and followed the instructions to the one she believed to be Porta Cerreto's home. If the woman was familiar enough with Zack to post his bail, it wasn't out of the question that she would send him to her home to dry out, away from the distractions of campus.

Or maybe he really had intended to leave. Maybe he was gone.

Norris Lane, downtown, was in an old district of houses that had the quaint look of a neighborhood stuck in the recent past. It was clean but outdated, quiet with the sounds of children who had grown and left their nests. The trees were large and full, crowding the streetlights.

Promise approached number 2310 with reservation. It was not the kind of place she would have imagined for Porta, who had been so quick to criticize Promise's own apartment. And yet how many Porta Cerretos could there possibly be in this town?

There was a light on upstairs, and the figure of a man in the window. He moved away when she saw him. She passed through the gate between the house and the public sidewalk, moved up the short path between a very small yard that was more garden than lawn, and rang the doorbell.

The man who answered the door was tall and slender with fine blond hair that fell forward around his face.

"Hi. I'm looking for Zack Eddy?"

He stared at her but didn't say anything. Maybe he couldn't hear?

She faced him directly so he could read her lips, if that was the issue.

"Is Zack Eddy here?" She enunciated without raising her voice.

A woman who looked surprisingly like the man — same hair color, same tall and slender build — took hold of the door and opened it wide enough for both of them. She wore runner's pants and ankle socks and a matching zip-front jacket. Her blond hair was pulled back in a tidy ponytail. Promise could see into the entryway now and noticed well-worn running shoes sitting in the hall by a bench.

She'd seen this woman before but couldn't remember where.

The man crossed his arms across his chest and stepped back. He started to pace at the foot of the stairs, one hand lifted to stroke his chin.

"Sorry, but maybe you have the wrong house," the woman said.

"Is this Porta Cerreto's home?"

"Porta? The woman who runs the gallery down the street?"

"Down the street?" Promise glanced at it.

"It's half a mile away. Right around the corner."

"You know her?" Promise asked.

"We've met."

"That's strange. I looked it up — 2310 Norris." She stepped back on the porch to see the house number. "The GPS brought me right here."

"I'm afraid you're on Morris Street. One letter off. It's an easy mistake to make with those little keypads."

Promise felt supremely annoyed with herself. "That sounds like the kind of mistake I would make. Sorry to have bothered you."

"She must come inside," said the man.

The woman glanced at him, then smiled and extended her hand to Promise. "I'm Chelsea Ellis. My brother seems to have been expecting you. Would you like to come in?"

"Oh. Well. That's nice of you, but I should go. I really need to find someone."

"You should not go," the man said. "Not yet. Wait. I have something that is yours."

Promise hesitated and tipped her head slightly to see him. "Do I know you?"

He was jogging up the stairs. "I have loved you with an everlasting love. I have drawn you with loving-kindness. I will . . ." The rest of the words were lost in the distance.

Chelsea didn't seem to think he was acting strange. She said, "He draws. Would you mind if he gave you one of his pictures?"

Waiting would be easier than protesting.

A breeze drifted down the street like a broom, pushing off the heat of the day. Awkwardness drifted in and out of the open door between the women.

Promise looked at Chelsea's feet, then at the shoes in the hall. "You like to run?" she said.

"Yeah. Training for a marathon in October. You?"

"No endurance for it. Walking is the most vigorous exercise I do." She showed Chelsea her sheepskin boots, the pair she wore without socks year round. No matter the state of Promise's health, having warm feet encased in softness improved her outlook on life.

Chelsea's eyes lingered on the footwear, then moved to Promise's cast. She didn't speak.

"What's your brother's name?" Promise asked.

"Chase."

Promise chuckled. "That's a hoot. Does he help you train?"

The woman blinked and then seemed to make the connection. "Uh, no."

Promise cleared her throat. "That's his real name."

"Yeah."

"I'm so embarrassed."

"Don't be." Chelsea smiled at her.

"I have to be! I'm sorry. This is a little strange."

"I'm sure it's about to get stranger. You sure you don't want to come in?"

Promise shook her head and looked at her watch. "Really, I need to get going." The night air tasted sweet.

She heard the sound of Chase's feet hitting the stairs.

"Does he do this a lot?" Promise asked at a volume that she hoped he couldn't hear.

"Depends on what you mean by *this.*" Chelsea stepped back to make room for Chase in the doorway. He held out a large sheet of black paper with jagged edges at the top.

"This is your tree." He pushed the paper into her hands.

She accepted it, wondering at his choice of words. It bore a simple but stunning picture, a huge leafless tree growing under a series of arches. The scene was lit from the back, creating an eerie but pleasing effect. She thought the drawing had required considerable skill.

"Blessed are those who wash their robes, that they may have the right to the tree of life," he said.

She didn't know the best way to be polite. "You're quoting something."

"The Bible," Chelsea explained. "Which book, Chase?"

"The Revelation of Jesus Christ to Saint John."

"He's memorized it in four translations."

"The Revelation?"

"The whole Bible. He especially likes the passages about trees."

A gentle breath of wind blew down the street again, soothing. In Promise's eyes, the branches seemed to sway safely under the protective shelter. She'd never read the Bible. It had simply never occurred to her as something she ought to do.

"It is a tree of life," he said.

"Oh."

"I am sorry that I do not know which species."

"That's okay."

Chase was rubbing his chin and gazing at the picture. He was handsome in a simple, boyish kind of way. His eyebrows were set wide, and there were lines at the corners of his eyes as if he squinted a lot. He was a kind and innocent soul, she thought — simple, incapable of being mean. She wondered what was wrong with him.

"This is a really nice gift. Thank you."

"It is a promise," he said.

"My name is Promise," she said gently. "Promise Dayton. I think I forgot to introduce myself."

"It is very good that you are not dead yet."

She supposed that was a *very* good thing, both for her and for the average person. "Do you ever take classes at the university?" Then she hated that she had asked, because obviously he had some kind of intellectual disability. "You're good enough to teach, actually. Drawing, I mean. I'm over at the fine arts hall sometimes. In class. For the students."

Chase didn't answer.

Chelsea eventually said, "That must be interesting work."

"I should go now."

"Please come back," Chase said. Under the porch light Chase's irises, the soft blue color of juniper berries, stared directly at Promise and made her uncomfortable. "I love you."

Embarrassment escaped Promise in a laugh, then shame for her meanness filled her. "Uh, well . . ." She took a step back and looked at Chelsea for escape. The woman's eyes shifted between Chase and Promise, and her face was crestfallen, which only confused Promise further. "Thank you again," she said.

The night seemed oddly cold. Promise no longer wanted to find Zack. She couldn't remember why it was so important she talk to him. The breeze rattled the thick paper in her hands as she returned to the car.

She dropped it into the passenger seat as yet another disturbance prodded her heart. She had forgotten to visit Michelle.

16

On the weekend nights the downtown buses ran late. Against Porta's protests, Zack left the gallery on foot, then hopped on a bus that dropped him off within a quarter mile of Promise's apartment complex.

The oleander bushes that lined her building were taller than a man and more poisonous, but less deadly. This is what Zack thought as he sat on the stoop of her illuminated front porch. He waited for her to come home, waited for his drug-induced haze to finally pass. Who planted such dangerous flowers where children played?

Why was he here? To apologize? To explore his mother's claims about Promise?

No.

Yes.

It didn't matter. He didn't care. Zack leaned his head back against the screen door. Minutes passed.

When Promise appeared on the short

walkway that led from the carports, Zack straightened. This was the first time he had seen her since paramedics and police had separated them for the second time. A cast wrapped her right forearm, a summer bag hung over her shoulder, a large sheet of black paper dangled from her good hand.

She was truly the most beautiful woman in Zack's world, perfectly proportioned and fair-skinned, delicate, happy, confident.

When he saw her, he understood why he had come. It was his own selfishness that had almost killed her this afternoon, his subconscious death wish, and it was some kind of injustice that he'd been spared. He needed her to put him out of his misery. She had the power to be his angel of death, and he hoped for a killing.

Please, hate me the way I deserve. I'll believe anything you say. Punish me.

Zack stood in front of the porch light, and the shadow of his body leaned toward her.

"Promise?"

She startled and came to a halt, even took one step backward before fumbling with her bag. For keys, he thought. Or a weapon. A weapon would be ideal. Her black paper slipped out of her fingers. He bent to pick it up. She didn't recognize him until he stood erect again.

Her face was in the light and his was in shadow. The divine and the devil. She placed her hand over her heart.

"Zack. I was looking for you."

She was?

"But I didn't think I'd see you here," she said.

"I was waiting for you."

Her eyes dropped to his hands. He thought she wouldn't have been surprised if he were holding a gun or a knife or a plastic bag. He held on to her paper but stepped aside so as not to block the path to her door. She didn't advance.

"Should I call 9-1-1 first?" she asked. The smile on her face matched the one in her tone. "Get them here before anything weird happens?"

"Why do you do that?" he asked.

"Do what?"

"Aren't you angry with me?"

"I'm a little . . . scared of you, I think. I joke when . . . never mind. No, I'm not angry."

"Why not?"

She shrugged.

"You should be."

"Why?"

"I might kill you."

"Well, you haven't succeeded yet." Her

laugh was light, a sandpiper running on water. Her gentleness broke him open. That and his own disappointment that she would not treat him the way he deserved. He loved her for it. And hated her.

Promise's smile faltered.

"I didn't know you'd be there," he blubbered. "You weren't supposed to . . ."

She fiddled with the purse strap on her shoulder and tucked her lips between her teeth but allowed his silence. He couldn't look at her.

"You are the most beautiful woman ever made. You don't deserve to be hurt. I'd never hurt you on purpose."

"I know you wouldn't," she said.

She was making him angry. She was pitying him, seeing his desperation and intoxication. "I wish you'd be ticked off or something."

"If anyone else had been hurt, I'd be catclawing your face right now. That was an incredibly stupid thing you did."

His anger retreated.

"You should go home and get a good night's sleep," she said, all undeserved kindness. "Sleep it off, you know."

"It's not what you think. I'm not . . ." He sniffed. "It's better now."

"When was the last time you ate?"

His eyes ached and leaked. He used his T-shirt for a blotter. Food? He couldn't remember.

She found her keys in the bag and marched past him.

"Come on. I'll make you something."

"I can't."

"It's no trouble. What do you like?"

"I'm not hungry."

She paused at the stoop, then returned and faced off with him. "Would it help if I was a little mad? I could manage that. You broke your word to me."

It took him a second to get what she meant. "Uh, yeah. About those pictures —"

"Why did you do it? What I asked you for was so simple."

"I couldn't help it."

She took a long breath.

"I wanted everyone to see you the way I see you," he said.

"Are you aware of how creepy that sounds?"

"I can't help it," he said.

"Your brain is a mess of crossed wires."

He nodded and wiped his face with his shirt again.

"You need some food."

Zack opened his mouth to object.

"No excuses. You owe me. Let me feed you."

Something about this demand didn't make sense to him. But those crossed wires . . .

"Come on," she said again. In three seconds she had her key in the door and was turning it. She held the screen open for him. "Going once."

Zack hesitated. He had wanted her to slip a noose around his neck. He didn't know what to do with a life preserver. He didn't trust himself not to turn it against her.

"Going twice."

"Someone told me you're vegetarian," he said, reaching for the door.

"Don't worry. I know how to order a pizza."

There was no time to sleep.

Chase brushed his teeth for two minutes, thirty seconds each top and bottom, front and back. He dressed for bed and pulled back the coverlet, then the blanket, then the sheet. It was 11:01 p.m. His mind, not a clock, told him this. He removed his slippers and stared at the pillows. The chain dangling from the ceiling fan kept time against its globe. He climbed into bed, and the sense of urgency diminished slightly. He closed his eyes.

His ears listened for the sound of rattling in the other room. It did not come.

Tink. Tink. Tink.

Though his eyes were closed, he saw Promise standing in front of him as she had stood on the steps of his home.

I love you.

I love you.

I love you.

He said this to her again and again, because it was true, and ever since it had become true — which was the moment he saw the image of her falling off a cliff — he had been able to think of little else. He knew that it was Promise in that photo, dying in an art gallery, dying under the wheels of that runaway car, as sure as he knew that the fourth tin from the right on the third shelf down at the left side of his window held two white Alphacolor pastel sticks.

He knew. Promise Dayton was his longing. She was his tree of life, the woman he was made to love unlike the way he loved any other person, the Promise he was destined to keep. And he had very little time in which to do it.

She was dying even now.

It bothered him a little that he could not say exactly how much time he had. Precision would make his work easier. He would have hoped for weeks or months. Now, with her sweet face at the front of his mind, real and fragile and very, very perishable, he considered that he had only days. Or hours.

Chelsea would not understand.

Chase opened his eyes. He sat up, then peeled back the layers of coverings one at a time and pivoted in the bed, dropping his feet into the slippers beneath the box springs.

In his studio across the hall, he heard the soup can fall over.

17

Zack awoke on a brown leather sofa under a window that faced east. A finger of sunlight reached through a curtain that hadn't been fully drawn and poked him in the eyes. He yanked the thin blanket up over his head. This exposed his socked feet, which annoyed him into full consciousness. He sat up to get out of the sun. In his dorm, black matte board in the windows protected his sleep no matter the time of day.

A greasy plate bearing a half-eaten slice of pizza stared at him from the coffee table. He was still at Promise's apartment.

She hadn't made him leave?

Oh yeah. She had declared him unfit for driving and demanded he hand over his keys. When she learned he didn't have a car with him — and might soon not have a license — she refused to take him home.

As he didn't have a home to return to at present, he gave in.

Zack stood, then sank back to the sofa cushions. His head hurt.

Big deal. Life hurt. He got up again, saw his skateboard shoes sitting near the front door, and slipped into them. He smelled his own stink on his T-shirt. He needed a shower.

"Hey there, sleeping beauty." Promise greeted him as she emerged from the hallway and went into the kitchen, carrying a plastic basket full of medicine bottles. She set them on the counter and withdrew a box of saltines and a cup from two different cupboards. Zack pressed down on his hair with the palms of his hands while she filled the cup with water and pulled the cracker wrapper open at the top.

"You been up long?" he finally said.

"Couple hours."

"What time is it?"

"Almost ten."

"The crack of dawn."

She laughed at that, and saltine crumbs fell from her lips onto the front of her T-shirt. "Aren't I lovely?" she said, brushing them off.

She was, of course. To have something to do besides stare at her, he reached for the blanket and began to fold it.

"You better now?" She tossed some pills

into her mouth and threw them back easily.

"Depends what *better* means."

"Want a soda?"

"Got any vodka?"

She leveled a maternal glare at him. "No."

The folded blanket looked more like a big wad of gum. He put it on the sofa and went to the kitchen counter, slid out a bar stool, and sat. She handed him a white cracker. He put the whole thing in his mouth. She set the full sleeve within his reach and then retrieved two glass bottles of soda out of the fridge.

"James told me you were dropping out of school," she said.

"Maybe."

"Why now? I don't know what else you're taking, but the life-drawing final is a week from tomorrow. Just a few more classes. You're so close to the end."

He shrugged.

"I'm modeling for it. You should come. Finish. Feel accomplished."

That wasn't the feeling Zack was going for. "That's a lot of medicine," he said, looking at her stash.

"You can't have any. Antibiotics and enzyme supplements wouldn't give you the kind of buzz you're used to anyway."

Zack laughed for the first time in ages. "Okay."

"I know when a guy's fishing."

"I'm not fishing! I've got plenty of my own stuff."

"You should get rid of it."

He stuck another cracker in his mouth to avoid answering. No go. She waited for him to finish. Most girls he knew would have filled the silence. But then, maybe he didn't know as many girls as he thought he did.

"Why do you have 'plenty of stuff'?" she asked after he swallowed.

"We all do what we have to."

"That's a nonanswer."

"Because life stinks. It helps."

"No, it doesn't. You know that."

"Life does so stink."

"I meant killing yourself won't help make it better."

Zack's grin must have been crazy, because Promise smiled too.

She said, "Okay. So spouting off wisdom isn't my thing. But you know what I mean."

"The problem is that it's impossible for *you* to know what *I* mean."

"Try me. Tell me what's on your mind." She dragged a stool to the other side of the counter and sat across from him, then twisted the caps off their sodas.

The invitation gave Zack something he could only think of as a paper cut on his brain, a stinging awareness. At once, his mother's demands that he win Promise combined with his unexpected personal desire to do that very thing. He spoke the words at the front of his mind.

"I have a lunatic for a mother."

"All mothers are a little crazy for their kids, don't you think? Mine can be like —"

"No. I mean really, really insane. Very dark."

"You're blaming your mother for your death wish."

"She has it out for me."

"And your father?"

"A sperm donor."

"Really?"

"Not literally. But I don't even know his name. And if my mother does, she'll go to her deathbed with it."

"Why?"

"If anything my mother did made sense, I might not be half as crazy as she is."

"So stay away from her. Right? Make your own way."

"It's not that simple, is it?" Zack said. "You know it's not that simple. 'Make your own way.' We try, don't we? What's your tale of woe?"

"I have amazing parents."

"There you go. How much of life is actually within our control to begin with?" He pointed the neck of his soda bottle at Promise's basket of meds. "You didn't ask for that, did you?"

"No, but I think we can influence what happens to us."

"A nice but useless thought."

She leaned in toward him, tilting her head so she could look up into his downcast eyes. This moment was strangely comical, like he was at a bar crying into his beer, without the bartender or the alcohol. How did he walk into this picture?

Promise said, "Everyone has something to live for."

"A poetic thought from a dying girl."

She flinched as if the words had burned her. Zack reached out for her hand and she withdrew.

"No, no. I can't believe I said that. Oh man."

Her lips were a line of self-control.

"Promise."

She got up and turned her back on him, picked up the meds from the counter by the sink and carried them down the hall. Zack followed her.

"I'm a jerk, Promise. Tell me what to do

to fix this."

"You can accept kindness when it's offered to you" — she turned into a bedroom at the end of the hall — "and quit slapping it down. It's not free, you know."

Sunlight filled the room, which was bright with hospital-grade medical equipment and a state-of-the-art computer setup. A screen saver of floating happy faces covered the large-screen wall monitor. A vest connected by vacuum cleaner-like hoses to a portable compressor of some kind lay on an inclined bench. Face masks and other plastic devices cluttered a counter built into one side of the room, and a large oxygen tank stood in the corner.

He wouldn't have known how to use any of this junk if Promise's life depended on it. Which it apparently did. This was some way to live.

Zack crammed his hands into the pockets of his skinny stretch jeans. Promise shoved the basket of meds into a cupboard over the counter.

"I don't even know you, but you're the only person who's ever been decent to me," he said.

She turned around and faced him, arms crossed. Her eyes were the color of his favorite dark beer — and if she ever found out he'd *thought* that, he'd die on the spot.

"I can't believe that," she said. He was staring. She held his gaze but shifted her stance. "What?"

Zack cleared his throat. "I don't remember anyone bothering . . . the way you bother."

"Well, maybe I'll stop. You're like a wounded dog that keeps biting."

"I am a dog, for sure. Want to see me froth at the mouth?"

She softened.

"I'll follow you around like a puppy," he said.

"You've got plenty of better things to do."

"Can't think of anything. You're going to be famous — I read the theater blog."

"You're stalking me, huh?"

"I'm a fan, not a stalker. I'll be your slave. You'll need a personal photographer. Someone to fight off the paparazzi."

"That's a bit premature."

"You gotta make your own way. No one else is going to do it for you, right?"

"Oh brother. That's not what I meant and you know it. If I get sick, it's all over."

"So don't get sick."

"I'll keep that in mind."

"And if you do get sick, there's always reality TV."

"What?"

"Maybe they'll create one just for you. You never know. We've come so far that America might like to watch a pretty girl die of a terrible sickness."

Her fair skin paled. "I guess that'd be one way to get my name out there."

"Wow," Zack said. "I really can't help myself, can I?"

He reached out and took her hand, trying to apologize yet again. He should just walk out, but he couldn't go. The skin of her hand was white under his fingertips. She squeezed back gently and released him.

"So this is your particular insanity, huh?"

"Twice a day. If I'm not hospitalized."

"How many times have you been in?"

"Every few months. All my life since I was four."

"That sucks."

"Five of my best friends have died in the last three years."

"No wonder you need to sing."

Promise nodded.

Zack pointed to a drawing that had been taped to the closet door at eye level. It was a fine illustration, white pencil or maybe charcoal on black paper. "So is that your inspiration?"

"What?"

"Is that what keeps you going on days

when nothing else will?"

"I don't know what you're talking about."

"This drawing." Zack moved to get a better look at it.

"That's what I brought home with me last night. I liked it. I taped it up. Do you know what kind of tree that is?"

"Tree?"

"And what are the arches over it? I was thinking it must be from a famous park somewhere. But in winter. The branches don't have many leaves on them, see? Honestly, it's a little spooky. But I like it."

Zack started laughing. "You're messing with me, right?"

She blinked at him.

"You don't know what this is?"

Promise looked again, shook her head.

Zack ran his fingers under the Scotch tape that held the corners in place and pried the image off the accordion door. When it came free, he rotated the paper ninety degrees and taped it back in place. His new friend took a step closer to it.

"It's a lung," he said, pointing. "The airways. And a rib cage. The right side. Who did you say drew it?"

Promise was still speechless, staring.

Zack said, "Maybe it's just that you've never had a good look at a healthy lung.

I'm no doctor, but those are the prettiest airways I've ever seen."

18

When Porta went to the gallery's front entry to lock up Tuesday evening, she noticed Belinda Morrow on the sidewalk, round and squatty as ever in a dreadful full-length skirt that did not flatter her girth. She was examining the sculpture of the boy in the front window, leaning from her hips so that the gauzy fabric pooled at her toes.

The unexpected guest made Porta suddenly weary and impatient. She stepped out of the gallery in order to pull the door shut. Belinda straightened and gestured to the artwork. "You never fail to surprise me," Belinda said. Her tone was complimentary and unnecessarily cheerful.

"Yes, well, he's only temporary."

"Why on earth? He's so welcoming."

Porta reached for the doorknob. "I was just closing."

"Perfect then! I won't be interrupting your work." Belinda inserted herself into the gap between Porta and the entry and went into the shop. Porta had to allow her passage or risk being squashed.

"I wasn't expecting to see you today," Porta said, shutting the door and locking it. "Or ever again, for that matter."

"Aren't surprises wonderful that way?" The stout woman was craning her thick neck to look at the skylights, which wouldn't completely dim for another hour or so.

Porta walked to the rear of the gallery, where she began to tidy her small desk. It was more a decoration than a true work space, but had collected a few new client folders over the last couple of days. Belinda took a slow turn around the narrow showcase, poked her head into the viewing room, and sniffed.

"Ah. That's creative. You always did have original ideas, Porta."

Folders in hand, Porta switched off the main lights at a panel behind the desk. Small floods highlighted the boy in the window and a few select pieces.

"At least that's what I always thought."

"What brings you all the way from New York, Belinda? I can't imagine you traipsed over here to make nice."

"Oh, Porta, honey, you know I think of you like a sister. I wish you hadn't left us.

198

Really, all the hard feelings would have blown over eventually."

"And have they?"

"Well, you know those women as well as I do. But we can always work things out."

Porta left Belinda in the gallery and entered the storeroom. The space was gray in the fading light that entered through a solitary window high on the wall. She turned off the coffeepot and carried the files to their drawers.

Belinda waddled as far as the door frame and stood under it, filling the space. She clasped her hands in front of herself. "I understand how you must feel, I really do. But if you could see things from their point of view —"

"Why would I want to do that?"

"You crossed a line. You have to admit that much."

"I don't have to admit to anything."

Belinda shrugged. "We have to have boundaries, don't we? Without rules, outsiders misunderstand. They think *witch* and imagine black hats and broomsticks, evil incantations." Belinda glanced over her shoulder and dropped her voice to a covert whisper. "Dark rooms filled with psychoactive incense." She grinned.

"You and I agreed to disagree. I don't see

that anything has changed."

Belinda opened her arms. "Let's not argue, Porta. I'm here because I'm deeply concerned about you. You shouldn't be working alone."

"I can't imagine why you're concerned." Porta, who had once invited Belinda to join her in the search for immortality, was not about to forgive her old friend for taking sides with the ones who threw her out of their sacred little community. Porta crammed the Jackson file into an open hanger behind the *J* tab. "Let me see if I remember your last words to me: 'Only the most selfish, arrogant rebels pursue eternal life, Porta. Death comes to all, and it should come to you first.' Yes, I'm pretty sure that was it." She slammed the file drawer shut.

"I think I was too harsh."

"You've come to apologize then? To what end? You want me to take you back on as a partner? You expect me to run back to that house full of silly women who think their highest calling in life is to make love potions for little girls?"

Belinda lifted her hand, a plea for calm. "Let me say my piece. Please? And then I'll go."

Porta took her summer wrap off the hook

and tossed the raw silk over her right shoulder.

Belinda said, "Some of our sisters have done you wrong."

The news was water on Porta's fire. Disbelief. "My *Ameretat*."

"Your sculpture is involved, yes."

"You have her? How did she get to you?"

"I don't know. Her crate was addressed to the house."

"The house on Rushford? I've never given anyone that address."

"Are you certain of it?"

"You exasperating woman! Why wouldn't I be certain? One of the girls stole her and sent me the hexed boy just to have her fun. Candace, or Althea."

"Anger never flatters anyone, Porta."

"Quit acting like a mother. Where is she?"

"Who?"

"The *Ameretat,* fool!"

Belinda ignored her insults — either that or Porta couldn't see her expression accurately. The light from the desk lamp in the gallery hit Porta's guest from behind and was mostly blocked from entering the small office space.

"The piece in your front window," Belinda said softly, "the child —"

"Came in the *Ameretat*'s box. Most certainly a prank. But I see you knew that all along. My money's on Althea now. Did you bring the piece with you?"

"I did." Belinda failed to move or explain further.

"Well?" Porta probed. "What is it? Are you waiting for my gushing gratitude? A reward? Why didn't you just ship it to me?"

"I thought if I was with you when you saw it, you might consider coming home."

Porta huffed. "Of all the illogical notions! Do you have it now?"

"Yes. I parked in back, but I wasn't sure which —"

"Thoughtful of you." Porta threw her rear door open and indicated that Belinda should lead the way.

Outside, a nondescript sedan was parked parallel to the building. The sun had not yet set, but dusk hovered over the alley. Belinda waddled around the car and opened the trunk. The compartment, illuminated from the inside, was lined with wool blankets.

"You just threw it in the car?"

"The crate wouldn't fit."

"I'll expect you to pay for damages."

Belinda muttered under her breath and Porta thought she said, "I'm sure you will."

"What's happened to it?"

Belinda leaned into the open trunk and

withdrew the top blanket. Porta cried out. The serene jade face of her stunning *Ameretat* had been smashed across the nose and lips. The wings that enfolded her pot of blessed soil were broken at the tips, and the bowl was completely empty. The injury caused the figure's blank, wide-set eyes to appear fearful.

"Where is the sacred soil!"

"No idea. I didn't cause the damage, I'm only trying to fix it."

"I'll take Althea by the throat!"

"No, Porta. She didn't have anything to do with it, I'm certain. We all know the value of this piece. Someone who wanted to harm you would have sold it, not" — she flicked her wrist over the *Ameretat*'s sorry state — "this."

"You underestimate how much they hate me."

"Porta, stop it." Belinda wedged her full body between Porta and the disaster, forcing Porta to step back. Belinda raised her eyes and lowered her volume. "I suspect the damage was supernatural. A warning of some kind. I fear for your safety out here, alone."

The boy sculpture's prophecy filled Porta's head with eerie chatter. *I have come out to withstand thee . . . thy way is perverse before me. In five weeks of five days . . . breathe her last.* She clenched her jaw and spoke to silence the voices. "I'm hardly alone."

Porta's birthday was less than three weeks away.

Belinda took a long, deep breath and placed her knuckles on her hips.

"You can't frighten me into returning, Belinda."

"I'm not trying to frighten you. I'm not." She gestured to the vandalism behind her. "What if this is from the gods? What will happen to you if you keep chasing your illusions? The true Ameretat never promised any human immortality."

"I never said she did."

"I wouldn't put it past you to make such claims to an unwitting patron. You place that *Ameretat* in the viewing room and give your customer a hallucination she'll never forget, the promise of something she can never have. She pays and pays for a repeat experience. You walk away rich. Let's count all the ways that would upset the spirits."

"Is that what this is about? You envy me my wealth? *You* stole my *Ameretat* and shipped that amateur work to me in its place. A fine joke made finer by the hex you put on it. So much money and trouble! You can't possibly care about my fate that much."

"I care about you more than you're willing to accept."

"And here you stand, accusing me of lies and deceptions."

"I'm telling you the truth. The *Ameretat* was shipped to me in perfect condition. I placed her in my living room. Tonya found the mistake funny and suggested we send the child to you in its place, let you stew for a week or so. The boy was a piece Althea's had for years. She was happy to contribute it to the prank, and I couldn't dissuade them from doing it."

"A prank, my foot. I would have called it a curse, but you seem to think they've got the corner on goodness."

"A curse? What are you talking about? The child was charmed to sing to you."

Porta leveled her eyes at the squat woman.

"Only you would think of a sweet little folk song as a curse, Porta."

"Believe me, the statue did not sing."

"Well, Althea will be disappointed. But that's irrelevant. This, though" — Belinda gestured to the shattered green stone — "this is desperately important. The girls never laid a finger on your jade. Last week, after a terrible sleepless night, I found the

Ameretat like this. Everyone was as shocked as I was. I brought her as soon as possible."

"I don't believe you. Anyone might have done this." But Porta sensed her own convictions destabilize.

Belinda sighed heavily. Her voice softened. "Why do you want it?"

"The sculpture?"

"Immortality. I've never understood. It's a life of loneliness and isolation."

"My whole life on this earth has been a life of loneliness and isolation."

Tears filled Belinda's eyes. "Please come home. You need the safety we can offer you."

"No."

"Don't be selfish. Your pride will be the death of you."

"I'm the least selfish person in the world. Do people who find immortality hoard it for themselves?"

"No one has ever found it."

"I know of one."

Belinda shook her head, pitying.

"Yes, a young woman who has more lives than a panther. She and I will share it with whom we please, and we'll hardly be lonely then. Don't expect to be one of the chosen few."

"With you doing the choosing, I can't imagine anyone would want to be."

Porta leaned into the trunk of the car and lifted her precious jade, cradling it like a baby. "Go home, Belinda. Go home to your fading life."

19

The following Saturday Chase left the house on Morris Street without his pencils or drawings. At the corner he stopped in front of Marlene's Sweet Shop and waited for Chelsea to open the door for him. He ordered a chocolate-chocolate chip ice cream cone and exited with it in hand.

Chelsea was overcome with relief. She held her breath as they approached ART(i)FACTS and didn't exhale until Chase passed by. She followed, allowing herself a quick look through the window. The sculptured boy was still gazing upward toward the sunny yellow canopy, and she was irrationally glad that the piece hadn't been sold.

The outdoor area of the Irish pub was still edged with yellow caution tape where the railing had collapsed and awaited repair. Chase didn't even look at it. They passed the cigar shop next door, and then a gift shop that sold silk dresses stitched by entrepreneurial Nepalese women funded by grants. There was a music shop that sold hand-hewn dulcimers, and a café known for its goat cheese omelets, and a children's clothing store called The Sly Stork. Reed's Menswear was three blocks down.

A couple was approaching them from the opposite direction. He was middle-aged and wore expensive leather shoes. She was clinging to his arm and walking with her head down. The man carried a large sheet of black paper carelessly, its edge wrinkled in his fist. Chelsea recognized them, taking note of the telling details simultaneously: the woman's pedicure-showcasing sandals, her untamed hair, her tiny nose, the scarf that in all likelihood covered a scar at her throat.

They seemed to notice Chase after Chelsea had noticed them: the woman's eyes widened and she gripped her partner's arm, squeezing. He lengthened his stride just enough to move ahead of her, protective, Chelsea thought.

She copied him, anticipating a conflict. The black paper forewarned her.

"What is this?" the man demanded, holding out the drawing Chase had given the woman on his first venture into

ART(i)FACTS, the woman who was a wild oak with a nesting bird in her throat.

Chelsea matched his tone. "It's a picture."

"Is this funny to you? Do you think we have come out here for your entertainment?"

"What?"

"Do you think we aren't human, with real human feelings and emotions?"

If the question had been an accusation rather than a plea, Chelsea might have tossed her ice cream on his casual designer shirt. But his shoulders were stooped. Chase's wrinkled drawing was limp in his fingers, and Chelsea saw the tattered edges, gone soft from overhandling, and the smudges across the sweeping lines of Chase's charcoal.

She said softly, "I'm not sure what we've done to upset you."

The sound that came out of his mouth was half sarcasm, half disgust. "You prey on people, you and that con. I should have looked into you all before we ever set foot in that gallery."

"I assure you, we're not associated with the owner in any way. The day we saw you there was the first time we'd ever set foot in the place."

"It was her first day open!"

"Sir, I'm still completely confused about why you're angry."

"How did you know about my wife?"

Chelsea's eyes darted to the woman. "I'm telling you —"

"You drew this before you sat down with us." Now the man was shoving the picture past Chelsea. The paper jabbed Chase's forearm. Her brother examined his bare skin. "Were you off in some room somewhere? Listening to that woman dig for our sad story and make all kinds of promises about how she could ease our pain? Does she wear a wire or something? Is that how it works?"

What? "Maybe if you —" Chelsea cleared her throat. "What is it that . . . I mean, what is so personal about this image? What is its connection to you?"

"She cannot speak," Chase said. He was rubbing the skin of his arm where the paper had poked it.

When the couple didn't protest, Chelsea pivoted to see him. "How did you know that?"

"He knew because we told that woman," the man said. "The owner. She knew. She said, 'Something here will speak to you. Something here will comfort your soul and fill your heart with music again!' Maybe we

211

were the fools, but we needed something. I'm ashamed to admit it now. We needed something to pull us through this. And then he waltzes in" — the man jabbed again — "like the answer to our prayers."

"You thought art would answer your prayers?"

"Not anymore!"

"I'm sorry," Chelsea said. "I'm truly sorry. But it's just a drawing. My brother's been drawing his whole life."

The man scowled at her. "The least you could do is deal with us honestly here." He held up the image square so Chelsea could see it head on and faceup for the first time. The little songbird in the middle of the beautiful, wild tree sang with a full throat and a wide beak. "What would 'just a drawing' say to you if you were a singer who lost her voice to the knife of a kid who needed the three bucks in her purse?"

Chelsea didn't know what to say. Her ice cream slouched shamefully in its cup. She glanced at Chase and saw that the rims of his eyes were brimming with tears.

"She will sing again," Chase said.

"Chase, you can't know that."

"It is true."

"When?" the man asked. "We've been waiting for a miracle these two weeks, patiently, like prisoners of war! And each day is worse than the last. I won't tolerate any more of this. We'd be better off if we'd never set foot in that gallery. So tell me if it's true: When will she sing? And how?"

"The time is not for me to say."

"Really? And what's the answer to that one going to cost us? Something more than this lure-'em-in freebie from an amateur? Next time we're going to have to spend seven or eight or nine grand on more snake oil? Is that how this works?"

Chelsea doubted that even ten times that much money would punch a hole in this man's net worth. She couldn't stop herself from saying, "Wouldn't you pay any price for your wife?"

"This is such a racket! Do you know how much money that woman got away with before they ran her out of her last town? Ten million. Ten freaking million in hearts and souls."

Now Chelsea kept her mouth shut. If Porta Cerreto was a criminal, authorities would find her soon enough, and it would be made clear that Chase was not affiliated with her. This man was a heat-seeking missile who'd been robbed of a target, and Chelsea saw no need to step into his path.

There was no argument to be won against grief.

"No one has any right to mess with someone else's hopes," the man said. "Not even good intentions can answer for the disasters caused by arrogance like that."

He reached for his wife in a manner that contradicted his frustration, taking her hand as if it were a broken wing. The woman was studying Chase, whose somber expression spoke of his own sadness for her.

"I only say the truth," Chase said to her as the couple moved past him. "I love you."

"Freak." The woman's husband pulled her away.

Chase started to follow.

"Chase. Leave them alone."

"Let him come," the man said. "We'll expose this charade for what it is."

"Chase, please."

He ignored his sister. The ice cream was lost to the sun. She detoured to the nearest trash can, tossed the treat, then jogged after him. Was this what her relationship with her brother would be reduced to now? Always running, never reaching?

They were back at the gallery in seconds. The man stormed in as wealthy people do: soundlessly and in full control of his body, with only his eyes screaming. After his wife passed through ahead of him, he let the door close on Chase, who caught it, entered, and let it close on Chelsea. She allowed it to close for the two seconds it offered her to compose herself, then she spent three seconds longer on a single breath. The boy child in the display window seemed to urge her in.

Porta Cerreto had noticed the man before Chelsea entered. The owner excused herself from a young woman who was examining a vase and crossed the sea-green carpet like a gliding gull.

"Mr. Bell," she said. "How kind of you and your wife to grace my gallery again." She registered Chase's drawing, and then its artist, with only the slightest tilt of her chin, smiling the entire time.

"A word, please."

Porta held out one hand, indicating the desk at the rear. "How can I be of service to you?"

"Perhaps somewhere private," Mr. Bell said. The courtesy was for his wife's sake, Chelsea thought, a promise made before they'd left their home.

"Of course. The viewing room is unoccupied. We'll be undistracted there." She led the way. Chase's drawing buckled in Mr. Bell's fingers and made a popping sound as he turned to gather his wife to him. Mrs. Bell had been distracted by an image on the near wall. That photograph of the person tumbling off a cliff.

"Darling," he said softly. She held up her right hand toward him, graceful, long-fingered. *Wait.*

Porta had paused. "Would you like a closer look at that? I'd be happy to bring it in —"

"We won't be spending any money here," said Mr. Bell. His fingertips brushed his wife's elbow. She turned her head toward him and this time mouthed the word that Chelsea had inferred: *Wait.* Her husband obeyed.

Mrs. Bell lifted her elegant hand to the soles of the falling shoes, the feet Chase had kissed. Without touching the surface, she followed the legs to the place where they vanished behind the bluff, then traced the remains of the broken fence.

"I can't see why this would interest you," Mr. Bell said. "It's like nothing we —"

"It is not for you," Chase said. His head was shaking back and forth. "It is not for you."

Chelsea silenced him with a hand on his forearm — a foolish, invasive move. He jerked away.

"We didn't ask for your opinion," Mr. Bell said.

"It's the same as yours," Chelsea muttered.

Mrs. Bell ignored this exchange. She was communicating with her husband in an intimate language shared by lovers who could read each other's smallest gestures.

"I assure you," Porta said, "you'll gain a much more objective assessment of this work's qualities once you spend some time alone with it. The woman who fell — she is a close friend of the family — she survived. I assure you, it's nothing morbid. Just miraculous."

Mrs. Bell looked at Porta for the first time since entering ART(i)FACTS.

"Remember why we've come," Mr. Bell said to his wife.

"Mr. Bell, please. As I explained on your first visit, the power of one's experience with a piece of art can hardly be comprehended by mere intellect. It is an emotional experience, a powerful experience that can awaken things within us we thought had died."

Mrs. Bell indicated to Porta that the photo should be taken into the viewing room.

"She's a charlatan, darling. She sells cut tulips to Danes. There is nothing here of any use."

"Mr. Bell, truly!" Porta exclaimed. Chelsea noted the ears of other patrons discreetly turning their way. "How could I possibly engineer something as complex as a personal emotional experience?" She lifted the photograph off the wall.

"No," Chase said. He raised his voice. "No!"

Chelsea didn't know what to do. Mrs. Bell made her way toward the viewing room. Mr. Bell sighed. "If that's what she wants, let's have a look."

"It is not for you," Chase insisted, calling after Mrs. Bell. There was an edge in his voice that was new to Chelsea and caused her some alarm. "It is not for you."

"I don't expect you'll be buying it yourself," Porta said under her breath.

"It is not for you."

Mr. Bell extended the black paper toward Chase. "This isn't for her either. Lucky for you we didn't pay anything for your promises."

"There were no promises!" Chelsea said. "It was a gift!"

"Take it or toss it," Mr. Bell said to Chase. "We're too old for false hopes."

20

Sunday night, in the banquet hall at the Doubletree Hotel, three hundred people from the state chapter of the Foundation for Autism Spectrum Disorder Awareness had gathered for its annual benefit drive. The dessert plates were being cleared away, and the penguified men and bedazzled women were stirring coffees and adjusting their chairs for a better view of the stage. Under the courteous volume of chatter was the sound of silverware bouncing on china and carts traveling into the distant kitchen. Servers refilled water glasses and coffee cups.

Chelsea, who had been an active member of FASDA since she and her brother were fifteen, leaned toward Wes to speak without being heard by the people who shared their table. She'd asked him to come because he was the most logical friend for her to invite. Maybe, in truth, the only friend she wanted to invite. He'd accepted the invitation more happily than she'd expected.

"I'm worried about Chase," she said.

"How do you mean?"

"He's changed. Distracted."

"You mean more than he was when he started handing out drawings?" Wes turned the stem of his water glass within a sweat spot on the tablecloth.

"But this is unusual. The degree to which he's deviating from his self-imposed routines, I mean. He didn't even stop to eat today. Far as I know, his lunch is still in the fridge."

"Chase is his own man, as I've said."

Chelsea placed her elbow on the table and leaned her cheek on her hand, facing him.

"Tonight when you arrived, did he tell you what happened this weekend? While I was finishing getting ready?"

"Something involving a woman, I'm guessing."

"Why such a good guess?"

"He keeps repeating himself."

" 'I love you, I love you,' " she provided.

"Well, I hadn't expected a confession here, tonight, but I love you too."

Chelsea laughed. Her neck felt warm.

"Oh! Sorry," he said. "We're talking about Chase." He smiled at her, a playful tease. "I have to agree, he seems pretty infatuated with someone. But he didn't talk to me about it directly. I was basically invisible to him."

"Her name is Promise." She explained how the girl and her brother had met.

"Can't say I don't know how he feels," Wes said.

Chelsea registered the implication and tried to step over it gracefully. "What are we going to do about it?"

"About my feelings?"

Chelsea slapped him lightly on the arm. "My brother thinks he's in love. Of everything he and I have been through together, this was a challenge I never saw coming."

"Just because a person has autism doesn't mean he can't love someone."

"Chase tells me he loves me all the time. He says it to most people. I'm talking about romance."

"That too. I can show you all kinds of romance between people with autism."

"All kinds? No, thank you. The autistic spectrum is pretty broad — you know that better than I do. I'd punch a hole in every example you bring to me. Chase is unique. Besides, I'm sure every couple you could present to me as proof share their affections for each other. Promise doesn't even know Chase."

"So maybe you should arrange for her to have a chance at that."

Chelsea let her mouth gape. "You're not serious."

"I can set it up if you want me to."

"Let Chase find her himself."

"Okay. You said she knows the art gallery woman. We could —"

"That girl will only reject him. It's the only possible outcome."

"How can I agree? I've never laid eyes on her."

"Wes, take me seriously."

"I am." He leaned toward her and took the hand she'd rested on the table. His palm was broad and firm. "Your brother probably has a bigger capacity for love than any other two people put together. One of these days someone's going to recognize that for the amazing thing that it is, and she won't reject it."

Chelsea slid her hand out of his, trying to stay focused on Chase. "But he doesn't have any way to express himself. Not in a way that would make sense to the rest of us. To someone like Promise. You can't love a person with pictures."

"Does that matter? Is that what love is

about? Saying all the right things and having all the right moves?"

A woman in an emerald green evening gown laid her hand on Chelsea's shoulder and whispered in her ear. "We're ready for you, dear."

Chelsea nodded and the hostess slipped away.

"Let him have his chance," Wes said. "It's something everyone wants."

Chelsea stood and pushed in her chair, irritated, plus annoyed for feeling irritated. She had introductions to make, thanks to offer, and a $50,000 check to present to FASDA on behalf of the brokerage firm she worked for, chosen because of her long-term connections to both parties.

"No one wants to be hurt," she said.

Wes only nodded as she made her way to the stage.

21

Monday afternoon Promise showed up at the university's fine arts building for her last modeling job of the summer term. Professor Dawson had made arrangements for her to model for the final life-drawing class weeks earlier, before the broken arm. When Promise arrived and showed her the cast, Dawson only shook her head and clucked her tongue.

"Let's do this anyway, girl. This group's good enough to see right through that."

"So long as they don't apply their X-ray vision to anything else," Promise teased. She'd posed undraped once before and decided it wasn't for her. Not in this broken-down body.

Dawson sent Promise away to change into a lightweight sleeveless chiton with gold clasps at the shoulders.

"So very Greek," Promise said.

"Away with you, my goddess!" Dawson

shooed her off.

By the time Promise returned, about a dozen students had arrived and were pulling drawing paper and charcoal pencils out of totes. Adam, a senior student Promise knew but didn't especially like, was helping Dawson erect a set of work lights at the front of the class. These would shine on Promise's pose and cast shadows for the students to recreate on paper. As he ran an extension cord to the nearest outlet, his eyes lingered on Promise's casted wrist.

"Heard about what happened to you," he said, nodding at her arm.

"Word gets around." Promise glanced around at the classroom, wondering if Zack would participate in the final today. She hoped he would come, for his own sake. The table where he usually sat at the back of the room was empty.

"Your arm okay?" Adam asked her.

"It's nothing. Just a fracture."

He shook his head and tore a piece of duct tape off the roll surrounding his wrist, then taped the cord to the floor. "That guy's been on the brink ever since I've known him. He's going to kill somebody one day and go on living just because that's his bad luck. Someone needs to lock him up."

The caustic words triggered Promise's

sympathy for Zack. "Maybe he just needs someone to talk to."

"Someone like a prosecutor. You should press charges."

"For what?"

The guy stared at her. "You're kidding me."

"It was an accident."

"That's like saying it was just luck that you were the only one sitting outside Blarney's on a Saturday afternoon. Nice people like you think everyone can be fixed with niceness. You should take advantage of the good publicity instead."

"I would never —"

"You'll change your mind when you hear the news that he shot up a classroom of your friends and then turned the gun on himself."

Promise recoiled. A woman eavesdropping, a sensitive soul named Allison, looked alarmed. "You shouldn't talk that way," Promise said.

"It happens. And it happens because nice people don't do anything about it."

"Look, he was arrested. There will be a hearing and —"

"Let's just hope it happens before the body count rises."

He stalked off, leaving Promise feeling

226

slightly bruised. She exchanged glances with Allison, who had always preferred drawing to speaking.

"I worry about the angry ones more than the suicidal ones," Promise said to her.

Allison's expression remained distressed. Promise worried. Maybe it would be best after all if Zack stuck to his plans to drop out.

"Got a pedestal for you today," Dawson announced to Promise, turning her toward the props.

"And a pool," Promise observed.

At the front of the room was a shallow acrylic tank filled with water. It was roughly seven feet square and half a foot high. Wooden blocks placed under the pool at the corners raised it off the ground a few inches so that lights could be placed beneath it. A battered cement pedestal that looked like it had been dragged in from someone's Greek garden stood in the center of the water.

"We'll do forty-five minutes with you lit from beneath and the side," Dawson explained. Promise saw low-wattage battery-operated lights, the kind sold on TV for closets and cabinets, underneath the clear pool. Dawson turned on the work lamps and adjusted the height and angle to hit

Promise low and from the side. "I want you to let the hem of the dress float."

"Poor students," Promise said of the challenge they'd face in drawing the light sources, the shadows, and the fabric of her dress lying on the water's surface. "I'd take a physics final over having to draw this."

"You're not a physics student."

"Exactly."

"This isn't too big a task for anyone here." The professor winked at a nearby junior, who replied by saying, "Well spoken, Great One."

Promise knew what to do with her props. As the last few students trickled into class, she went barefoot into the water, then rested her hip on the pillar and leaned slightly, her legs extended in the opposite direction. The chiton formed an elegant drape below her bare neck, was cinched at the waist, and then followed gravity into the water.

With her back to the audience, Promise turned her jaw in profile, lining up her chin with her forward shoulder. She could see the classroom from the corner of her eye. She braced herself on her good arm and placed her cast in front of her, out of the students' sight. A strand of hair escaped the pile atop her head and grazed her cheek.

"Good, good," Dawson said to Promise,

then to the students: "Now's the time to show off all that you have learned." While the woman gave instructions, she activated the small lights underneath the tank, then dropped the blinds over the classroom windows and turned off the overhead fluorescents.

The classroom became like dusk, and the delicate blue cloth of Promise's dress took on new hues. The water refracted the light and followed the fabric's movement. The artists, sitting in shadows, bent toward their drawing pads and applied themselves to an advanced study in chiaroscuro, an assessment of light sources for the purpose of creating shadow, dimension, and texture.

Promise adjusted her hip to prevent her leg from falling asleep later. She relaxed, preparing her body to settle. One of the lights from beneath, though soft, shone directly into her face. She closed her eyes.

The scritching of pencils on paper was like the hushed conversations of friends. Dawson moved around the room, graceful, nonjudgmental, almost invisible. When she spoke her words were discernible only to the student they were intended for. Pencils danced and chairs creaked and students breathed. Familiar, unthreatening noise, the sounds of concentration.

Promise coughed once. The sound shouldn't have been odd to her but was at that moment. She realized that she hadn't coughed for . . . days. Her coughing never seemed louder nor more frequent than it did during her modeling sessions, and yet it never seemed to bother anyone but her.

A rustle that was different from the other sounds drew Promise's attention. Without moving her head she opened her eyes and directed them toward the noise. She saw Zack enter the dim room at the rear door, eyes on her. Promise's first instinct was to look for Adam, to hope he wouldn't notice Zack's arrival. The silhouette that was Adam was wetting a pencil tip with his tongue.

Zack wore the trench coat today, though it was the end of August. He took a stool at the empty worktable to the rear of the room and sat, laying a portfolio on the desktop. A beam of weak light from the door he'd neglected to close fell across his belongings and his face. Zack made no move to begin working, though he studied Promise attentively. He nodded at her once, offered her the slightest of smiles. She matched the gesture, and his posture relaxed. He leaned forward and opened the flap of his bag.

"Nice of you to leave your car outside

where it belongs," someone muttered. Adam.

There was a stir and a few snickers as people looked around, matching the remark with Zack's arrival.

"Dr. Dawson," Adam said, "doesn't the school policy call for students to be expelled for reckless behavior?"

"Let's resume our concentration," Dawson said.

"No, really, I want to know why someone who's got it in his head to kill himself and take a few people out with him is sitting *here* rather than in a shrink's office."

"Adam, that's enough," Dawson said.

"No one died," Zack muttered.

"I wasn't aware that was a criteria." Adam.

"Criteri*on*." Zack.

The tone of Dawson's voice took on a warning. "Would you gentlemen like to step outside and discuss this privately?"

"The correct grammar is *criterion*," Zack said. "No need to discuss it."

Promise coughed again. She didn't mean anything by it; it was entirely involuntary, but Zack turned his head toward her.

"This is a *life*-drawing class," Adam said. "I have no idea why you're here."

"Because it ends today," Zack said.

Silence came over the room. Promise held

her breath. *Please, please don't. It's not funny.*

He chuckled. "What?" he said. "I meant the class. Everyone's so uptight."

He reached into his portfolio, and Allison, the normally silent woman who seemed to hang on Adam's every word, screamed.

"He's going to shoot us! He's going to kill us!"

The classroom erupted. Promise jerked upright on her pedestal. Her toes dangled in the water. The women were shrieking. An easel clattered over and stools toppled.

"Stop!" Promise yelled.

The work lamps glared in her eyes and made the dim surroundings all the more confusing. The sounds of yelling, of bodies colliding with furniture and other bodies, swallowed her cry. Frantic forms rushed for the door behind her and for the rear exit near Zack. She thought she saw someone lunging at him.

A frantic student splashed through the pool and pushed Promise out of the way. The force tipped her off the pedestal, and her bare foot, searching for balance, slipped on the smooth acrylic. She went down, smacking her elbow on the rim of the tank. A sharp pain electrified her triceps. The concrete prop teetered and fell out, crashing onto the classroom floor. Someone tripped over it and fell into the sloshing water, onto her, pinning her shoulder. Promise thrashed and sputtered. Water rushed her nostrils.

She felt her filmy dress pooling around her thighs. She tried to rise, but the man was crushing her under the brilliant spotlights that Dr. Dawson had set up, the large electric work lamps. They were blinding her.

Falling on her.

The lights crashed into the small pool, and Promise heard the cages surrounding the huge bulbs strike bottom and wink out. She heard electricity crackle and lash out. She heard steam sizzle and smelled hot plastic. She felt the shrieks of the man on top of her as hot breath on her cheeks. She sensed his flailing limbs go rigid, couldn't resist the solid and muscular torso that bore down on hers. He outweighed her.

Survival instincts commanded Promise to breathe. Her adrenaline caught him by the waist and threw him over her body, then rolled them both out of the roiling water.

22

Chelsea was in her office Monday, watching a webcast interview with the financial markets analyst Clifton Savage, when Rena called. It was 4:50. The NYSE had closed hours ago, and her day was winding down.

"Chelsea, it's your brother. I'm afraid he's gone off."

"What do you mean, gone off?"

"He left the house. He's very upset."

Chelsea rose from her desk and began to gather her things. "What upset him?"

"I have no idea. I was making a wrap for him for dinner. The news was on in the eat-in. He came in for water. Everything like usual."

"Then he just stormed off?"

"Something flustered him, but he wouldn't say. Maybe something on the TV? It's the only thing I can think of, but honestly, I wasn't paying attention to it. He went up to his room, then came down a few minutes later, went straight out the door."

Chelsea exited her office with her purse on her shoulder, then spun and went back in for the laptop she'd left open on the desk. She closed it without shutting down, then scooped it into her bag.

"Did he say where he was going?"

"No. But he headed toward downtown."

"How long has he been gone?"

"Just one or two minutes. I called right away. Should I try to find him?"

"No, stay there in case he comes back."

Out in the hall again, Chelsea remembered her keys. Back to the office. They lay by an empty Styrofoam cup where she'd dropped them that morning.

"Where's Wes?" she asked Rena.

"He left at four, as usual."

Right. She knew that.

"Okay. Stay put. I'm coming now."

It would take Chelsea less than a half hour to get from the heart of the city to the Shore. Even so, once her car was on the highway, she called Wes.

"Do you think he went to the gallery?" she asked him.

"That all depends on what set him off."

"If he's been anywhere alone in the past decade, he's kept it a secret. It's the ice cream shop, or the gallery, or anywhere in the universe."

"You might be surprised."

"What do you mean?"

"I stopped for coffee with a friend on my way home, so I'm not far from ART(i)FACTS," Wes said. "I can be there in ten minutes."

"Wes, what are you not telling me?"

"We'll find him. Don't worry."

"I'm sorry to interrupt your date."

Wes belly-laughed. "He's my pastor. He'll understand."

"Then tell him I said thanks. And call me."

"Sure thing."

But Wes didn't call, and when Chelsea pulled into the metered parking space at the front of the gallery twenty minutes later, he was waiting for her on the sidewalk.

"You checked inside?"

"The owner hasn't seen him. 'And if I had, I'd have thrown him out,' " Wes mimicked.

Chelsea put a hand on her head and the other on her hip. She longed for her running shoes instead of these heels she was in. She looked up the street toward home. She looked at the gallery window. The sculptured boy — her brother, herself — smiled at the sun that never stopped shining above his head.

"When was the last time you called Rena?" Wes asked.

"Two minutes ago. He's not back yet."

"Would he go to look for Promise?"

"Why?"

"Kid in love —"

"But Rena said he was upset."

"Just for the sake of argument. Where would he look?"

Chelsea closed her eyes and tried to remember. "She said something about drawing classes at the university."

"The bus runs that way."

"You've been teaching him to ride the bus?"

Wes looked at her. "He's been riding it for three years."

"What? Why?"

Wes took her gently by the elbow, then steered her toward his car. "If you weren't worried sick, the answer would be obvious to you. Let's go see what we can find at the campus."

"My car —"

"Meter maid clocked out at five. It's fine."

"I need my running shoes."

"Chelsea." He opened the passenger door for her, still holding her elbow, keeping her anchored. "Your brother is not incompetent, or lost, or being hunted by assassins."

"He needs me," she said.

"We all need each other. I'm sure Chase knows exactly where he is, even if he didn't tell anyone where he was going. Trust him. Trust me. Please."

Chelsea lowered herself onto the front seat, not sure at all how to trust anyone.

23

Within an hour the incident in the art room was known to everyone on campus and many people off campus. Emergency workers milling around the red brick fine arts hall appeared to outnumber the students and staff. Several people were recording events with their cell phone cameras. Reporters were broadcasting live. A crowd of the curious had gathered outside of the area cordoned off by investigators.

The entire building had lost power, thanks to the surge that blew circuits when the lamps fell into the pool.

Promise was eager to leave. She had grabbed up her belongings on her way out of the room, then had exited the building and run across the lawn, dripping wet in the Greek gown that sucked at her skin. She ran like a rabbit, half distracted by the fact that she could run at all. Then a police officer stopped her without really explaining why she couldn't leave. She supposed it was self-evident.

So she waited, standing on the grass and gripping a wool blanket tight around her shoulders. There was no place to change into dry clothes. She felt like she'd survived an oceanic confrontation with Poseidon rather than a spill in a four-inch pool of water.

Her entire body vibrated, waiting to launch. Her fingertips tingled and her lungs seemed twice their normal size. One half of her head tried to convince her this was adrenaline, still teasing her nerves. The other half sensed that something less easily explained was responsible for her agitation. She wanted to sprint to the beach. She wanted to dive deep into the ocean.

An EMT had declared her to be wet but otherwise fine, given her the blanket and told her to wait for an investigator, then moved on to the injured. She knew of a broken arm, a sprained ankle, a goose egg on someone's forehead. No serious injuries, except to Zack, who remained at the center of the chatter even though he was no longer present.

He'd been taken to the hospital on a gurney a half hour ago. As far as Promise had been able to sort out, two male students, one of them Adam, had tackled Zack in the dark classroom and beaten him unconscious. Police had separated the two attacker-heroes from the other life-drawing students but were questioning everyone. If the wildfire rumors were true, authorities had seized the messenger bag abandoned on Zack's desk and found nothing in it but sketchbooks, pencil cases, and a biography of Vincent Van Gogh.

No gun. No shots fired. No deaths.

She was worried about Zack. She wanted nothing more than to leave this place and find him, make sure he was okay. Her busy schedule of the last week, which was filled with rehearsals and brainstorming meetings for a new video and marathon songwriting sessions, had prevented her from seeing much of him, though he texted her and called daily. He was sweet on her, and she didn't want to lead him on, but there was certainly no harm in being nice to someone who needed a little kindness in his life. She'd even managed to squeeze an hour out of last Saturday to have lunch with him.

She fidgeted. Tried to figure out who was in charge of the questioning and how she could move up to the front of the line.

Her powers of observation decided on a female in blue slacks and a Windbreaker that said POLICE across the back. Promise took a step toward her.

"They're not buying my story," someone said, right next to her. Promise jerked around.

A guy she recognized from class was bent over next to her, peeling wet socks off his feet. His carpenter's shorts were damp and sagging. His shirt was as wet as her dress. No blanket.

"What story is that?" she said.

"The one in which I was turned into a human power station and a little gal saved my skin without getting hurt."

"I'm not sure I buy it either."

"But is that how you would tell it?"

Promise wrinkled her nose. "Essentially. You're Chris, right?"

He faced her, held out his hand. "Good memory."

"My name's Promise."

"I know. Police talk to you yet?"

"Still waiting."

"We should both be fried fish. What do you make of it?"

Promise really, truly didn't know. She didn't even know if she *wanted* to know. "Maybe the circuit blew before it could really harm us."

"Not a chance. I *felt* it."

Promise glanced back at the detective. Near the entrance of the building, the woman had been joined by a man in black slacks and shoes. Both of them wore white gloves and were looking through a small book.

"Women are more susceptible to electrocution than men, did you know that?" Chris said.

"No." She bounced lightly on the balls of her feet.

"It's a body-weight thing. I've got to be at least fifty, sixty pounds more than you. And I was seized up, completely frozen. I'd swear my blood stopped moving. So how'd you flip me out of the water like I was a guppy?"

"Is that what happened?" The event had slipped away from her memory like a dream upon waking.

He eyed her as if uncertain whether she was teasing or genuinely asking. "My mind is a steel trap."

"Are you sure you didn't heave yourself out without knowing what you were doing?"

"Is that the way you remember it?"

She sighed. "I don't remember much at all."

"Those detectives over there are telling me that stress can mess up a person's recollection. That what I thought happened was delusional, impossible."

It was. Truly, nothing made sense.

"It doesn't take much electricity to kill a person," Chris said. "That many amps in water stops hearts. Lungs. You and I are a walking medical mystery, but they just think I'm a liar."

Promise only nodded.

"Don't take this wrong, but you're not the picture of health to begin with, from what I hear."

"I'm feeling pretty good right now. Maybe I've stumbled upon a revolutionary therapy."

Chris wrung the water out of his socks. "Maybe you can explain what really happened but don't want to tell me."

"Seriously! How could I know any better than you? And why wouldn't I tell you?"

He dropped the socks onto the grass. "I think the charge blew off my shoes."

The image of Chris's shoes, whatever they might be — she pictured pool slides — bobbing in the water struck Promise as funny, and she started giggling. Chris cracked a smile.

"It's not that funny," he said.

"I know. It's really not." She tried to sober up.

"My dad was an electrician. You know a

person can get electrocuted and not even know they're injured? They'll bleed inside for a while and die later. Maybe that's what we're in for."

"Thank you for that lovely possibility."

Promise's fingers ached. Her joints burned. The power of suggestion, she thought.

The police detectives who were holding the small book carried it to Dr. Dawson and showed it to her. The instructor opened it carefully and flipped through the pages.

Chris said, "They seem to think we got out of the water before the lights actually fell in it."

"That's the easiest thing to believe."

"What do you believe?"

Promise pulled her blanket tighter around her arms. She didn't know what she believed, and she couldn't put the ideas that were tripping through her mind into words. "I already told you," she said.

Chris said, "I hear all kinds of stories about people who lived through something that should have killed them."

"Why do some people get miracles and others don't?"

"Is that what you think we got? A miracle?"

"I don't know what to call it. But

lately . . ." She pulled her casted arm out from under the blanket and showed it to him. It was water-resistant fiberglass, not in the pool long enough to damage it. She hoped.

"I heard about that. Does Zack Eddy get the credit for that too?"

"What do you mean?"

"You know what I mean. Does he have it out for you?"

"Of course not."

"So he's a friend of yours?"

"What are you driving at?"

Chris shrugged. After a few seconds of silence he asked, "Do you believe in God?"

"Not a capricious one."

"What I mean is, who else can say when it's your time to go? Zack wants out bad, but he sure isn't having any luck."

"What a terrible thing to say!"

Dr. Dawson was holding the book and scanning the crowd. The man and woman did the same, heads swiveling slowly on their necks. Dr. Dawson saw Promise and nodded at her, then pointed.

"Thank you, Promise," Chris said, noting their intentions. The couple retrieved the book from Dr. Dawson and headed toward Promise and Chris.

"For what?"

"For hauling my butt out of that water."

"Uh, sure. Anyone would have done it."

He grinned. "No one *could* have done it. You shouldn't have been able to do it."

Promise blushed and glanced at the art building.

"You're the hero of the day, girl. Not Adam, not Shawn. They need muzzles, not attention." Promise figured Shawn must have been the other student who jumped Zack. "Zack's head is a little cockeyed," he said, "but he's harmless. Sort of."

The woman holding the little book called out to her. "Promise Dayton?"

Chris waved off as the officers arrived.

"Are you Promise Dayton? I'm Detective Halston." She gestured toward her companion. "My colleague, Detective Rimes."

Rimes said, "You're quite the rising star. I saw your video."

"Thank you," Promise said, which was a lame response. For all she knew he thought it was amateur.

"You like the spotlight?"

Promise wasn't sure what he was getting at, but his tone was almost accusatory. She didn't answer.

Detective Halston held out the book to Promise. It was a leather-bound journal, worn down on the corners and the spine.

"We were wondering what you could tell us about this."

It was the first time Promise had seen the volume. She took it, and the wool blanket slipped off one of her shoulders. She opened the cover and started turning through the pages.

"Do you know Zack Eddy?" Halston was asking.

She nodded, shocked to see herself on every page.

"Are you close?"

The drawings were indisputably her, soft and sometimes smudged images. Kindly but honestly represented, more honestly than any other student (to her knowledge) had drawn her. Here, her face, her profile, her eyes, her hands. Her clubbed fingertips and thick knuckles, unapologetically rendered.

"I'm a model in a class he takes. Is this his?" Promise asked.

"Tell us about your relationship with him."

On this page, she stood on a bluff holding a fluttering scarf over her head. The figure was nude and disturbingly accurate. She passed it quickly.

"Relationship? He drew these for class."

"That one too?" Rimes said, and Promise knew he referred to the nude.

"I can't say what he does with his imagination."

"Would he have any reason to harm you?"

On another page, he'd drawn a set of shriveled lungs behind a pair of perfect breasts. The image was compassionate and tasteful and confusing to her. The air felt cold on her damp dress where the blanket had slipped away.

"No."

"But last week you were almost killed by a car he was driving under the influence."

"A freak accident. It could have been any-one."

"Why did he come to class today?"

"Because he's a student, I'd guess."

"He's missed the last several sessions. What made him come back? Was it because you were there?"

She turned the page. Here, her figure was crushed by a car. She was an inhuman, disfigured collection of bones and skin under the mangled body of a rusty Honda — a horrifying, bloody mess identifiable only by the pretty hair and deformed hands. Promise slammed the book shut. Obviously, he had drawn these after the accident. She saw only Zack's heartrending guilt on those pages, not a plan, not a threat. But she also saw how this kind of loneliness must look to detectives like these two, trained to see the sinister in everything.

"I don't know why he came," she said. "I can't help you. I don't know what any of it means."

"Have you spent time with him outside of class?"

"Not much."

"We hear that you were dating, that you might have had a falling out."

"What? That's not true."

"That you were dating or that you had a falling out?"

"Both!"

"Was Zack suicidal?"

"Of course not! How should I know? I said I can't help you!"

The detectives exchanged glances that annoyed her. She bent to pick up her bag of dry clothes.

"Miss Dayton," Rimes said, "if you are withholding any information that would help us get to the bottom of what happened today, please consider what might happen when everything comes to light. I would hate for your promising young career to be set back."

Promise digested his words. "Are you saying we . . . I . . . had something to do with all this?"

"Did you?"

"No! That's crazy! *He's* crazy. Can't you see?" She gestured to the book. "That's psycho stuff. He's been following me around. That's all I know."

Detective Halston placed the journal in a plastic bag.

"Those pictures are sick." Promise was shaking. "I wouldn't trust him."

24

Chase took bus number 47 because it was the one that went from the Shore to the university four times a day. He sat as close as possible to the door, then tapped his pointer finger on his knee at the same speed his father's light chain struck the glass globe, counting off the sixteen minutes that the schedule said it would take him to arrive.

When sixteen minutes passed he stopped tapping, then stood and began to pace, and the driver shouted at him to have a seat.

Chase didn't want one. He could see the university on the green hills ahead, illuminated by the falling sun. The flashing lights of a fire truck moved along one of its roads. The red vehicle followed a downward slope and then passed between two buildings, leaving Chase's sight.

The fire truck would lead him to Promise.

That afternoon Chase had stood in Rena's kitchen and watched the early edition news. He saw a fire engine in front of a building bearing the name F. Samson Davis Hall of the Fine Arts. Promise had told him about this hall when she came for her picture. So he was not surprised to see her there in the news report's footage. She was standing alone, wet like a sea otter, and her hands were on fire, flaming at the tips where she clutched a blanket. Her beautiful hands.

No one moved to help her. Not even Promise seemed concerned that she was burning.

The image vanished and the photo of a man named Zack Eddy blocked Promise from view, and that was when Chase left his home as quickly as possible. There were hands on fire and a world standing around gawking, allowing a woman to burn. That Zack Eddy would not help Promise. That Zack Eddy had lips that turned downward in the same way Porta Cerreto's did.

Zack Eddy appeared in Chase's mind like a strangler fig, a hemiepiphyte plant, a killer that grew on top of other plants and overtook them, surrounding them with a death grip, choking off the light and air.

The frowning bus driver let Chase off at the front of the administration hall, and from there Chase hurried along the road that the fire truck had taken. A police sedan passed in the opposite direction, as did a media van and several other passenger cars. He saw several people, many of them on bicycles or on foot, going the same way the fire truck had gone.

Would so many people be looking for Promise?

Chase walked faster.

After ten minutes, Chase passed between the same two buildings the fire truck had rushed by. On the other side of these structures, which seemed to be dormitories, the road took a sharp right and dropped low under a long canopy of trees with bright white blossoms clustered on the leaves. It would make a fine picture, but he had not come in search of subjects. He committed the scene to memory and then ignored it as he passed through.

The road bent for one more curve, dropped into a depression in the land, and finally approached the F. Samson Davis Hall of the Fine Arts. Chase stood at the highest point on the hill and saw that detectives and medics and workers in blue jumpers from the electric company still walked all over the lawn. Students stood in clusters like tree flowers outside of yellow-tape barriers. Reporters spoke to cameras. But

Promise was not where she had been on TV, standing on the knoll that rose gently in front of the entrance.

The hall itself stood in the shelter of two towering *Quercus garryana.* Each white oak was likely twice the age of the structure it protected and three times as tall. This beautiful detail had been omitted on the television.

Near the bottom of one of the great trees, Promise was walking away from him, stepping over the bumpy roots, going toward a parking lot on the other side of the detectives' barriers. Her hands seemed to have recovered from the flames. She was wearing jeans and the same sheepskin boots and a fluttering yellow blouse. A large turquoise-colored straw bag hung on the shoulder of her good arm. He stooped under the barrier tape and jogged to meet her. He reached her in fifty strides and touched her on the shoulder.

She jumped away and her hand went to her stomach. Her bag slapped her side.

"You are dry now," he said. He smiled the way he did when he and Chelsea ate ice cream.

"I . . . uh . . . they finally let me change."

She walked slightly faster than she had been. "I saw you on TV," he said. "Your

255

hands are hurting."

"What?"

"You are dying. No one will help."

Now Promise looked at him. "You're the guy who drew me that picture. What are you doing here?"

"Finding you."

She pulled her hair to one side of her shoulder. The strands were shiny and flat. "Why?"

"I knew you needed to be found, the way you did when I saw your picture."

"The picture you drew?"

"Those are pretty boots."

Promise glanced at her feet. "I need to talk to you about the picture."

"The picture on the television?" Chase hurried to catch up. She was moving very fast.

"What television pic — oh. I mean the picture you drew for me. The lung."

They approached the edge of the lawn, where a broken asphalt drive led into the parking lot. It was crowded with cars, some of them double-parked.

"I drew a tree for you. A tree of life."

"It looks like a tree, but it's a lung. Airways."

Chase stopped walking and recalled the picture by holding his memory of it out in front of him. He moved his hands to shift the picture to a new angle, then shifted again, and once more, and he saw it in his mind's eye. A full lung.

"Ha ha! That is very good! A good surprise."

"There's a car coming."

Chase left the street and joined her in the parking lot.

She said, "You didn't know it was a lung?"

He shook his head. She moved swiftly among the cars, looking for something.

"Did you know my lungs are sick?"

"You are dying."

"Yeah, you keep saying that like I had no idea," Promise said. "People have been telling me since I was four years old that I'm going to die young."

"Everyone dies young."

"Now there's one I haven't heard. Usually it's 'everyone dies.' "

"Methuselah was 969 years old."

"Who?"

"Son of Enoch. Father of Lamech, an ancestor of Noah —"

"You are very sweet, Chase, but you're freaking me out a little bit."

"You could never be a freak."

"I have cystic fibrosis. A terminal genetic disease. No cure."

"Those boots will not last forever," Chase said.

"What?"

"I am sorry you are sick."

"Actually, I've been strangely healthy, which is why I wanted to know about that picture. It's a good lung."

"Thank you."

"I mean you drew one that appears to be healthy."

"I did."

Promise turned around in front of an old champagne-colored Camry. She crossed her arms. "I don't mean to sound impatient, but it's been a pretty upsetting day for me, and I need to find my car and get out of here. Something happened in there that I can't explain to anyone" — she pointed at the F. Samson Davis Hall of the Fine Arts — "and my lungs feel practically brand new, and things are getting downright weird. So I just need to get to the point here: Why did you draw *that* picture? What does it mean? And how did you know it was for me? Like, even my meeting you was a complete accident."

All the words shouted at Chase. She was angry over a nice picture, and this was confusing. He placed his hands over his ears and took a step back. He tried to remember what the bristlecone had said about the picture, and why it might make Promise upset. She tossed her hands up and started moving again.

"You are looking for the wrong thing," Chase said.

"I'm pretty sure I know what my car looks like."

"You want people to remember you. You want fame."

Promise stopped walking and turned around.

"How do you . . . ? I mean, what are you talking about?"

"Fame is not love. It does not remember the way love does. Not forever. No one can remember forever."

"I really don't know what you mean."

"There is your BMW Roadster. It is a very nice car." He pointed.

She looked at the convertible, one aisle over. She looked at him. She twisted away and squeezed between parked cars to get to hers. "You have a very strange way of talking with people."

"I am telling you something important."

Promise reached her car, which had no top, and slowly lowered her turquoise-colored bag onto the backseat.

"So did they say that on the news? That I

259

almost died?"

"Maybe. I did not hear."

"How did you know, if you didn't hear it from someone?"

His knowing was like his breathing, like his love for this beautiful woman with the sleek hair and the fingers like slender tree branches. It simply *was*. He did not question it.

"I can see it."

"No, you can't. Someone told you, or you heard about it, or —"

"You are angry at me again."

"I'm confused!"

"I saw your boots. I saw you falling. I saw your broken arm. I saw your burning fingers."

"Burning fingers?"

Chase pointed.

Promise stared at him, and he did not like the shift in her eyes. They looked like Chelsea's eyes when Chase talked about their dad. He tapped his thumb on his thigh. One tap, one second.

"On your fingertips," he said.

When she did not move, he reached out for her hand that did not have a cast. It was a fist, but she let him lift her wrist and turn it over so that he cradled her wadded fingers in his open palm.

Her skin was soft like his favorite paper, which could be easily damaged. Chase moved his chalk-marked fingertips over her hand the way he prepared a surface to receive an image from his mind. With tenderness he grazed her knuckles and let his touch slide over her nails into the center of her closed hand. Her muscles slowly opened of their own accord.

Her fingers were so perfect. The tiny pads of her fingertips were bright pink. The color of Chelsea's favorite lipstick.

She removed her hand from his and brought it up to her eyes. There was a line between her eyebrows. "What happened?"

Perhaps Promise, like Wes, was not always a good listener.

"I didn't even know this," she said. "How could you?"

"How could you not know you were burning?"

"I couldn't have been *burning* burning."

"Sometimes I see pictures that other people do not see."

"Like, you saw a picture of my fingers?"

"They are like strong branches."

Promise laughed, but the sound was not happy. Chelsea did this sometimes, and also cried but said she was glad, and the contradiction made no sense to Chase. She held her hands out in front of her and examined them the way Rena did after washing dishes a long time in the sink.

"Branches. I guess that's one way of putting it," Promise said. "I'm not going to start growing anything under my nails, am I?"

Chase was not sure what she meant.

"Shoots? Buds? Leaves?" She was shaking her head.

"You have beautiful hands."

Promise shoved them into the back pockets of her jeans. Her lips formed a crooked line, but this was very different from Zack Eddy's lips.

"You must stay away from Zack Eddy," he said.

Her legs and lips both stiffened. Her eyes turned to look at the F. Samson Davis Hall of the Fine Arts. "How do you know Zack?"

"His mouth turns down like Porta Cerreto's."

Her eyes slowly came back to him. "His mouth?"

"Also, you should not die until you love."

"Wait a second, Romeo. Let's finish with Zack."

"A good idea."

"What do you have against Zack and Porta?"

"We are finished with them, you said. We should stay finished."

"We? I didn't mean —"

"I love you," he said. "That is more important. I want to tell you all about the trees."

Promise placed her hand on the door handle, then took it off. She said, "I love my parents. I love my close friends."

"I am glad."

"Is that what you meant, about loving someone before you die?"

"I think you should love me too."

"Oh really? Is this your usual approach to picking up women?"

"I have never picked up any woman. I think I could lift you."

Promise graced his ears with a musical laugh that sounded like love.

But then she left.

The sun was below the watery horizon by the time Chelsea and Wes drove off the university grounds. They'd searched for more than an hour, and in the process of showing Chase's photo around (no one had seen him) were educated on the incident in the fine arts hall. The knowledge didn't tell Chelsea anything about her brother.

Wes pointed his car back toward the

downtown shops at an even speed with one hand on the wheel. Chelsea's mind was miles down the road, reckless and swerving. They were weighing the pros and cons of filing a missing persons report when Rena called Chelsea's cell phone to say Chase had returned and gone directly upstairs.

The news sent Chelsea's thoughts skidding off her mental racetrack. She closed her phone, exhausted and — to her surprise — disheartened. She had fantasized about being furious with her brother, lecturing him once he was safe, even though Wes had always said lectures were inadvisable.

Wes's voice butted into her head. "This is a milestone event. We'll get Chase a phone, teach him to check in. He might get so good at it that you go crazy."

At the crest of a hill, Chelsea could see the ocean's distant shipping lanes. The lights of a large boat were steady stars floating on the water.

"Someday he's not going to need me, Wes."

"Chels —"

"He's going to walk out of our house and never come back."

"You sound like a mom who's just dropped off her five-year-old at kindergarten."

"Five? I've given Chase more than three decades. My entire life. What will it be without him needing me?"

25

Promise drove straight to the hospital, not sure if she'd be able to see Zack or if she really wanted to. What she did want to know was whether his presence at all three of her close brushes with death was genuinely accidental. Such a terrible coincidence would be impossible to explain. She kept glancing at her red fingertips, which hadn't felt tender until Chase pointed them out.

She almost preferred the truth to be that Zack was malicious. It would be emotionally easier to cope with.

In the parking lot, she called her mother for the third time since reclaiming her cell phone and street clothes from the authorities. When she first picked up her phone, it had logged twenty-seven missed calls, and twenty-three of them were from her mom. When Promise finally reached her, they both burst into tears, and Promise decided not to tell her about the lights falling into the water with her and Chris. Instead, she agreed to check in by phone at least each hour until she was safely home again.

"Your father and I are coming down tonight," her mom had said. "We're already packed."

Promise didn't object. She explained her plans to visit a friend at the hospital.

If she ran into anyone there who asked, she'd say she was there to see Michelle.

She really needed to see Michelle. In fact, one of the missed calls was from Michelle's phone. She'd likely seen the news and was worried. Chelsea made a mental note: after Zack, Michelle. In the craze of the prior week she'd dropped in only twice — a real slouch of a friend. But she was so busy, she'd cut corners on her own therapy regimen too.

Promise put up the top of her car, changed from her boots into flip-flops, pulled a university sweatshirt over her head, and then stuffed her long hair into the hoodie. It wasn't exactly a disguise, but it wasn't her usual look either. There was no point in announcing to anyone that she was here.

A volunteer at the information desk told Promise that Zack was still in the emergency room. It took Promise several wrong turns to reach the ER and pass through security.

By then she was so disoriented that she didn't see Porta Cerreto until the gallery owner reached out to touch her arm.

"Promise, sweetie."

"Porta. I didn't expect to see you."

"It's a mother's duty."

"A mother — you're . . . ?"

"I know, I know. Most people are surprised when I tell them. I waited a lot of years for my one and only."

"Why did he introduce you to me as a friend? And you have different last names." The questions popped out before she thought of them as being too personal.

Porta linked her hand into Promise's arm the way a girlfriend would. Her fingertips were cold and sent goose bumps rippling up Promise's skin. She turned Promise away from the ER and out into the hall toward a café. The scent of fresh-ground coffee beans surrounded them.

"Let's just say we have more than a generation gap between us at present. Nothing that can't be closed, my dear. It's very dear of you to come see Zack. He'll be happy about that."

"Is he all right?"

"He has a possible concussion and a very unattractive face, but he's going to be fine.

268

Can you believe they didn't break any bones?"

"That's a relief." Promise thought her politeness must look as strained as it felt.

"Of course he had no intention of harming anyone."

"I would hope not."

"Oh, they'll call a battalion of therapists into this one, you can be sure of it. I came out for a coffee while we wait. Come join me."

"They're calling therapists to the ER?"

"No, no. They say they're going to discharge him, but it can take hours, you know."

"They're not going to arrest him?"

"On what grounds! I'd like to know. They should be arresting those boys who attacked him. What's that law about screaming 'fire' in a crowded theater?"

"Can I see Zack?"

"Soon enough. But quickly, before we have to endure Zack's interruptions, I want to hear your version of what happened. I hardly trust the news anymore, let alone my son."

"What did he tell you?"

"That some rogues looking for their fifteen minutes of fame decided they could call him a terrorist and become superheroes."

Promise waited.

"That's all," Porta said. "He's a man of few words."

"I'm not sure I trust my own perceptions sometimes," Promise said. But then — maybe because she was sitting down at a small, intimate table with Zack's mother, who would be sympathetic but not frightened like her own mother, or maybe because Porta seemed to be a woman of a broad and uncritical mind — Promise told what she'd seen and experienced. She started with fielding Adam's critical comments before class and finished with throwing Chris out of the electrified water. Porta listened without interrupting.

"Everything happened so fast. Less than a minute. I probably imagined half of it."

"It's astounding. Just astounding."

"I guess it's not really that important, compared to what Zack went through."

"No, no."

"I have a lot of questions for him about things that have been happening to me when . . . while he's around." Promise made a motion to leave the café.

Porta held up her hand. "You and I must talk first, sweetie."

"About what?"

"I had a buyer for your picture this weekend."

"My picture?"

"The one of you falling."

"You sold it? I asked you not to even put it up."

"Yes, yes, yes. Let's not stomp over old paths. Listen: I want you to know what people had to say about it."

"I'm not really interested in that. Zack —"

"The merely curious spend their time wondering, as you thought they might, if it's a composite, a photo illustration. But the truly interested don't even ask the question. They see that it's not, or they don't care. They point out the weather, the bright orange wrap flying free, the sensation of falling. They relate to that on a figurative level."

"Why do you keep ignoring me?"

Porta said, "When I tell them you survived the fall, they stop telling me what they feel. This is a private moment between a person and the art, and I've learned to respect it."

"Porta! Why do you tell them about me? That's irrelevant." Promise stared at Porta, feeling used.

"Irrelevant to what? Their experience with the image? Not true. You have everything to do with it, Promise. Do you think it's accidental that death has teased you all these years and yet spared you? We're all dying, as you said the night we became acquainted — but why not you? Why not yet? I find the mystery intriguing myself. The moment I laid eyes on that picture I knew that there was something about you that the world needed to hear about. Something worth immortalizing. Do you follow me, Promise?"

They were alluring ideas, pretty words. Words that eclipsed the reality of Promise's frustration.

Porta lowered her voice. "Your ability to cheat death could inspire great art and many people. You could save whomever you want, as you saved the boy in the water."

"You mean Chris? I didn't *save* him."

The old woman's eyebrows raised a challenge to that claim and caused Promise to question it herself. Had she prevented someone from dying?

"Life itself will stand up and take notice of you. Perhaps I could interest you in exploring how it works."

The offer came across as a temptation, a suggestion that they embark on some illegal, profit-seeking venture. Seeing it this way was unreasonable, Promise felt, somehow unfair to Porta, and yet she said, "I have a much more traditional career plan in mind."

Zack's mother laughed. "You think singing for a couple people for a couple months is going to give you what you're really after?" She reached across the table and laid her fine-boned hand on Promise's arm. "Some lives are more remarkable than others. Worth saving. Other people pass through this existence without a care. But you — I sense that you want something more from your experience. Don't you? Don't you see how you've been set apart?"

"No. No, I don't." But it was a wonderful possibility. "I don't know what you mean."

"You have a gift, child."

"I'm just . . . lucky. A freak." Chase's words popped into her head. *You could never be a freak.* "If I had a gift, I'd know it."

"Not necessarily. I'm an old woman, child. I know things you've never even dreamed of. I can teach you, Promise."

Promise wavered. "Teach me what?"

"How to harness your power. Today your gift not only saved you — it saved another life. Isn't it wonderful? Imagine what you could do with that."

Imagine. Oh, Promise could imagine beating this Grim Reaper disease that had shadowed her from childhood. She could imagine saving friends. She could imagine being desired and being powerful and being sought out. Really, what if . . . ?

What if w*onderful* was the wrong word, a criminal's description for getting away with a heinous violation of the law — a metaphysical breakdown of the natural law? This was insane talk.

"Absolutely not." Promise stood. She needed to speak to Zack. He'd bring her back down to earth. "Ask the questions of someone else. 'Why haven't you died? Why not yet?' Ask anyone but me."

A new voice jerked Promise's ears toward a nearby table. "Excuse me, Ms. Dayton?" Promise saw a fair-haired fortyish woman in glasses watching her and Porta. The frames of her glasses were thick and bright red, the color of cranberries, and decorated with rhinestones. A small spiral notebook and paper coffee cup sat in front of her. "I see you know Zack Eddy's mother."

Porta said, "I'm sorry, you are . . . ?" at the same time Promise said without thinking, "Yes."

"You are Zack Eddy's mother?" the woman said, apparently needing to verify what she merely suspected.

"I'm about to become your editor's worst nightmare," Porta said, eyeing the notebook.

"Which would make for a great drama, as I'm her dream writer. Danielle Dean, the *First Word*." She extended a hand, which Porta ignored. "Ms. Dayton, I have no intention of keeping you long. But I was wondering about your relationship with Mr. Eddy's mother in light of your claims that you and he hardly know each other."

"She's here as a courtesy, because she's a more-decent-than-average human," Porta said.

"You are the only student to pay him a visit," Danielle said. "Did you know that?"

Promise was still wishing her first audible answer back into her mouth. She bit her lip.

"A source tells me that you made a phone call just moments prior to the incident in which Mr. Eddy struck you with his car. May I ask who you called?"

Porta said, "No."

"By chance did you place a call to Mr. Eddy, informing him that, for the moment, the sidewalk was clear of bystanders?"

Danielle's suggestion ran over Promise like a truck. "What is *wrong* with you?"

"Securing phone records is more a matter of good connections than court orders these days," Danielle said. "It will be an easy matter to —"

"Please, do," Promise said. "You won't

275

find any calls from me to Zack."

Not that day, at least. When had they called each other to set up the session on the bluff? Days ran together in a sickening blur. What if . . . ?

"Are you aware that Internet hits on your music video have tripled since word got out that he tried to kill you? Twice?"

"My son hasn't tried to kill anyone." Porta's tone was strangely level.

It was the part about the tripled viewings that Promise took note of.

"I wasn't aware . . ."

"How do you explain his presence at each of your —"

"My son has the right to be anywhere at any time," Porta said.

"— accidents that could have led to death, but cost you little more than a Band-Aid?"

"It's not like that," Promise said.

"Like what?"

"Zack Eddy has been stalking me," she blurted and wished she hadn't.

Porta reacted to this claim by facing off with Danielle and avoiding Promise's eyes.

"He scares me. He needs help." Promise hated her compulsion to lie, despised her reflexive survival instinct.

"You can see why I reached out to Ms. Dayton," Porta said to the reporter.

Promise stared, disbelieving Porta's support.

"I am highly interested in any information that would help me to help my son. Go now. Assure the world that it is a safer place, now that Zack Eddy is guaranteed to receive the best possible mental care."

"And what about Ms. Dayton? Are you confident that she is not in need of similar care?"

"More confident than you are in your writing skills."

"May I —"

"Get out. Or I'll call security."

Danielle Dean made a slow-motion show of stowing her notebook and pen, keeping her eyes on Promise as she rose from the café table. Promise's feet were icicles in the flip-flops. She quaked, but not from cold. What had she done?

26

Behind the curtain of an emergency-room bay, Zack rolled onto his side so that his back was to his mother. After being pressed by police and prodded by doctors, all he wanted was painkillers.

Porta pushed her small wheeled stool around to the other side of the bed, chasing him. The close-quarter curtains clung to her linen suit. She unstuck herself, then sat.

"You know what this means," she said to him in a low voice.

"What on earth are you talking about?"

"Promise, of course."

"Would you drop your obsession already! She could have died today."

"How do you know she's telling the truth about what happened? No one really saw it. There are dozens of alternative explanations."

"What? Does she strike you as a liar?"

"Everyone lies."

Zack raised himself up on one elbow, which hurt his ribs but gave some impression of being assertive. "She looks death in the face every day. She is *not* some goddess from your fantasies. She has no motive to lie about something like this."

"Plenty of people think she might."

"I don't give a rip about what other people think."

"She told a reporter you're a kook. Said you've been stalking her and should be locked up. Shall I lock you up?"

Zack sagged back onto the mattress. She had really said that? The girl who told him to accept kindness had smacked it out of his hands? "You can't lock me up. I'm not going home with you," he said.

"I see. If you'd rather return to your dorm I'll gladly feed you to the wolves."

"Maybe I'll be lucky enough that some vigilante will shoot me in the hospital parking lot first."

"That would be some luck." She crossed her arms. "Or you could do something worthwhile for once. Redeem yourself."

Zack didn't miss Porta's tone, which was the seductive voice she put on for clients oh-so-close to making a purchase.

"I want you to try to kill her," Porta said. "I have to be sure she's the one."

279

Zack popped upright. Blood rushed out of his skull, but not fast enough to prevent him from finding his feet.

His mother said, "My usual means of determining these things is presently unreliable."

He tried ignoring her. *She* was the one who needed to be locked up. "Where's my shirt?"

"It has to be you."

"I'm not a killer."

"It only makes sense for it to be you."

"Why? Because you want to keep your hands clean? Because you think it will just fit right into what everyone expects of me already?"

He took the heart rate monitor off his forefinger and then silenced the alarm by punching a button on the machine.

"Yes!"

"I'm *not* a killer."

"You're a closer fit than I am."

Zack saw a bag that might contain his shirt and shoes. He dumped it on the bed. The shirt in the bag was bloody and had been cut off of him. No shoes.

"You'd kill yourself easily enough if you were smarter and braver."

"With you believing in me like that, is it any wonder why?"

"You care for Promise," she said.

"Not anymore."

"Then what have you got to lose? It will cost you nothing. It will fail, like everything else you've ever done. No one will have to know what you did, except Promise and me. And then, what possibilities! You'll be the one who proved the truth about her. She'll fall at your feet."

"I can't believe I'm listening to this." Zack tried to open the cabinets in the wall behind the bed. They were locked.

"If we're wrong, if she actually dies, it doesn't matter. She's going to die anyway. In a year, two years."

"There is no *we* in this discussion."

"It would be a mercy. The end of life for people with cystic fibrosis is no walk in the park."

Zack leaned over his mother, who sat as calmly as if discussing plans for a dinner party. "You can't have it both ways."

"Oh, I'm not going to. She's exactly what I think she is, and you're exactly what I know you are. It's only a matter of time before you both buy into it."

Zack spun, barefoot, and threw open the curtain. He walked out wearing only his threadbare jeans.

Porta pursued him, walking swiftly, her

high heels clacking. "I know you, Zack. Love on your terms is all you've ever wanted. You can't find it in yourself to meet anyone halfway. Which means you won't forgive her for turning her back on you."

No, he wouldn't, but holding a grudge and killing someone were entirely different matters.

Weren't they?

He punched his way through the doors between the treatment area and the waiting room. Porta held back as the doors slowly closed.

"I don't forgive," he said loudly enough for his point to be driven home over his shoulder. "But I can level the playing field. *My* side of things is that she set up all these stunts to kick-start her own publicity. She came to me. *She* staged the cliff dive, the car crash, the big act at school — it was all her idea. Let's see how she survives *that* revelation."

Zack padded by the sole member of his waiting-room audience, a middle-aged woman who was writing in a spiral-bound notebook and looking at him over the tops of her rhinestone-studded reading glasses.

27

Promise closed the door on her home and leaned against the solid wood, something that would hold her up. The possibilities Porta had placed in front of her mind made her feel breathless.

"Promise!" Her mother rushed out of the kitchen, where she'd been cooking something. Food? Under these circumstances?

Her father stood from the sofa and embraced his daughter, kissed her on top of the head, then released her.

"Thank goodness you're okay," Mom said. "It's been all over the news."

"It was just a misunderstanding," Promise said.

Dad said, "Things like this can't be blown off. The administration had better get to the bottom of it quickly."

"I think it's out of their hands." Mom rubbed Promise's back, small and distressed circular motions. "The FBI is all over the place."

"Is it true that this boy Zack has been harassing you?" Dad asked.

Promise's stomach dropped. "Who said that?"

"Some talking head. I don't remember. But if you have a problem with him, that's something we can help with."

"No, no. It's not like that."

Her mother laid a hand light on Promise's cast. "You told me you broke your arm skating."

Promise played dumb.

"They're saying it was a car accident, and this Zack was involved."

"I didn't want to worry you. Really, it's no big deal." She pulled away from her parents. "Smells good in here, Mom." But she wasn't hungry for anything.

"Honey, do we need to talk?"

"About what?"

"About today, about this young man —"

"What happened today has been blown way out of proportion. Things have been so great for me — I feel stronger than ever, I've got the dream role in *Wicked,* my video found an audience and an agent! I'd rather talk about that stuff. Please?"

Her parents didn't exactly relent, but they

gave her what she asked for as if it were a new dress or tickets to a hot concert. Promise soaked her voice in brightness and optimism and choked down what would have been a delicious meal, though tonight it was tasteless. As early as possible, and as graciously as possible, she escaped their company.

In the silence, Porta's voice emerged larger than life. It bounced around in Promise's head as she went through the motions of her evening routine.

If death at a young age was not her fate, everything would change.

Promise had never wanted to die. She was not suicidal. None of her friends, many of whose lungs had given out in their teen years, was suicidal either. Hope for cures, for longer lives, for accomplishing something meaningful within the shorter time allotted to them had always outweighed death wishes. People outside of the CF community often seemed surprised to learn that suicide rates among patients were lower than among healthy populations.

The reason why, in her opinion, was simple: people who were sick like she was understood the urgency of life. Time was like money. People who had less of it knew not to squander it. Not without consequence. And they certainly wouldn't put it through a paper shredder.

What if she had more time than she thought? All the time in the world? What if she couldn't be killed, not even by this brutal disease?

What if she wasn't going to die? Ever?

How could she even entertain an idea like that?

Porta hadn't actually said Promise couldn't die. That was Promise's brain, running around like someone who thought she'd won the lottery. What were Porta's actual words?

Something about a gift. A gift worth immortalizing. Which was a strange way of putting it. Promise wasn't even sure what that meant.

In her therapy room, Promise strapped her chest therapy vest on and hooked up the hose to the generator. She checked the frequency settings, then reached out toward the switch that would turn the machine on and disrupt the death in her airways. Her finger hovered over the plastic button.

Maybe all the time she spent doing this therapy was pointless.

Maybe it was completely unnecessary.

What if? Porta's murmur sang to her.

Promise withdrew her hands and looked

at the burns on her fingertips. They were so mild that they were hard for her to see in the room's low light. Barely pink. The electricity had to go somewhere, she supposed. But why hadn't it fried her heart, or her nerves? She should be a charred corpse.

She unbuckled the vest fasteners and slipped out of it. For her parents' benefit, she ran the machine anyway. At the desktop system sitting under the large flat-screen wall monitor, she woke up her computer and clicked on her default search engine. She typed in *electrical burns* and then, after a moment's hesitation, added *images.* A link over several small photos came up. She clicked on it, and a catalog of grotesque exhibits lined up for her. At a glance, she could see that the smooth tips of her fingers bore no resemblance to any of the disfigured, bleeding, and splayed layers of tissues captured in these pictures.

Her stomach started a dispute with her meal. She closed the link and returned to the search engine. Her fingers hovered over the keys until she chose her next words: *fatal fall height.*

Within a few clicks it became clear that death wasn't the inevitable outcome of her fall from the bluff. Many people had survived higher, harder falls, typically with severe injuries. Shattered legs. Crushed lungs. Exploded hearts. She found a case in which a woman who fell from a height similar to the ocean bluff landed in a plot of tilled soil, then got up and walked away. Promise's mind went to the sand of the beach. She didn't know enough about physics or anatomy to calculate what the most likely outcome for her scenario ought to have been.

As for the car accident, anything could explain what had happened there. Or what had not happened there. She'd need a scientist's analysis to show her why nothing but the guard railing and her radius had broken, why the rear tires came within an inch of her belly and the front tires had missed her completely, why the frame hadn't cut her arm in two as if it were made of wax.

Who can say when it's your time to go? Chris had asked her. It was a fair question. She and Michelle and their friends had kicked it around among themselves many times without ever landing on a sensible answer.

Michelle. Promise needed to return her calls, assure her friends that she was okay. She looked at the clock in the corner of her screen. Michelle would be sleeping. Promise put off the call until morning and shut off the computer.

The only explanations for why she hadn't died in the pool of water at the arts center were thin theories suggested by everyone but her and Chris: The lamp's cord had been yanked from the wall in the stampede. The circuit blew before the charge caused any damage. Promise and Chris weren't in the water when the electricity hit.

But they were in the water, and she'd heard the bulbs shatter. The currents had paralyzed Chris and energized her, Wonder Woman style, and she knew as sure as she needed oxygen to make it through the night that nothing logical could explain why.

The only way she could know for sure was to test it.

Confront it head on. Try dying. A bullet to the head. A stuffed exhaust pipe in a closed car.

No no no no no!

All she wanted out of this life was to do something that others would find worthy of remembering, and to do it before she died. Some said she wanted fame, but this is what she thought artists like Kurt Cobain or Sylvia Plath had wanted. Fame, and escape from pain. She was not one to shy away from pain.

An extra-large bottle of acetaminophen. A noose.

Promise let out a grunt and clapped her hands over her ears. Her cast pounded the side of her head, reminding her that she had indeed been injured during one of her standoffs with mortality. She had never had a more wrong idea. This pestering notion that she was invincible was juvenile, the fantasy of youth. Everyone died. Everyone.

E-V-E-R-Y one.

She shut off the therapy vest, left the room, entered the hallway, and couldn't decide where to go. Her parents' low voices at the front of the apartment prevented her from going to the kitchen for water. What if? What if? Behind her were chest-therapy devices and antibiotics and nebulizers and the ever-present hope that she'd live one day longer than anyone said she could. Ahead of her was a dark bedroom and an oxygen concentrator and — eventually — a long, slow decline into eternal sleep. This was the timeline of her life, as short as the hall itself, lived out in a small world where she had access to everything she needed when she got sick.

If sickness were no longer her enemy, she'd be free! Promise placed her good hand over her heart, charged with fright and excitement. She'd sing and sing. She'd tour, she'd do interviews, she'd find some cause that would justify her celebrity status. She'd start her own version of Make-A-Wish for kids and adults who had CF. She'd give money to research for a cure. She'd save lives.

But Porta had suggested she could save lives even now. Was she really Chris's savior? This, for some reason, was not a happy thought. If she had some woo-hoo voodoo witch doctor skill that could have *done something* to save her friends' lives — or to extend their lives by even a day, a week — her grief over having lost them without lifting a finger would smother her.

Promise walked into her bedroom and stared for a long time at the oxygen concentrator she had relied on every night for several months.

Perhaps she no longer needed it.

Without changing her clothes, she fell onto her bed and turned her back to the machine. She curled up in a ball and waited for daytime to bring sure answers on its wings.

28

Chelsea couldn't sleep. In spite of the long day that stretched ahead of her, she rose at four after an hour awake and tugged on her CW-X running gear. The hyper-engineered running tights promised to boost her oxygen efficiency, but she hadn't decided yet whether they were worth the cost.

Her four-mile route took her through the old neighborhood and across the highway to a beachside frontage road, then back over streets and past homes she'd known since childhood. The predawn air was full of ocean fog that would soon burn off. On her way toward the water she passed a sedan moving slowly down one side of the street, headlights like twin suns. The driver tossed newspapers into driveways.

This morning Chelsea changed her route so that it cut back through the downtown area. She headed for ART(i)FACTS, compelled to see if anyone had purchased her boy yet.

She couldn't remember when she had started thinking of it as hers, nor when she first perceived him as an amalgam of herself, her brother, and — because of Wes's suggestion that it looked like a piece her father might have made — her dad. A family portrait. Beyond that, she couldn't explain what kept bringing her back to this child. She had long ago set aside any notion that she would marry or have her own children. It wasn't that she had never wanted to but that she made a conscious choice. She turned her back on these common paths to do something uncommon: protect and provide for her brother.

Caring for Chase was the highest purpose she could aspire to, and she had found her way through every challenge so far. But she had no idea how to address Chase's fixation on Promise Dayton. Promise was the first thing that had ever distracted him from his safe world of trees and Bibles.

When Chelsea arrived at the gallery, she paced on the sidewalk until she caught her breath. The soft spotlights overhead and at the statue's feet gave the metal a reddish cast that glistened like something molten.

"What would you tell me to do, Dad?"

Chelsea said this aloud.

She had never blamed her father for his disappearance, which was worse than his deployment because it marked the end of communication and comfort and, eventually, hope that he would return. There was no time for anger, or even grief, both of which she'd once experienced over her mother. Her mother, the runaway. Chelsea didn't have any feelings about that loss any more. It was too long ago.

For the last ten years, her life had been so full of Chase and young adulthood and the need to survive in her new role that emotional living had become an indulgence she could not afford. She started moving, fearing paralysis. She started doing, fearing that nothing would get done. She started running, fearing sleepless nights.

She'd held the fear at bay. But now Chelsea needed her father not to be dead.

"Do I protect Chase or let him go?" The damp air chilled her now that she had stopped running. The fog felt heavier than her sweat-soaked layers of gear. Goose bumps rose at the base of her neck under her ponytail.

"A longing fulfilled is a tree of life."

The voice was so like her father's that Chelsea spun around, looking for him, then felt foolish. The morning was so silent that the thoughts in her head had taken on volume.

She sighed and glanced back at the boy. Maybe she ought to name it.

Also foolish. Naming an inanimate —

"Blessed are those who wash their robes . . ."

The boy's lips had moved. Chelsea took one step back from the window. Her heart had resumed its full-tilt-running rate. She looked again for her father. Or rather, for some other explanation for the voice.

". . . that they may have the right to the tree of life."

"I'm going crazy," she whispered.

"That's what I thought too, first time I came here."

Outside the oak door of the gallery, face pressed close to the frosted glass, was a woman who might have been a grandmother or great-grandmother, fragile and stooped and leaning on a cane. She nodded at Chelsea. Had she been there when Chelsea arrived?

"Sorry to startle you," the woman said. "Is that the piece that grabs you?"

"What?"

"Ms. Cerreto says everything in this place calls out to just one person. Is that the one that's been talking to you?"

"Did you hear it?"

"My hearing isn't what it used to be. I thought that woman was full of it the first time I came in. But there was this one oil pastel that I couldn't take my eyes off. A boat in a harbor. An ocean liner, really. I finally let her take it down for me, had a look at it for a time. And now I can't get the voices out of my head."

"What kind of voices?"

"If I bought it, do you think they'd leave me alone? Or would they be noisier?"

Chelsea craned her neck to see if she could identify the painting herself. "What do the voices say?"

The cane wobbled under the woman's right hand. "They say that it was a mistake for me not to get on the boat all those years ago. I should have got on the boat, but I was stubborn."

"Then maybe it's good you didn't buy it."

The old woman shook her head. "Some regrets are too big to walk away from."

Was she supposed to comfort this woman? Commiserate with her? Chelsea was at a loss. "Is that why you keep coming back? To look at it?"

"I figure it's better to be about getting some exercise than sitting in an armchair not getting any sleep."

Chelsea swallowed. "Maybe you could take it home and see. Get rid of it if that doesn't work for you."

"Maybe. Except it's not leaving me alone now. I'm not sure what it would do in my own house."

"Let me walk you home. It's dangerous out here alone."

"Except for people like you who run, eh?" It was a friendly accusation. The old woman ambled in Chelsea's direction. "What about you? What's that boy? What does he say to you?"

The boy's lips had not budged again. "I'm not sure yet."

"You're too young for big regrets."

"How is it, then, that the woman who owns this place talks so much about how her art saves lives? What does she say about that boat picture and you?"

"Nothing, since I told her I can't afford it! But I don't know, honey. At my age, there isn't much worth saving."

"I'd think people your age have loads more worth saving than people my age."

The woman lifted her eyes to Chelsea. "Now there's a thought. I don't know. We've got more litter on the highways of our lives too."

"Comes with the territory, I guess."

"But you might be right. Out of the mouths of babes."

Chelsea glanced at the motionless child. "Maybe so."

"I'll think on it."

The right to the tree of life. But this time the voice was only a memory. Still, she'd take this kind of haunting over the ghosts of regret any day. Poor woman.

"You going to buy that boy?" the woman asked.

Chelsea looked at him. She couldn't afford to part with five grand. And she hated to give a woman like Porta Cerreto a dime of her hard-earned money.

"Yes," she said. "Yes, I need him to come home with me."

29

A wind full of heat and sand plowed into Promise's back. She stood on a treeless plane, potato-skin earth beneath her feet, white-hot sky on the three-sixty horizon. She squinted against the glare and held her breath as the grit tore through her hair from behind.

When the gust died down, a woman was standing in front of her. Michelle. Her cheeks were flush with rosy health, and her jet-black curls danced around her eyes.

"I could have saved your life," Promise said to her.

Michelle laughed and threw her arms open. Promise fell into them, feeling a despair that was out of sync with her friend's happiness. Michelle's warm hug lifted the weight of her heart like a balloon rising. Promise sighed.

The sigh became a hiss, and then a rush of air, and Michelle's body deflated in

Promise's grasp. Her face, still laughing, sank and distorted first, drooping as if her neck were jointed. Her chest caved in, her hands dragged the ground, her legs gave way. Her skin turned blue.

"Michelle? Mickey!"

The wind swirled around them again and grabbed her friend by the hair, tearing her out of Promise's arms and up into a twister. Promise lunged, reaching.

She fell.

She woke. Fully clothed, breathing deeply, alert with the wakefulness of hours. Her clock said it was eight in the morning.

The dream slipped away from her mind, leaving only a sense of urgency behind. Michelle needed something from her. She needed to call Michelle.

Promise rolled over in bed and groped for the phone on her nightstand. There were three missed calls. All of them from Michelle. No messages.

How had Promise slept through them? She should have called her back last night, but this whole thing with Porta —

What was she going to do?

No answers. Right now, all she was going to do was dial her best friend's number. And wait for the phone to ring. And wait for Michelle to pick up.

"Yes?"

It was not Michelle, and Promise hesitated, sorting out the surprise.

"Promise?"

"Mrs. Graham?"

"Hi, honey." And then a pause.

Promise did not like that pause, that silence that said, *I will linger here, on endearments, because I don't want to move on to what must come next.*

"Michelle tried to call me a few times last night. I'm sorry I couldn't —"

"Oh, honey, that wasn't Michelle. It was me."

More silence. Promise couldn't stand it.

"Is she there? I'm sure she was worried about —"

"No, Promise, Michelle isn't . . . Michelle's lungs . . . She went very peacefully. Around three in the morning. I'm sorry, honey."

Now Promise owned the silence. There was something wrong with Mrs. Graham offering this comfort that the mother of a dead child should be able to have all to herself. It was confusing.

Michelle was dead? Promise's bedroom looked the same in this second as it had ten seconds ago. Shouldn't it be vastly different? Ransacked, like the Graham family's reality?

Promise had received similar news in the past. Never had it felt like this.

Mrs. Graham said, "I don't want you to feel bad for not getting here. It was sudden, and Michelle wasn't conscious. Even if you'd come . . ."

Promise started to sob. Michelle's mother let her cry. Michelle's bedroom was right next door, five steps away, waiting for her to come home.

Promise eventually mumbled, "I could have done something."

"There wasn't anything anyone could do, Promise."

"I could have saved her life."

"You've been through so much, honey. So many friends . . . Michelle loved you more than any other."

"She didn't want it to end this way."

"None of us did."

"I'm so sorry. What can I do?"

"Right now, let's just let her go without worrying about that."

"Okay."

"We can sort out what needs doing later."

"Sure." Promise was sniffly and snotty. Her eyes ached.

"I'll call you, honey."

"Okay."

"Bye now."

Promise closed her phone and slouched on the edge of her mattress, propping up her head with one hand on her forehead. She sat that way for a long time, breathing as normally as a healthy person, free of coughing even, while her best friend's borrowed lungs were being sealed away with the rest of her body in some mortuary refrigerator.

Oh! Michelle!

For no reason at all, not because of fairness or justice or equality, Promise had strength and air enough for both of them, and no way of sharing it.

There must be a way. There must be a way to share the life.

There it was. This, truly, was the answer Promise had been seeking through the subconscious corridors of her mind: saving a life was superior to destroying it. She'd be a fool to test herself by trying to commit suicide. That would make a mockery of Michelle's courageous attempts to live! But to test the ability Porta claimed she had by trying to save someone . . .

Promise stood, resolved: in honor of the friend whom she failed, she should see if she had the power to save a life.

Yesterday's clothes hung limp on her body. She ignored them. She needed to tell her parents about Michelle.

She went out into the hall and was enveloped by the scent of cooked bacon. Her mother was standing at the entrance to the kitchen, looking out across the mouth of the hall toward the front door. Promise heard voices. Mom turned to see her, and her worried expression deepened at the sight of her daughter's rumpled clothing and swollen eyes. The lines in her forehead rose and asked, *What's wrong?*

Promise reached her mother and turned to see what had held her attention at the open door. Her father was standing before the screen, legs spread, arms folded. Once a soldier, always a soldier. He seemed to be barricading the apartment. His voice was firm, low.

A woman on the other side of the screen noticed Promise.

"Perhaps your daughter would like to make a statement," the woman said. It was the reporter who'd cornered her at the hospital the night before. Danielle something, with the red rhinestone-studded glasses.

"What is she doing here?" Promise said, as if her parents would have the answer.

"Ms. Dayton, I thought you'd want to reconcile the remarks you made to me last night with the new information that has come to light regarding yesterday's incident at the university."

"What new information?"

"What's your reaction to those who are calling for your expulsion?"

"Why would I be expelled?"

"That's unnecessary and extreme," her mother said from the kitchen entry.

"Many of your fellow students and several faculty members are of the opinion that you and Zack Eddy should be expelled. How do you respond to this outcry?"

"Why are they saying that?"

The woman's rhinestones caught the morning light and gave her a cartoonishly wicked appearance. "Have you been accident-prone all your life, or is this a recent development?"

Dad said, "You have three seconds to start making sense, and then I close this door."

"Yesterday, Ms. Dayton, you denied any part in orchestrating the car accident or the terrorist plot."

"There was no terrorism," said her father.

"Do you deny staging any of the accidents in which you've been so recently involved?"

"I don't know what you're talking about!"

Promise said.

Danielle kept her eyes on Promise. Their intensity would bore a hole in the screen. "Mr. Eddy claims the two of you staged your numerous brushes with death in order to increase your . . . popularity."

"That's a lie. Zack would never . . ." A flash of understanding passed through her as swiftly as that electrical current. "You told him what I said last night."

"In fact, Mr. Eddy made these allegations spontaneously. We hadn't even been introduced. He has since made further accusations publicly, on a blog. At times people will do this; it's cathartic for the conscience."

"It's not true. He's — he must be upset."

"Why would he be upset, Ms. Dayton?"

Promise's parents were uncharacteristically silent. Her father was staring at her, lips parted in a question.

"Would you like to respond to his confession?"

"I had nothing to do with any of this!"

"You don't look well. I imagine you didn't think things would go this way."

"You have no idea what you're talking about. Zack's lying."

Promise's father snapped back to the moment. With one hand he reached for the door and with the other he gently pressed Promise aside. "We're done here," he said.

Her mother said, "I'm calling the administration."

"You should also call an auto detailer," Danielle said as the door closed on her. "Looks like someone egged that pretty Roadster of yours."

The door latch clicked into place.

No one said anything. Promise's eyes were glued to the closed door. It was blue, and she could see the hardened streaks of the paintbrush that last touched it. She heard her mother flipping through the phone book she kept in a drawer under the landline. Her father sighed and sank onto the sofa, then got up again and fetched his cell phone off the coffee table. He'd want to call his lawyer.

Promise said, "Michelle's dead."

Everything else seemed meaningless.

30

Chase paced on the back porch. The boards underneath his feet groaned. His portfolio lay open on the patio table. Lined up in order were five drawings of Promise's tree of life in the different stages of being overtaken by a strangler fig. There were twenty-three others upstairs in his studio. Whether it was a lung or unidentified tree made no difference to Chase. Both would be suffocated, and he was distressed.

There were many species of stranglers, nearly a thousand, nearly all of which could be found in the tropical world. Not even the Pacific Northwest was humid enough for the many varieties of *Ficus* to grow epiphytically, that is, by sprouting from seeds dropped by birds and such onto a host plant. In the tropics — where the precise species of wasps required to pollinate their correlating species of stranglers also lived — a healthy *Ficus* sent aerial roots from its host's top branches to the earth, took hold, formed an inescapable cage, and then closed in on the unwitting plant in a long and deadly embrace.

There were no tropical figs in Chase's backyard. Only cultivated species of fig could survive here, outside of shopping malls and office planters, and even those were rare. They lacked the proper wasps this far north.

In any other territory, the uncultivated strangler could be considered a threat. A deadly invader. Not unlike *Ailanthus altissima,* that stinking sumac.

The Great Basin bristlecone had not visited him for several days.

The glass door that led into the house slid open in its track, and Wes came out. Chase knew it was Wes because his steps were heavier than Chelsea's. The porch boards groaned more loudly. Chase stopped pacing and looked out at his guardian trees.

Wes stopped at the table where the drawings were laid out. Bright white trees dueling on sinister backgrounds. Chase had used the square tip of an Alphacolor pastel stick for these, and the smaller, textured Mi-Teintes sketchbook paper. The images looked more hastily done than his usual work. Broader strokes, less definition.

More fear.

"This is different," Wes observed.

"Different from what?" Chase asked.

"Your usual method, detail."

"The *Ficus* will kill the arborvitae. That is the only detail that is important."

"I thought *Ficus* trees were office plants. Nice little figs."

"Not in the jungle."

"Are you drawing people, Chase?"

"I draw trees."

Wes left the drawings. In his usual easy stride he joined Chase at the top of the porch steps and stood to his left. Chase allowed Wes's arm to touch his arm. It was a stabilizing sensation. A fearless calm.

Chase leaned into his friend.

"Tell me about the girl you love," Wes said.

"She is beautiful," Chase said. "But she is dying."

Wes nodded.

"I do not want her to die," Chase said.

"Why do you love her?"

"I was made for her."

"I can understand that."

These kinds of remarks were strange to Chase. There was nothing to misunderstand, so Wes's need to say so seemed unnecessary.

Wes said, "I feel that way about someone too."

"Is she dying?"

"Not in the way you mean."

"I was made for her because I can save her."

"From dying?"

Chase frowned. What else would he save her from?

"I suppose love is a kind of salvation. For people who accept it. Does she know she is dying?"

"No. She thinks she will live forever."

"That's tricky then. Does she love you back?"

She had not said so aloud, but she had not objected when Chase told her of his love.

"Yes," he said. "But I think we should have more time."

"Then you should take it," Wes said. "Do you know where she lives?"

Chelsea said from behind them, "Please stop encouraging him to do things that will hurt him."

Chase felt Wes turn around. Their arms disconnected. Chase tried to recall if he had heard Chelsea come through the glass slider. She might have come around the side of the house. The sound of paper bending as she lifted it off the table told him she was looking at his drawings.

"Love isn't harmful," Wes said.

"I didn't say *harm*," Chelsea said. "I said *hurt*. There's no need for hurt that can be prevented."

"Love does not hurt," Chase said.

"You two are quite the romantics. Maybe love doesn't hurt when you're drawing pictures. Or when you keep your distance, okay? So let's leave it at that."

"I have to save her," Chase said. He turned around on the porch and went to the table. He collected his drawings and put them in a pile. He needed to draw Promise's tree free of the strangler, but he would do that on the Stonehenge paper. The pencils he needed were upstairs.

Chelsea crossed her arms. "Chase, do you remember the sculpture in the window of the art gallery?"

"Yes."

"Wes thinks it looks a little bit like the piece we've got in the living room. The one Dad did all those years ago when we were kids."

"Yes. It is the first tree I ever drew."

"What kind of tree is it?"

"It is his own design."

"Do you know what he called it?"

"No."

"Well, I was thinking about buying that boy. It's similar to the tree. I think it would fit."

"You should not buy it."

"I know you think Porta's of questionable character, but I could negotiate a fair price for it —"

"You should not buy it."

"Don't you like it? I think he looks like you."

"What do I look like?"

Wes leaned against the porch railing, smiling at Chase's sister.

"Carefree. Secure. Why don't you want it?"

"I want it."

"But you said —"

"You should not buy it. It is already ours."

"What?"

"Dad made that sculpture."

"What?"

"You should remember things like that."

Wes laughed.

"You're the one with the memory of an elephant," Chelsea said. "Can you prove the sculpture is ours? How long have you known? Why didn't you say something?"

The problem with so many questions at once was that deciding which one to answer first took too much sorting out. Also, he was not an elephant.

Chase left the porch and entered the house. He walked into the living room and passed through it to the right, following a carpet runner into the den where he had searched for the species name of Promise's tree.

Six cupboards stood under the built-in bookcases that lined one wall. He opened the second from the left and withdrew a short stack of photo-archive boxes. At the bottom was one labeled *1983.* He carried this one to the desk that had been pushed under the rear window. He removed the lid and set it aside, then walked his fingers across the tops of variously labeled dividing tabs. Behind the one labeled *First Bikes,* Chase started going through each picture one at a time.

Chelsea was behind him now, looking. She slipped her hand into the box and withdrew a group of snapshots from behind a different tab.

"I haven't looked at these in years," she whispered.

Wes came over, and Chelsea showed him one from her pile.

"You two looked a lot more alike back then," he said.

"It was the haircuts," Chelsea said. "Princess Diana bobs. Even on Chase."

Chase found the photo he was looking for. He pulled it out and held it close to his face. Yes, this was the one.

The shot had been taken at the top of the narrow asphalt driveway. His father had taken this picture; Chase remembered Dad standing there with the chunky camera pressed up against his nose.

Chelsea, on a red-and-yellow Roadmaster Action-Rider tricycle with an empty blue bucket on the back, raced down the center of the drive toward their father, pedaling so hard she ought to have unbalanced the bike. She was gritting her teeth and leaning over the handlebars, chin jutting.

The garage sat deep behind the house, and Chase was to the side of it, filling the bucket of his matching trike with a collection of leaves and sticks. The mouth of the single-car garage was open. Pressed tight against the right wall was the family's 1978 Ford Fairmont Squire station wagon, white with brown paneling. Both three-wheelers fit into the back for trips to the park.

At the left, Dad had squeezed in a workbench under a grimy window. The yellowing of the photo and the murky lighting blurred the details slightly, but the facts were unmistakable. Metal trash cans under the bench held scrap metal, and a Peg-Board held tools. A welder's mask lay on its side on the ground.

On the bench was the statue from the ART(i)FACTS gallery, not quite completed. He had not been mounted on his base yet and was propped up by a vise.

A figure at the garage stood with her back to the camera. Their mother. Chase placed his finger over her tiny photo body and imagined what the picture would look like if she were facing them. She seemed to be looking at the statue.

"Here." He placed the picture on top of the pile Chelsea was browsing. She fumbled to hold it in place with her thumbs.

Chase returned to the bookcases. There were several he had not browsed yet that might be able to tell him more about Promise's tree of life.

"Unbelievable," Chelsea said.

Chase ran his fingers over the spines. *Identifying Trees: An All-Season Guide to Eastern North America* by Michael D. Williams. *Meetings with Remarkable Trees* by Thomas Pakenham.

"Even if I remembered this photo, I don't think I would have noticed the statue," she said.

"Do you know if he made this before or after the tree in your living room?" Wes asked.

Tree Finder: A Manual for the Identification of Trees by Their Leaves by May Theilgaard Watts.

"No."

"He's like a child come home again," Wes said.

"I guess he is."

"Where has he been all this time?"

"Maybe Mom took him with her," Chelsea said.

Dirr's Hardy Trees and Shrubs: An Illustrated Encyclopedia by Michael A. Dirr.

Chase did not like the story Chelsea was about to tell. He pulled out *The Meaning of Trees: Botany, History, Healing, Lore* by Fred Hageneder and opened it to the middle but did not look at the pages. His ears were in charge of his mind right now.

"When did your parents divorce?" Wes asked.

"She left in the fall of 1983. Chase had just been diagnosed."

"You mean she left because of the diagnosis?"

"It's hard to say. Dad didn't talk about it. But I'm pretty sure. You know — back then we didn't know as much as we do now

317

about autism. There was some stigma attached to it. A lot of unknowns."

Chase turned a page, and then another. Page after page to create noise, but it wasn't loud enough. He did not like stories about his mother. Fortunately, there were few.

Mothers were supposed to be strong, well rooted, sheltering and shading. Like *Ulmus americana,* the elm tree that was graceful and had a high tolerance for environmental stresses. It could grow in almost any kind of soil, resisted disease, tolerated drought, and lived a long life. Chase's mother was no such tree.

"She sent me a letter once, when I was a teenager."

Chase stopped turning pages. Their mother had never sent him a letter. He closed his book and placed it back on the shelf. When he turned around, his sister was watching him. He avoided her eyes. Wes was still looking at the picture Chase had located.

"She wanted me to come live with her. She said she had found a community where she really belonged. She wanted me to be a part of it."

"What did you do?"

"I shredded it. I know that sounds unbelievable — what daughter would shred her

mom's mail no matter what she'd done,
right? But it was the right thing to do. I
belonged here with Chase and Dad. Mom
belonged here too."

"A mother is not supposed to leave,"
Chase said.

Chelsea said, "No, she's not."

"Our mother's name is Althea," he said.
"Althea is really just a shrub. *Hibiscus syriacus.* It is pretty. Some people call it a tree,
an Althea tree. But I think it is not."

Wes nodded at him.

"If our mother were a tree, she would not
have uprooted herself."

"I'm sorry, Chase."

"Love does not leave. Love does not
pretend not to love."

Chelsea's eyes were wet.

"I love Promise," Chase said. "I will not
pretend not to, even if it hurts."

"Okay, Chase," his sister said.

"Not loving hurts more."

"Okay. Okay."

31

Porta waited. All the events of the week conspired to place their hands on Promise's back and shove her in Porta's direction. The child would come to her without need of force or fear. Perhaps without need of attempted murder either.

Still, Porta sensed that the pages of her mental day-by-day calendar were being ripped off and tossed into a bonfire. Twenty-one days had burned up and vanished, just like that. Her birthday was four days away, on Monday, and she still had not unearthed *her* truth about that silly prophecy prank. It bothered her to feel doubt over what might befall her when the time came.

Friday morning Porta bent over her sagging front porch and picked up the newspaper, which had been tucked into a plastic sleeve in anticipation of the forecasted rain. She carried it inside and followed the gray path of a matted carpet past the front rooms

— a parlor to the right and a living room to the left — which contained no furniture. Large moving boxes had been stacked in an organized fashion against the walls of the front hall and dining room, in which there was no dining room table or chairs. Porta simply had no use for them, as she never entertained and saw no point in pouring her money into anything less valuable than artwork, a worthy showcase for it, and the car and clothing necessary to represent the image.

Throughout the old house, beadboard and wainscoting in need of fresh paint peeked out from behind the boxes. The guesthouse on the north side of the property had similar details, but it was a completely unnecessary amenity. Porta was considering having it torn down. In truth, she had purchased this house for two reasons: the French-paned windows of the eat-in kitchen formed a panoramic wall that faced the ocean, and the basement was ingenious.

So she lived in the kitchen and practiced her craft in the basement, unpacking boxes only when she needed what was in them.

She withdrew the newspaper from its rain bag and spread it on the table. Thanks to Danielle Dean, Porta had been rewarded through the week with confirmation of

Zachary's and Promise's suspensions from the university, pending an investigation into the so-called terror scandal. Tuesday Promise became cloistered by her parents, who reportedly had hired a very expensive attorney. That same day Porta's son had vanished. She was unconcerned about this. The boy had too few resources to stay away for long. Left to simmer, he would likely come around to his mother, if not to her original plan. In the meantime, she would exploit her alternatives.

Wednesday Promise lost her lead role in the university's musical production, a consequence of her suspension. "We can't have distractions and potentially problematic outcomes hanging over our heads," the director was quoted as saying. Thursday Porta searched for Promise's music video online and learned that its skyrocketing popularity was in part due to the inflammatory comments posted by viewers. Truly, some of the sentiments bordered on criminal.

Today, Friday, there was no news of Promise. Instead Porta caught hold of a detail that would ultimately be more helpful: an obituary for a cherubic young woman named Michelle Graham who'd succumbed to a valiant battle with cystic fibrosis. In lieu of flowers, donations could be made to the Cystic Fibrosis Foundation. The family, however, welcomed cards and memories of people who had known the young Michelle. The address of a funeral home at a small coastal town an hour or so away was provided. Memorial services would take place Saturday. The public was welcome.

Porta had seen this girl before. The picture in the newspaper was flattering and had been cropped from a larger image, which included another woman. Porta knew this because she had seen the original. When she and Zack had first paid a visit to Promise, this very picture had been hanging in the bedroom where they'd spoken together.

Now was the time that Promise would come to her. Of course, encouraging the girl in that direction wouldn't hurt.

Promise went to Michelle's funeral alone, against her parents' advice, because in spite of having spent her life trying to stand out in a crowd, she believed she could blend in just as well. She wore black slacks and a black summer trench and a black scarf in her hair. Black umbrella, black sunglasses. Nothing worth noticing by anyone who loved Michelle Graham.

She looked like Zack Eddy. Her betrayal

of him had put her here, in need of being incognito for all the wrong reasons. Promise didn't know where to direct her regret about that.

She sneaked out Saturday morning while it was still dark. Her parents didn't stir. Promise had opted not to ask her friend Jenny to go with her.

"It'll be best if I lie low until this all dies down," Jenny had told Promise in their last phone call. Jenny had not returned Promise's texts or e-mails since Tuesday.

Acquaintances who were not as close as Jenny, on the other hand, texted and e-mailed Promise regularly, advising her to take her singing career and her only fan to Siberia, or to electrocute herself right this time, or — and this was a gem — to go jump off a cliff.

Zack was not responding either, though she had put more effort into reaching him than anyone else. Her numerous voice mails and texts would probably come back to haunt her when investigators dug into these records, and that was the thought that finally put an end to her attempts. Through the rumor mill she learned he had left town. Some said he had finally killed himself, perhaps by wading out into the ocean. She hoped this was not true.

Her agent had not contacted her at all, nor accepted any of Promise's attempts to contact him.

Promise eventually shut off her phone and her computer. Today she left them both at home.

The view from the coastal highway on this Saturday morning was similar to the conditions on the morning she had met Zack at Vista Park Bluffs. The sun was weak at the early morning hour, too weak to beat back the advancing clouds. They hovered over her as she drove.

Rain started to fall just outside Michelle's hometown.

She had brought some of Michelle's personal belongings for Mr. and Mrs. Graham. The things that were most important to her friend — the photos, the journals, the teddy bear, the favorite pillow, the comfort blanket, the laptop — had gone to the hospital with Michelle as they did for every visit. On the CF ward, bed spaces were like dorm rooms; patients moved in and marked their territories, personalized and defended their space. But Michelle had left a few mementos at the apartment: a scrapbook, a dog-eared copy of Leonard Pitt's *Walks Through Lost Paris,* a shoe box full of cards and letters and printed e-mails, her high school mortarboard and tassel, a chess club trophy.

Hidden from busybodies behind the curtains of her home, Promise had more time than she needed to sort through Michelle's belongings. She lingered, looking for the most important treasures. The Grahams would box up the rest after the sting of death subsided to a chronic pain. She found two T-shirts of her own that she thought had been lost and a pair of earrings Michelle had forgotten to return. It was these earrings, which Michelle could keep forever if she'd only come back, that kept raising tears in Promise's eyes.

While she sat at Michelle's bedroom vanity she'd opened a drawer, expecting it to be filled with cotton balls and eye shadow applicators, but found a box of stationery. Under the plastic cover of the box, the top sheet was addressed to her, Promise, and was dense with Michelle's tiny handwriting.

The unfinished letter, now tucked into a special zippered pocket inside Promise's book bag on the passenger seat, had been speaking very loudly to her ever since.

Dear Promise,

As you can see by the date up in the corner, it's Christmas, and though I've just received the most amazing present ever, I'm feeling a bit torqued about it. After all, you're with your spectacular parents in BELIZE, and I was SUPPOSED TO BE WITH YOU, diving the Blue Hole and picking up Mayan hotties to do our calculus finals come January. Though I personally think the whole thing about their being great mathematicians is a load of stinky cheese, you've got to use the pickup angle that works! (Did it work? Tell everything.)

When you get back I'll have to ask the real question that's eating at me: Are you still stuck on NEVER getting a transplant? Because here's the thing: I FEEL GREAT. You would not believe the high you get off an oxygen exchange that works the way it's supposed to. Really, you should reconsider. Now, in the interests of full disclosure I must say you would not believe the number of medications they are cramming into me right now. Swallowing and injecting and inhaling everything I'm supposed to takes up several hours of each day. A small price to pay, though.

Of course, this could all go south. I get that.

Okay, I'm being entirely selfish. I

admit that the Big Truth about my funk is that I just don't want to feel great alone. I'm suddenly, completely, literally freaked out for you, over the new truth that I've got these lungs that will keep me going another five years — or whatever it is these days — and you don't, and what does that mean for us? That one day I'm going to be out there in Belize (or France!!!) and you're going to be in here, and our paths will stop running parallel to each other FOREVER? I'm really not up for that, my friend.

Being in here alone — well, that's a farce considering all the hovering the parental units are doing, and the doctors and their armies of nurses, but you know what I mean — it's made me think hard about what I really want out of life, and for me, it's come down to this: there's just nothing like the love of a good friend, and you've been that for me, and I don't want to lose it. I mean seriously, I'd rather be stuck in this old town with you than go to Paris by myself. I just wanted to say that. It's stuff like this we take for granted and somehow never get around to saying. So, there it is. I guess if you stick with swearing off your own chances of a transplant we'll have to book our Air France tickets pretty soon.

There's sentimentality for you. I would have e-mailed this, but my computer crashed yesterday and I'm dying of boredom. No wonder all those Jane Austen epistles went on and on. Writing by hand takes hours and at least passes the time. But can you imagine? Their fingers must have been hideous compared to ours, all cramped up like that from gripping and dipping their quills all day. That's a nice thought to end on — the possibility that others in the history of the world had uglier hands than ours!

Don't let me forget to tell you the story about

It was possible that Michelle had told her the story at some point, though she'd abandoned the letter. Michelle's initial rejection symptoms kicked in a mere month after the transplant, though she rallied several times before her final slide. Promise tried not to dwell on possible reasons why Michelle had never given her the letter, because one kept jumping out of line to scream at her:

As Michelle's body rejected her lungs,

Promise's tolerated hers . . . and Promise never gave Michelle any indication that she'd rather sit by her side in the hospital than sing and talk about her own dreams.

Promise purchased a coffee at a drive-through and waited in the parking lot of the funeral home. The service wouldn't start until midmorning.

The world was a backward place. Michelle, who should have lived longest, died first. Promise, who should have been singing, had been silenced, while Michelle spoke from the grave. The woman who once had the true friends now walked alone. Her very efforts to save her own reputation by diverting attention to Zack's had killed it.

Her coffee was acidic and bitter. She drank quickly.

At the cemetery Promise stood separated from Michelle's family. She held the small box of Michelle's trinkets against her body with her casted arm, covered them with her coat. She let the light rain fall on her without the umbrella to protect and waited while the Graham family took turns heaping damp earth on the casket.

When they began to scatter, she kept her shaded eyes on Mrs. Graham and approached on the margins, waiting to be noticed. Then she walked toward Michelle's parents with the box outstretched. A peace offering. A buffer.

"I thought you'd want these," she said. "Sooner than later."

Mr. Graham took the treasures, and she felt exposed. His eyes were bloodshot, his mouth grim.

Mrs. Graham extended her left hand and placed it over Promise's fingers, clasped together in a pointless grip. Michelle's older brother, whom Promise once had a crush on, passed them. He glared at her, but — maybe for the sake of his parents — didn't make a scene. That one glance, however, brought the condemnation of the world down on Promise's head. She tried to pull away from Mrs. Graham's touch. Her friend's mother wouldn't let go.

Promise said, "I'm so sorry I wasn't there. With her. I should have been there."

"You are blessed with such health," Mrs. Graham said. "I don't understand it. I don't understand why you'd abuse such a gift. It doesn't seem fair."

Shame stuffed Promise's throat. She studied the grass, tethered to Mrs. Graham until the woman released her.

The Grahams moved on to their idling cars.

Promise stayed in the rain and thought about her chances of getting pneumonia. She hadn't taken her medications since getting news of Michelle's death. She hadn't needed them. Maybe this exposure would do its work.

Promise didn't know where to go. She wasn't welcome here, though it wasn't clear now why she'd thought she might be. She didn't want to go home and sit with her parents in her hideaway until they decided they could afford to return to their lives. She couldn't tolerate their unspoken question: had she really done such terrible things for *fame?*

Promise trudged to the terrible hole Michelle had been laid in. Already the world had moved on without her. Promise decided not to be one to bury her memory in dirt.

She lifted her head. On the other side of the grave, sheltered by both an umbrella and a thick old shade tree, Porta Cerreto smiled at Promise and extended a hand toward her. *Come.*

Promise went.

32

Though Chase had asked Promise to come back when they first met, she did not return. Though he had given her a gift, she did not reciprocate. Though he had told her he loved her, she did not accept his love.

He stood at his drawing desk in front of his studio window and waited for her to pull her handsome BMW Roadster to the curb and walk up the path that cut through their small front yard. He waited for several days after finding her at the F. Samson Davis Hall of the Fine Arts, and during that time he ignored Wes's urges to study or read or walk. Chase did not speak to anyone. He ate little. He did not draw even one doodle, and then he decided that he had waited long enough.

A longing fulfilled is a tree of life. She was his longing.

It was time to go find Promise Dayton and remind her of his love and her beauty, and of the fact that she did not have to die.

He came to his conclusion at 11:36 in the morning on a Saturday, and at the same time he made the choice not to wait for Chelsea to walk with him at 2:15. He turned away from the window and walked downstairs, sat on the bench, and tied his shoes while reciting a passage from the apostle Paul's letter to the Romans. He seated his baseball cap on his head and slipped his arms into a light jacket that would repel the rain.

He heard his sister on the phone in her room.

Chase left the house and walked toward Porta Cerreto's gallery, which was his most immediate connection to Promise. He stared straight ahead and moved swiftly. His hands felt strangely unoccupied because he did not have his pencils or portfolio with him. This should not have been so uncomfortable, however, because he had only started taking those with him about a month ago, and for years prior to that he and his sister had walked mostly empty-handed, except for ice cream.

He let his arms dangle at his sides. Raindrops dripped off the slick sleeves and tickled his bare fingers.

Chase arrived at ART(i)FACTS and

reached for the oak-and-glass door, placed his hand on the knob, turned it, and pushed.

The gallery was locked.

Chase tried again. When the doorknob did not turn, he took a step backward. Water plunked off the scalloped edges of the yellow awning. Wind had freed one side of the GRAND OPENING sign so that its soggy mass folded in two and slouched at the corner.

There was no one inside, no sunlight penetrating the clouds or domed roof. The sculptured boy that his father had made continued to walk under perpetual summer.

He stepped to the door and pressed his face into the glass, scanning the wall. The picture of Promise falling had been replaced by a closely cropped photo of white chrysanthemums. His breath obscured UNEARTH YOUR TRUTH for two seconds and then vanished. He breathed again, watched the fog stick and then lift again. He did this several times and then disconnected his forehead from the door.

Chase called up information in his mind about Porta Cerreto and reviewed it, paging through details the way he paged through his many books, looking at the pictures.

He saw the ax in the stinking sumac.

He saw Porta whispering in Chelsea's ear

while the women looked at the sculptured boy.

He saw Promise falling off a cliff on Porta's wall.

He saw Promise coming up the path to his front door.

And Promise's tree of life.

The strangler killing the tree of life.

The picture of the strangler, that Zack Eddy, on the news when Promise was burning.

He saw Promise standing on his front porch, asking if Zack Eddy lived there.

If his home was Porta Cerreto's home.

Zack Eddy's lips and Porta Cerreto's lips had the same downturned shape.

Stinking sumacs and strangler figs were both invasive plants.

Chase saw Promise step back and look at his house number, 2310 Morris.

He saw his sister say, *It's an easy mistake to make.*

He saw a city street map that he had memorized when Wes started teaching him how to ride the bus.

Chase turned away from the empty gallery and started walking toward 2310 Norris Lane. Porta Cerreto or Zack Eddy would tell him where Promise was.

■ ■ ■ ■

The journey took Chase two hours. His shoes were squishy and the noise was consistent as he walked. The light chain hitting the globe of his father's ceiling fan was also consistent. A pace for moving. The scent of ocean salt grew stronger than the scent of damp earth as he moved toward the address.

The house at number 2310 Norris Lane sat at the end of a dirt driveway on a very large property at the edge of a grand ocean vista. The structure was big and old and separated from the neighbors so that it was not necessary to share views of the cliffs and waves. A variety of native trees sheltered the house: Sitka spruce and canoe cedar and Pacific yew. Many, many Pacific yew. *Taxus brevifolia.* Doctors loved and hated these evergreen trees. The cinnamon-colored trunks were covered with peeling bark that reminded Chase of shaved chocolate. The yew contained Taxol, which was derived from its inherent poison taxine, and was a valuable component of many cancer chemotherapies.

The Pacific yew could heal. It could also kill. The taxine was present in the leaves, the bark, and the seed inside the red *Taxus* seed coatings. Many horses and children had been harmed by the tree's alluring features.

When no one answered the front door, Chase descended the porch and circled to the back of the house. The cliff-top yard was sandy and landscaped with shrubs, not grass. There were few trees here compared to the street side.

A structure separate from the house needed a new coat of paint. The wind lifted latex flakes that peeled like the yew tree bark, and the rain had washed some of these chips into a border on the ground that circled the tiny building.

A curtain in the front window shifted. Chase went to the door.

Rain started to pour instead of drop.

Chase stood close to the entry, which was not sheltered, and waited for the person who had seen him to open the door. He waited for a long time. The curtain shifted again.

"I am looking for Promise Dayton," Chase announced to the window. "Is she here?"

A floorboard inside squeaked.

"If she is not here, please tell me where she is."

A voice came through the door. "I don't

have any idea."

"The people who live here know Promise Dayton and know where I can find her. Do you live here or are you a visitor?"

Rain slid off Chase's hat and down into the collar of his jacket. He felt rivers on his back.

The door opened two inches, and the dark eyes that Chase had seen on the TV news appeared between the edges. Zack Eddy's eyes. The strangler fig.

"You can bet I don't live here."

"Did you know that not all strangler figs grow epiphytically?" Chase asked.

"What?"

"They can be cultivated. They can be rooted in their own space in the ground and can grow without needing a host. I find the *Ficus macrophylla* to be one of the most beautiful trees in the world. The largest one in the United States is a few hundred miles down the coast from here, at 201 State Street in Santa Barbara, California. It is more commonly —"

"How do you know Promise?"

"— known as the Moreton Bay fig. Each *Ficus macrophylla* is called this, and not only the one in Santa Barbara."

"Are you stalking her?"

"The Moreton Bay fig provides protection

to humans from sun, and fruit to many species of birds, and is an essential mating site for wasps. Most people do not fully appreciate wasps."

"Why don't you tell me what you want with Promise?"

"I want to save her life. She is dying. You should not kill her."

Zack Eddy's eyes widened a tiny bit. "I would never hurt her. What I did — I was angry, but I couldn't hurt her. Physically."

"The strangler figs kill their hosts by suffocation. Promise is a tree of life. It is her calling to live."

"Well, I won't be the one suffocating her. It seems her body's set up to do that all by itself."

"I am not talking about what her body will do, but what you will do."

"I'm not going to kill her."

Agitation finally abandoned Chase. He took a long slow breath while keeping his eyes on the paint chips scattered in the dirt by his feet. The rain was causing them to jump around.

"That is good. That is what I want."

"You going to donate your lungs to her or something?"

"No. But I drew a picture of a lung for her. That was my gift."

340

Zack opened the door farther. Water ran over the bill of Chase's baseball cap to the right and left of his eyes. The rain sounded like tree leaves in a strong wind.

"I saw that drawing," Zack said.

"I love her."

Zack did not reply.

"Where is Promise?"

"I couldn't say."

"Why not?"

Zack laughed in that way that was illogical, because he was not talking about anything funny. "Because I don't know where she is, Einstein."

"My name is Chase Ellis. Do you know where Porta Cerreto is?"

"No."

Rain was going in through Zack's door and splattering the old carpet inside. The place smelled moldy.

"I will go find Promise somewhere else," Chase said.

"Fine."

"But if she comes here, please tell her I am looking for her."

"I doubt we'll speak."

"You do not have to avoid speaking to someone in order to avoid killing her."

"I'll keep that in mind."

341

"You could be a stunning tree," Chase said.

"And you could be a fine sideshow at the circus."

An image came to Chase's mind, not of the circus. "If I were to draw for you, I would draw a Moreton Bay fig that is larger than the one in Santa Barbara, California. It would be loaded with birds and surrounded by a beautiful park that people from all over the world would come to see. Would you like a picture?"

The door slammed so hard that droplets of rain water flew off the surface and struck Chase in the eyes.

But Chase no longer worried about Zack Eddy.

33

Porta led the drive back to her home, one eye on the road and one eye on her rear-view mirror, making sure that Promise didn't change her mind along the way. She felt as if she were in possession of the Cullinan diamond, whole and raw, priceless and fragile. Verifying Promise's true nature and simultaneously urging the girl to consider Porta a trusted friend would require the delicate skill of a diamond cutter.

The rain came hard, and though her home stood close to the ocean, she couldn't see any water except the gray weights falling from the sky. As she turned onto the lane, she passed a sopping fool in red basketball shorts and a baseball cap who'd been unfortunate to be caught in the deluge without an umbrella.

Promise's car followed closely enough that Porta couldn't see her headlights in the mirror. Only the hood of the car. Necessarily dangerous. Or perhaps just needy.

They pulled onto her property and followed the long drive down to the garage attached to the side of the house. There was room for two cars. When Porta parked, she got out and punched the second remote opener for Promise, then motioned that she should pull into the empty bay. She closed the overhead doors, and the women were sheltered from the drumming drops on the hollow-sounding garage.

They entered the kitchen through the garage door. "It's a terrible day for burying a friend," Porta said.

Promise sagged into a dining room chair in front of the window. The guesthouse was just visible at the edge of the yard. The grayness of the outdoors seemed to have come inside, and the dull yellow paint was defenseless against it. Porta decided not to flip on a light. They wouldn't sit here long.

"Do you believe in heaven?" Promise asked.

For some people. "I do."

"It's easier to believe in heaven on sunny days."

"Maybe so."

"If there is such a place, Michelle belongs in it."

"Of course she does." Porta rested one of

her hands lightly on Promise's head. In the past month, her hands had aged more than they had in the past decade. They had become loose and papery and fearful of Porta's looming birthday. Even now, they quivered. Porta hated them.

"Tell me about your friend, about all the things you'll never forget."

Promise's sigh was heavier than the rain.

"She wanted to go to France. Took three years of high school French and two in college and completed every audio course you could buy. Lots of time in the hospital for that. She taught me a few phrases to use when the nurses were in the room." The corner of Promise's mouth lifted. "I think she could have been an interpreter for the UN or something if she wanted."

Porta let Promise's thoughts go unguided. They would lead to her desired destination because there was no other place for this conversation to go.

"This world needs another recording artist like it needs another car on the road," Promise said.

"Now, Promise —"

"But it doesn't have enough peacekeepers. We really could use a few more of those."

"You can't value one life over another,

345

dear." Porta didn't believe this for a second, but grief didn't have the stomach for truth. And it would have hurt Porta's campaign.

"Well, she was better than me in every way that mattered. She was selfless and optimistic and cheerful. She blogged and volunteered when she was healthy enough to do it. I had a dream the night she died. I dreamed I could have saved her life, but didn't. I was too busy with my own stuff."

"Do you think you could have saved her?"

"If what you think about me is true, I could have."

Porta let that remark sit out in the open for a moment. Then she said, "Do you think I am right?"

Promise didn't answer. Out at the guesthouse, a beam of a lamp or flashlight illuminated the bedroom window for one, two seconds, then blinked out. Porta's surprise turned to knowing as quickly as the brightness had passed. Zack — without a car to drive or a dollar bill to fold into an origami swan — had come home. She wondered if he had seen Promise sitting here.

"The thing that really scares me is that I might forget her one day. I might wake up one morning and not have her at the front of my mind the way I do right now, and I might get all the way through the day — or two or three days, and realize I haven't spent a single thought on her."

"You loved each other like sisters. You spent your lives together. What are the chances of forgetting that? It's like forgetting a part of yourself."

"There are so many days of my life that I can't remember already, and I'm only twenty-two. If I can't die — if I don't die — how many more days will I forget? How many more people?"

Porta said, "Let me show you something that might cheer you up."

Promise turned her face away from the kitchen window. The girl really was a child in so many ways. Still, she was a favored child. Porta helped her up and, encircling Promise's shoulders with a maternal arm, directed her toward a closed door that appeared as if it should have led outside. Instead it opened to reveal a narrow and steep flight of custom-cut mahogany stairs and a solid, shiny rail of the same material. The women descended.

Porta called the lowest level of the house the basement for lack of a better word. The label didn't fit the traditional definition, but more fitting words escaped her. Somehow the area had been cut down into the rock of the high bluff on which the house was built. A great body of rock was exhumed from the cliff, creating a hole topped by an unremarkable, rundown house. The hole itself had been outfitted for a queen. Or a witch not easily impressed, who had a personal investment in physical beauty. It had been lavishly carpeted, formally decorated, and kept in pristine condition with a system of air purifiers and dehumidifiers.

The mostly round space, supported by three pillars, had a great picture window rather than a wall about thirty feet across — roughly ten o'clock to three o'clock wide if the basement were a clock face. On a clear day, a person standing before the view could imagine she was alone in the world on its first day alive, when green and blue light took its first breath. Today, however, gray clouds oppressed all color, and a mixture of rain and ocean spray dotted the thick glass.

The person who'd lived here before her, the original owner, was an eccentric who had the place built for his dying wife, who loved the ocean. Porta loved the basement not for the view but for the fact that the man was of a mind similar to her own, pouring every resource into what mattered most and letting the rest fade away.

She had replaced the classic seafaring oil

paintings with tributes to the deities she worshipped, done in lighter, brighter pastels and acrylics. She had installed cabinets and a counter and a fire pit where she could cook when necessary without going upstairs. She had cleared out the expensive imported furniture to make room for a laser-cast ceremonial circle similar to the one that could be projected in her gallery's private viewing rooms. And in the center of this circle — though it wasn't presently il-luminated — she had placed her damaged *Ameretat.*

She did not know yet how she would repair the figure's wing tips, the scarred lips and nose. The lost soil had been of far greater importance, and so Porta had se-cured, at terrific expense, new soil and a blessing from a Zoroastrian mobed she hardly knew and therefore didn't fully trust. The priest lived nearby, which was the only reason she agreed to his blessing; she was forced to. This meant that her confidence in the *Ameretat* was at an all-time low. The purity of the soil was in question, and what the vandal might have done to curse the jade itself was still unknown.

An attempted murder would have been a much more reliable test, overall.

"You buy into all this." Promise was gazing at a painting of Artemis, Greek goddess of the hunt, who knelt at the side of a tree with her strung bow pulled taut alongside her cheek.

Promise had made a statement, but Porta heard the reluctant question behind it. "We all must put our hope in something."

Promise appeared to be pale, but that might have been the poor lighting.

"I'm not sure I even believe in God. Or gods, goddesses" — she waved her hands over the paintings — "let alone living forever."

"Why would humans have any hope at all for a life that transcended the cycle of birth and death if it didn't exist?" Porta said. "Or another way of asking it is: why do you want people to remember you after you die?"

"I want to know I mattered. That my life had meaning."

"Yes."

"If I'm immortal the way you say I am, wouldn't I know it?"

"Not necessarily. The gods rescue the ones whom they love, but they often don't announce their verdict until after the death."

"I hope you're not planning to kill me with that end in mind."

The words held dissonant notes of black humor and genuine alarm. Porta allowed this fear to linger, as fear was always useful. Then she placated Promise with an indulgent smile.

Porta opened a small storage cabinet against the wall. She withdrew a clean lancet, the type a diabetic might use to prick her skin, from the top shelf. "Sweetie, that would be a terrible last resort. There are easier ways to tell."

"You understand how dumb this all sounds. No one lives forever."

"And yet here you are."

"Morbidly curious, I guess. Do I have anything to lose at this point?"

Porta watched her move to a more optimistic image of Gaia, goddess of the natural world.

"Why would these people — I mean gods — pick me for something like this when I don't even know if I believe they're real?"

The girl's candor was slightly annoying. Porta supposed she had assumed that an immortal would be more educated in these matters. "The gods deem it right that all of us die, but they bless people like us who defy that notion. We're not animals to roll over and sink back into the earth."

"So you, like, flip off the gods who are going to judge you, and they like that?"

"There's a fine line between disrespect

and boldness that commands admiration. We are in a contest with the rest of humanity for favor. There is much strategy involved."

Promise's eyes glanced off a shadowy portrait of Hecate, goddess of the crossroads between life and death. Porta had to admit it was rather gloomy as images of the three-headed guardian went. But life wasn't all sunshine and roses — not even the afterlife. The sooner Promise realized this, the better off she would be.

"So . . . what are these 'easier ways' that you mentioned?" The girl had noticed the *Ameretat* and went to examine her.

"The obvious one is that we could try to kill someone else, and then see if you could prevent the death."

Promise swung around sharply toward Porta.

"But I wouldn't ask that of you," Porta said. Then she lifted her fingers toward the *Ameretat.* "This is the easier way."

"What does it do?"

"That will take some time to explain. Let me simply show you instead. Give me your hand."

The girl extended her palm upward. Porta took hold of her knobby fingers with the tiniest bit of revulsion, applying enough pressure to tip the pointer slightly down-ward. Swiftly, Porta pricked the soft pad of the tip with the lancet and held on.

"Ow!" Promise's tug was ineffective. The squeeze drew a drop of dark red blood from the lanced spot. "What was that?"

"A blood test. Simple, quick."

Promise frowned, but she quit tugging. Porta passed the girl's bleeding finger over the top of the *Ameretat's* full bowl and twisted her wrist so that the drops of blood fell into the soil. She counted seven and then released her. Promise sucked on her fingertip. The blood seemed to sit on top of the earth.

Porta tossed the lancet toward a small lined trash can. The quivering in her hands had increased, and the device missed. She let it lie on the floor, feeling her own anticipation churning like the ocean.

"What's it supposed to do?" Promise asked.

"Patience."

The sign didn't come. It might take time, though Porta had expected something im-mediate. It was more likely that the damage to *Ameretat* had interfered with the process than that Promise was not chosen. She had meant this test to be an easy confirmation of what she already knew, not a challenge.

Promise coughed, a deep and productive spasm. Startled, Porta faced her.

"It's cold in here," Promise said.

Porta took Promise by the hands. They were indeed chilled. "Child, do you understand the gift of immortality? Do you know that it means bearing the responsibility of choosing others worthy of living?"

"I don't feel well."

"Listen: I will teach you what to do. I will teach you all that you need to know. You can save your own life, but you can also save the lives of others. Of people like Michelle."

"Okay."

"In exchange for this help, will you make a vow to remember me? Will you promise to give me your gift?"

She lifted Promise's punctured fingertip and squeezed it so that the blood oozed again.

Promise nodded. "I promise."

All Porta's worry left her in a sigh of relief. Nearly all of it. She closed her eyes and lifted Promise's finger, then pressed it against her wrinkled forehead between her eyes, sealing their agreement. "Thank you."

Promise coughed again. And again. Her hand slipped out of Porta's grasp.

The tiniest doubt turned Porta's head back to the *Ameretat.* There was no life sprouting in the soil yet, though the blood had dropped down like a seed.

"I believe she was cursed by an old nemesis of mine. You can help me restore her, yes?"

Promise leaned against one of the pillars. "What do you need me to do?"

"I'll show you. It's a simple ritual of purification. Let's prepare."

34

Promise woke gasping for air. She'd fallen off a cliff into the ocean and was drowning; her lungs filled with water and she sank, unable to swim. Her limbs were immobile and heavy. Sculptured jade.

The uncovered bedroom window showed a black starless sky. She rolled out of bed and onto her hands and knees, spewing water that didn't exist, coughing up nothing, dragging in barely enough air to stay conscious.

She wondered what Michelle had felt like when her lungs finally stopped working.

The rain had stopped. Porta's old house was still, silent except for Promise's hacking. The dust in the room had been stirred up when they'd put sheets on the bed the night before, and now her lungs felt heavy. She needed her oxygen, her inhalers, her therapy vest. How long had it been since she'd taken her medications? Why had she stopped? Promise couldn't remember. Maybe she should go home.

If she did, she couldn't return here. Her parents were there waiting for her, worried. She'd called from Porta's house to explain that she'd gone to the funeral. She said she needed some time alone and agreed to call daily, then hung up the phone. When they tried to call back, she ignored the ringing. Promise knew her mother wouldn't leave the apartment until Promise came back, even if her father returned to work.

When her breathing finally leveled out, she decided to go down to the basement, recalling the air there being strangely clear and sharp, like mountain air.

She stood slowly and was not dizzy. She moved quietly, not to bother Porta's rest. The old woman had been kind to her. Promise left the bedrooms and moved down the stairs, whisper quiet. She wore an old robe of Porta's that smelled like vintage cologne but was soft and clean and exactly her size. She reached the landing and rounded a corner into the long hallway that cut through the center of the house toward the kitchen. The old hardwood floors were coarse under her bare feet. She reached the stairs to the basement and turned on the light.

She coughed several more times before beginning her descent. The lack of oxygen had weakened her to a familiar state of feeling a little unsteady. It had been a few weeks since she'd felt this way. How long, exactly? Her doctors might want to know. The last time, in fact, was the day she'd climbed the hill to model for Zack's painting.

A blue glow was the only light that guided her feet. The light came from the electronic circle that Porta had shown her how to cast the night before. It was like a hologram, and Porta had decided they would keep it lighted after finishing the purification ritual, allowing the energies to remain inside after the women cut and closed the circle's door, so that the healing of the statue might take its full effect.

At the bottom of the stairs, Promise took a breath. The air was cleaner, but her lungs didn't operate any more easily. Climbing the stairs to return to the kitchen at this point was out of the question. She sank to her knees in the thick carpet.

Porta's consecration procedure had been a little on the creepy side, but Promise was willing enough to follow the old woman's instructions in hopes that this little green statue might be able to tell them what it was supposed to tell them.

She wondered how it had been broken. She wondered what it was supposed to do.

Another coughing fit rattled her.

Her sudden return to illness made her think of that picture of health drawn for her by Chase. Such a strange man. She wondered where he was and what he was drawing now and if — oddly enough — he would be the type of person to call her friend even after what the rest of the world thought she had done.

She hoped the spells Porta had cast on the statue were effective. Now more than ever, she did not want to die. Not in this lowly place of failure, of loneliness, of shame.

The circle of blue light winked once and then became steady again. A chunk of jade from the *Ameretat*'s pot fell out of the side and landed on the carpet without making a sound.

Early Monday morning, at the desk in her bedroom, Chelsea replied to one last e-mail, her mind only half engaged in the content. She was decided: having given herself the weekend to consider a final decision, she determined to confront Porta this afternoon about the statue in the window of her gallery. She'd make the case for it having been created by her father and then, expecting Porta to be ungracious and unmoved by the story, would offer a fair price to buy it back.

Chelsea shut down the e-mail account and dropped back to her home page to check local headlines before signing off and heading into the office. One captured her attention fully: SINGER'S SUICIDE BLAMED ON PHOTO.

She clicked on the link, read quickly, and printed the article, then went looking for Chase. She found him in the kitchen, where he was eating blueberries. A short stack of his drawings lay in the middle of the table. Rena was at the butcher-block island chopping vegetables for the afternoon and evening meals.

"Chase, something sad happened over the weekend," she said, placing the printout and her purse on an empty chair.

"I know."

"You know Mrs. Bell died?"

Chase lowered his spoon to the bowl and looked out the window. "No, I did not."

"Something else sad happened?" Chelsea poured herself a glass of orange juice.

"Yes."

"What? Is this about Saturday, when you went out in the rain?"

"It is all about everything. Tell me about

360

Mrs. Bell."

Chelsea placed the juice on the table and picked up the article. She pulled out the chair and sat next to her brother. She read:

The body of a woman found early Sunday morning at the base of Vista Park Bluffs has been identified as fifty-three-year-old former folksinger Brandy Bell. Assistant County Coroner Donald Rand is calling the death an apparent suicide. A full autopsy is pending. Harlan Bell, Bell's surviving husband of twenty-two years, says she had suffered from chronic depression triggered by the physical assault of a gang initiate that took her voice nearly five years ago.

Mr. Bell says he will file a lawsuit against Porta Cerreto, owner of the ART(i)FACTS gallery on Main Street, for selling a photograph to his wife of a jumper leaping from the same spot where Bell is believed to have taken her own life.

Pending lawsuits of undetermined claims have been filed against the art dealer in California, Texas, and New York. Authorities have taken additional interest in the case because Cerreto is the mother of Zack Eddy, who was recently accused of a terrorist plot that is currently under investigation. The photograph purchased by Bell is rumored to involve Eddy's alleged accomplice, Promise Dayton, but federal investigators on that case stated that there is insufficient evidence at this stage to warrant an arrest. None of the parties was available for comment this weekend.

Mrs. Bell produced seven albums over the course of her career, the last of which was the Grammy-winner *Painting My Peonies.*

The blueberries had trailed purple juice up the sides of Chase's white bowl. Chelsea said, "I'd forgotten about that album until now. There was one song on it I really liked."

" 'Auburn Leaves,' " Rena provided.

Chelsea turned in her chair. "Yeah, that was it. About the end of summer. How did you know that?"

"Everyone liked that one," Rena said. "As much as 'everyone' can like anything."

"This is all so sad." Chelsea laid the printed article on the table and slid it over to Chase. "I thought you'd want to know about this, because of the picture you drew for her."

"Death always leads to more death,"

Chase said.

There was a hiccup in Rena's chopping rhythm. Then it resumed.

"What do you mean?" Chelsea asked.

"There are Pacific yew trees in Porta Cerreto's yard."

"You've been to her house?"

"Those trees are highly poisonous."

"When did you go to — is that where you were Saturday?"

"Everyone is going to that house."

"Everyone. As in, everyone liked 'Auburn Leaves'? Don't go there, okay? Everyone can go there but you." Chelsea finished her orange juice and carried the empty cup to the sink, then put her bag on her shoulder.

"I found Promise's home on Sunday. But she was not there."

"Why don't you stay here today? You and Wes can watch the PBS concert we recorded last week."

Chase didn't react to the suggestion.

"Until people can figure out what's really going on with those three, you should stay out of their business. Stay here. No more death-unto-death or whatever it is." She wished she'd kept the news to herself and glanced at his pile of drawings. More trees. "What are you going to draw today?"

"Mrs. Bell did not have to die," Chase

363

said. He pushed the bowl away from him.

Chelsea sighed.

"It is possible to choose to live. 'I have set before you life and death, blessings and curses. Now choose life, so that you and your children may live.' "

"I know this is hard for you."

"It is possible to choose to be a cultivated fig instead of a strangler fig, and a mother instead of a witch."

"Chase, I have to go to work now."

"Good-bye."

Chelsea hesitated before leaving. Chase wasn't behaving abnormally, and yet he wasn't himself. In the hallway, she fetched her summer jacket out of the closet and draped it over her arm. She watched her brother pick up the drawings off the table and study the one on top.

"That's your best one yet," she heard Rena say from her position within the kitchen.

"The bristlecone drew this one," Chase said. "That is why it is the best."

"Tell me what it's about. I like those trees of yours."

"I have to go to work now," Chase said.

"You can tell me later then, okay, Chase?"

He left his breakfast on the table and

364

walked out of the kitchen past Chelsea,
turning up the stairs to his rooms.

35

Late Monday morning Porta rose with new resolve. The girl was increasingly sick, and the *Ameretat* had not bloomed. After thirty-six hours, it had not even sprouted! After all the mountains she had climbed to find Promise Dayton, the possibility that she was not immortal after all disgusted Porta.

It was not out of the question that the *Ameretat,* and not the coughing girl, was the one giving the wrong signals. There was only one way to be certain, and she would have to be careful how she went about it. She herself had no qualms about killing anyone. In this season of her life, unloved — in fact, despised — by the world in general, she had little to lose. And if Promise was not what she hoped, she had absolutely nothing to lose.

But there was considerable risk in the possibility that Promise was a goddess after all. Promise and her immortal host would frown upon any lowly human who tried to kill her, even to prove her status. The attempt would need to be made by someone else, which was why she had originally nudged Zack toward the task. Porta moved to her bedroom window and looked out upon the guesthouse.

Today she would make her plans, then she'd let them work overnight. Her son would be more amenable to her suggestions now that his wounds weren't so fresh. He was no less impervious to the effects of her psychoactive incense than any of her gallery clients were.

Freshly invigorated, Porta dressed quickly and then left the room. Promise had been up half the night gasping, insisting she was fine, until Porta finally talked her into sleeping in the basement as she had the night before. The air was purified, she argued, though the truth was Porta just wanted an hour of uninterrupted sleep.

Porta went downstairs and to the kitchen at the rear of the house. She withdrew a bottle of mineral water, a box of salt, and a bundle of braided onions from the pantry. Her eyes passed over a gap between a box of instant oatmeal and a bag of natural granola. She did a quick inventory of her shelves. She seemed to be missing a box of muesli, a jar of peanut butter, and several apples. She smiled. Her son apparently had no immediate plan to strike out on his own.

She took a sharp carving knife from a drawer under the counter. The rest of what she needed was downstairs.

She went below, glanced unhopefully at the worthless jade statue as she descended, and saw that Promise was still propped up by a hill of pillows on the benches in front of the huge window. She placed the items on top of the cabinet where she kept her supplies, then withdrew a cast-iron skillet from underneath a portable kitchen island.

The skillet went onto a stand over the basin of a portable outdoor fire pit, the kind that sat on patios, which she'd installed indoors against the manufacturer's instructions. In the chimney hood that dropped from the ceiling over the skillet, Porta opened the vents to the outside. Death by carbon monoxide: prevented. She lit the wood in the basin with a match.

As the pan warmed, she opened the cabinet and withdrew a box of cigarettes she had rolled herself with the same herbal blend she used in the viewing room of her gallery. She preferred to smoke the mixture, but sharing it in incense form was more effective for the average person, such as her patrons. Or her son.

Lacking time to prepare a new batch or to go to the gallery for her existing supply, she planned to take what she needed from these smokes. She'd slice the papers and warm the contents in a pan, steep them in a solution of purified water and linseed oil, then fill the little guesthouse with the suggestive aroma tonight while Zack slept. She counted out a dozen rolls, about a third of the stash, and laid them on the counter.

A crash upstairs diverted her. Promise stirred. Still holding the box of herbal cigarettes, Porta went up to check out the noise, considering possible causes. Perhaps Zack had come back for more food and dropped a jar of jam.

She emerged into her kitchen expecting anything but what she saw: a rock on the traffic-stripped hardwood floor, shards of glass surrounding it like flower petals, and a hole the size of a cantaloupe in one of her window's French panes.

The obnoxious young man who had caused her so much trouble at the gallery stood outside, looking in through the hole. The glare of sun off ocean water behind him cast the scene into angles of light and dark that were hard on Porta's eyes, but the cap on his head was unmistakable.

"What's this?" she cried. "You come to harass me at my home just because my shop is closed?"

"I have come for Promise," he said.

Porta stepped over glass daggers and reached for the phone on the counter. She set down her cigarettes next to the base. "I'm calling the police," she said, raising the handset. She started punching buttons.

"The police would like to speak to you."

Porta stopped. "About what?"

"Mrs. Bell is dead."

"Who?"

He pushed a piece of paper through the hole and let it sail to the ground. "That picture was not for her. I tried to tell her."

"Sounds like the police need to be talking to you, if you know so much about it." She left the phone and picked up the paper. It was a news article, dated this morning. She read quickly, then cursed. Another wrongful death suit hanging over her head. Not that anyone had been able to prove anything. For one, sorcery didn't hold up well as evidence in court. For another, though she was indeed one of the most skilled witches ever to walk the face of the earth, she couldn't force human will. Not even the gods could. They were all only influencers.

Mr. Bell's claims were absurd. The whole

point of Promise's photograph was that a person could fall from a great height and survive. That Mrs. Bell had found a different message in the image was not Porta's fault.

"I'm not responsible for this." She threw the paper into the trash can near the sink.

"I want to see Promise."

"She's not here."

"She is."

"I'm not about to get caught up in an argument with an imbecile."

"Then it would be wise to stop."

Porta laughed at that and picked up the rock on her floor. "The police will come soon enough to talk with me about dear Brandy Bell and my wayward son, now that they've connected all those dots, and that's no trouble to me. But what will you say when I have them arrest you for trespassing?"

She hurled the rock at Chase's face, missed, and broke the pane adjacent to the one he'd struck. *Blast.* Chase didn't even flinch.

"I will tell them you have kidnapped Promise Dayton."

"I haven't kidnapped anybody."

"And I will tell them that Zack Eddy is living in your guesthouse."

371

This detail could present a problem, if the police were of the mind to keep closer tabs on her son. Depending on what charges were ultimately brought against him, she had no time to waste being charged for harboring or aiding or abetting or whatever they would accuse her of. It would be better for her that they not know about Zack until tomorrow. At that point, it wouldn't matter what happened to him.

"Promise is here of her own will," Porta announced. "I'll show you, and then you'll leave us both alone. Is that clear?"

"I would rather Promise left with me."

"You would? I'll tell you what, if you can convince the girl to leave with you, she can go. How's that? Deal?"

Chase stepped away from the window and walked around the side of the house. Porta swore again and kicked a piece of glass into the baseboard. The shard stuck. She stomped down the hall and threw open the front door. Chase emerged at the side of the porch with a portfolio under one arm and a clutch of sharpened white pencils upright in his fist, a cartoonish idiot.

He walked past her and down the hall as if he knew where he was going. Into the kitchen, over the glass, through the open door to the basement. Of course, he would have seen her come out of it.

The sounds of Promise coughing came up the staircase as if through a megaphone.

"Promise Dayton," he called out, "a tree of life cannot grow underground. You must come home with me."

A crash of waves and then the sound of her name awakened Promise to the scene of the ocean caressing the earth. Her waking thought, again, was of Michelle and her love for the Pacific and her longing to see the Atlantic, preferably from the coast of France. She took a taxing breath.

Her second thought was that Porta was losing faith in her, even though she continued to insist that these things take time. They'd get their confirmation, she'd said last night, but her lips were set in a thin line. Porta spoke without looking at her. Promise would be affirmed, she said; they would initiate her into an exclusive sisterhood of secrets, and then they would perform the rites and incantations of immortality.

Why can't we just jump to that? Promise had wanted to know. *Why do we need the confirmation?* Porta had grown angry then, frightening Promise into silence with accusations of being more ignorant than a novice and completely unworthy of the gift she possessed.

She was not unworthy. Promise said this to herself again and again, a prayer of desperation to no one in particular. Porta apologized later and offered a brief, condescending explanation that didn't give Promise any confidence or clarity. *It's not for mere mortals to tinker with spells too far out of their reach. We had better know exactly who we are before trying to claim what is ours.*

If Porta really knew what she was doing, Promise thought, that statue would be working properly by now.

"It is time for you to go home."

Promise startled and jerked her body away from the view. She slipped off the bench and landed on her tailbone. Chase Ellis was standing over her holding drawings and pencils and looking right at her.

"What are you doing here?" she asked.

"Finding you."

They'd had this exchange once before. This time Promise found it to be less odd. Behind him, on the other side of the room, Porta stood at the foot of the stairs, arms crossed. The *Ameretat* between them was unchanged.

There was a fire in the fire pit, warming a pan.

"How did you know I was here?"

He juggled his possessions in order to hold out a drawing to her. Promise took it from him. On the black page, a white tree grew in a cave under a hillside. On top of the hill, two more trees sent their roots down into the cave and were choking the sheltered tree.

"The bristlecone drew this," Chase said. He pointed to one of the trees, which had an ax in its side. "*Ailanthus altissima.* And a *Ficus.* The tree of life cannot grow where trees of death take root."

"It would seem that not all your fans have abandoned you," Porta said to Promise.

"Chase, I know you mean well, but this is where I need to be."

"You will not find life here."

"I'm pretty sure this is the only place I'll find it," Promise said. She covered her exposed legs with the robe Porta had loaned to her and realized she'd been in it for more than a day now. Her breath was an audible wheeze.

"No."

Those juniper-berry eyes begged her to listen. She looked away.

"That stinking sumac is a liar. She has told you stories."

"She makes sense to me."

"She said you can live forever."

To hear him say it that way made Promise feel like a child who'd just learned that Santa Claus wasn't real, and that she'd been a fool for ever believing he was. The wound caused her to snarl. "Wouldn't that be something?" Then she wondered how Chase knew of the claim at all.

"Porta Cerreto is a charlatan. She does not love you."

"She's the one friend who didn't run off when the whole thing with Zack happened."

"I am your friend," Chase said.

"I don't even know you!"

Chase lowered his portfolio to the ground and crouched in front of Promise. "You do not have what she wants. She will kill you when she knows for sure."

The old woman rolled her eyes.

He took hold of Promise's hand. "You will not find life here," he repeated.

"She *is* life," Porta spat.

Chase twisted like a rising corkscrew and hurled his pencils across the room at Porta. She raised a hand and deflected one. The rest made light wooden music against the stairway rails and then fell at her feet. His extended fingers pointed at her, accusing.

"Behold, I have come out to withstand

thee," Chase said, "because thy way is perverse before me. No man or woman hath ascended up to heaven, but he that came down from heaven, even the Son of man which is in heaven. She that believeth on him is not condemned: but she that believeth not is condemned already."

Porta's face turned white like a moon in a dim sky. Promise got to her feet.

"*He* is your life!" Chase shouted. "Neither is there salvation in *any* other: for there is none other name under heaven given among the people, but the name of Jesus Christ of Nazareth, whom ye crucified, whom God raised from the dead!"

"*Promise* is life!" Porta shrieked, but she took hold of the banister like it was her only tether to the earth. "She's going to save me and throw you onto the rocks!"

"Mrs. Brandy Bell is dead," Chase said to Promise. "She jumped from the Vista Park Bluffs after living with the picture of you dying. You could not save Mrs. Brandy Bell. You cannot give anyone life until it is first given to you."

Promise could find no sensible words.

"Here is the truth," Chase said. "Porta Cerreto will kill me, and you will not be able to save me, because you do not have life. Then she will kill you, because you do not have life. But we do not have to die."

A fierce cough squeezed Promise's lungs and shook her in its fist. Her eyes moved between Chase and Porta, not knowing which one to believe. She couldn't believe them both. She didn't want to call either of them a liar.

"I gave you a promise. Do you remember it?" Chase said. He clasped both her hands in his. His fingertips were soft, and the creases of his skin were filled with chalk dust. "The promises of love are the promises you keep. The promises of liars are worthless. Throw those promises away."

"How?" Promise whispered.

"Get out of my house!" Porta unwrapped her knuckles from the rail.

Chase said to Promise, "Blessed are those who wash their robes, that they may have the right to the tree of life and may go through the gates into the city."

"Get out!" Porta took long strides across the room, seizing the *Ameretat* as she passed it. Soil from the jade bowl spilled onto the carpet.

"The tree of life is evergreen," Chase said. "It outlasts us all."

"Porta, no!" Promise yelled. She pulled Chase toward her.

The jade sculpture came down on Chase's

head while Promise still cried out. His blood spattered across her cheek as he went down.

36

From inside the musty guesthouse, where the week of his self-imposed isolation was starting to sour, the sound of breaking glass dragged Zack out of his rumpled bed. He lifted the edge of a curtain and saw the man in the red-and-white ball cap, the crazy who had come looking for Promise two days ago. Had he said what his name was? The guy stood in front of Porta's kitchen window holding a folder and a bunch of pencils. The hole in the window was big enough for him to stick his face through.

Zack watched the exchange that followed. He saw his mother emerge from the basement and speak with the nutcase, who put a piece of paper through the window. She threw a rock in return. It busted a second pane and didn't get a reaction.

This made Zack smile. His estimation of the strange artist grew.

Chase something. That was the name.

Chase left the broken window and walked around the side of the house. Was he leaving? For some reason, Zack didn't want him to. Some reason to do with Promise that he couldn't put his finger on.

Zack dropped the curtain and crossed his arms, thinking that Chase's appearance meant something important. But thinking was hard these days, and his logic was a tad skewed. He had thought several times about Chase's offer to draw him a picture and vacillated between feeling insulted by the gesture and hopeful like a kid.

The picture Chase had drawn for Promise was remarkable and ironic and magical, and thinking of it made Zack sad that he had ever lied about her, regardless of what she had done. She was only protecting her dreams. Zack wanted a picture like hers, a picture for himself that he hadn't created and no one else would care about, except maybe that it would make another person see him in a different, more hopeful light.

Like the way this dude Chase saw him.

What did a Moreton Bay fig look like, anyway?

In that second, Zack wanted this picture more than he wanted his next high. And the fact that Chase was handicapped somehow made it okay for Zack to ask if the offer still stood. He threw open the door to the guesthouse and rushed out into the glare. He shielded his face with his arm.

When he regained his sight, he saw Chase inside the house, heading toward the door that led to the basement, and Porta following, which was when Zack first thought that the importance of Chase's visit had nothing to do with him.

Of course it had nothing to do with him! Chase would only come back for Promise. Promise must be here.

Porta's plans to kill her went straight through Zack's heart. Had his mother found someone else to do the job? Was Promise even alive? Would the artist die too?

Zack stumbled back into the dreary little apartment and fumbled through his dwindling supply of hits, needing something to take the edge off this moment. He ransacked the coffee table, the dresser drawers. Nothing, nothing, nothing. He'd burned through everything.

It was time for him to clear out. If Promise was dead and Chase was next, police would swarm to the kill like flies.

If only he could clear out with a little mental stimulation.

While upending the contents of his backpack — it wasn't like he had much in the way of possessions to go through — his dead phone tumbled out. The charger was in the confiscated Honda, and he'd run down the battery reading and rereading Promise's text messages, listening and relistening to her voice mails.

I'm sorry I didn't stand up for you. Are you okay? Where are you? Please call me.

By the time Zack finally lined up his courage with a moment of sobriety, the opportunity to connect with her, at least by this phone, was gone.

Now the sight of the dead cell was all the stimulation he needed. Promise — beautiful Promise who sang cheerful songs that he loved even though they pushed against his image — didn't deserve anything that had happened to her. This guy Chase, the bumbling encyclopedia of trees, was the better man when it came to helping her. Maybe the better man in all ways.

Zack wondered if it was too late — again — to rise to the occasion.

He ran out the door and across the scrubby wind-battered yard, up around the sloping path at the side of the house, and jumped over the three dry-rotted steps onto the porch. His feet landed like mallets on a drum. The front door was unlocked, and he went through it with the same urgency that had carried him up the hill. He slammed the door and pressed into the house. If he hesitated he'd never follow through.

The sound of cars rolling over the unpaved drive stopped him like a wall. Sunlight reflected off the red-and-blue on top of each car and cast the colors into the living room. The fingers of light stopped inches from Zack's shoes.

He thought Chase must have called the police before coming in.

Zack heard his mother's voice rising from the basement, distressed, angry. He could go there, become a third fatality — or accomplice, as the cops might see it — or he could turn here: go up the stairs, find a possible escape from one of the bedroom windows.

A car door slammed. Zack peeked. Two police cars, two officers.

He was shaking. He was sweating. His stomach wanted out of his body. And none of it had anything to do with a need for weed.

Zack turned up the stairs, everything loud and pounding. Feet, heart, breath. He darted into the room that faced the guesthouse because he had seen during endless hours of staring out through the crack in the curtains a perfect exit: a slider window, a drainpipe within arm's reach, a safe drop onto a narrow lip of sloping roof. It almost didn't matter if the drainpipe was stable. Even a catastrophic descent would put him squarely onto a juniper hedge.

In the room, he got his head level. He took deep breaths. He closed the door to cover the sounds of his leaving.

Though his mother lived alone, this room had been occupied. The bed had been slept in. A woman's outfit hung in the open closet. A set of keys lay on the dresser. On the flimsy wooden rocker by the window, an orange shawl had been draped over the back. On the floor, a pair of sheepskin boots had fallen over on their sides.

The officers pounded on the front door and punched the doorbell, heavy handed, as if already doubtful that they'd get a straightforward answer to a simple inquiry.

Zack crossed the room and picked up the shawl. By the light of the cheerful sun, he could see tiny grains of sand still clinging to one corner, in the fringe. He ran his thumb over the granules, then felt compelled to stand there and pick them out. They were stubborn. He turned his back to the window.

That rapping sounded again. That chime.

Impatience making noise.
   He gave up. He buried his face in the wool.

37

Promise dropped to her knees beside Chase. Her hands moved around in the air, seeking something helpful to do. He lay facedown over his drawings, and his cap had been knocked off to the side. Ruddy blood caked the blond strands of his hair at the back of his head.

She reached for the blanket that had covered her during the night and pressed it against the oozing. Her breaths came shallow and fast. "What did you do? What did you do?"

"I saved your life is what I did!" Porta's jaw jutted out, defiant.

"What for?" Promise screamed. "You said I can't die!"

"Do you understand *nothing*?" Porta threw the *Ameretat* down with such force that the statue broke in two. The lip of the jade bowl was slathered with a gruesome stain where it had struck Chase. She stormed off toward the stairs.

Promise couldn't tell if Chase was still breathing, if his nose and mouth had access to air or were suffocating in carpet fibers. He seemed unconscious. His back didn't rise or fall. She pushed on his arm, then stood and used her body weight to raise him onto his side. He was too heavy. Fear and illness made her breathless. Gray dots danced in her vision.

She knelt again and gently placed her hands on either side of his head. Fearing she could harm him further, but not knowing what else to do, she lifted and turned his neck so that he faced her, free to breathe without obstacles.

Chase's eyes were still open, but she knew he couldn't see her.

"Oh, Chase. Oh no. Oh no." The flesh of his cheeks was soft and trapped her hand between him and the stiff paper of the drawing he had brought. It bent slightly under their weight. She didn't want to pull away. She brushed his face with the fingers of her casted hand. "Please, no."

"Let's pull ourselves together, shall we?"

Promise jerked away from Chase and clutched the old robe closer to her body. Porta stood over her holding a carving knife, and except for the fact that her shiny silk blouse had become untucked at the waist-band of her slacks, she was the picture of composure.

Porta smiled at Promise, maternal and compassionate, and only a small twitch in her chin gave away her pretense.

An eternal moment of knowing came between them.

The older woman licked her lips. Her bright pink lipstick had feathered at the corners of her mouth. "Though this was never the scenario I had in mind, it may prove to be the perfect opportunity," Porta said. "For you."

Promise's mind went to Chase's claim that Porta would kill him, and then her.

Porta gestured to Chase's body with the knifepoint. "I myself have never believed that Jesus Christ of Nazareth was the only one with power to raise the dead."

Wary, Promise groped for the bench directly behind her and pulled herself onto it, letting her shoulders lean back against the cool glass of the thick window. She focused on Porta, and on regaining her breath and her balance.

"What do you want me to do?" she asked.

"Let's see your hand." Porta extended her own.

Promise looked at the knife, then at Chase.

"He needs your blood. If you've got what he needs, it's in your blood."

"What if I don't have it?"

Porta didn't react. Her hand remained outstretched.

Promise said, "You killed him to *test* me?"

"So let's have at it. Quickly now, or you'll be responsible for his death."

"Chase didn't deserve this. No one deserves this."

"He was going to keep you from becoming who you were meant to be."

"He saw me the way I hope to be."

"As do I. The longer you put this off, the lower your chances of succeeding."

Promise stood. "I thought it wasn't unusual for the gods to raise humans from the dead, if they want to."

"To immortality, not to their puny old existence."

"Is there a deadline? A time limit?"

"A little education in pagan history will clarify everything when this is all over."

"If I'm a goddess, you'll be the one getting the education." She coughed.

Porta spread her arms and bowed her neck. The knifetip caught the sun. Promise thought the gesture mocked her, but she couldn't be sure.

"I am your humble servant," Porta said.

"You'll pay a price for this."

"Nothing is free, sweetie."

Not only that, but everything came with a price too steep for Promise to pay. Not even her parents' money could buy her way out of this situation. But that was not why she wanted Chase to live.

"I'd prefer the lancet you used on me for the sculpture."

"For this, we need more."

"Of course we do." She leaned forward and reached for Porta's knife. Instead of giving it to Promise, the witch dropped the blade so that it slashed her open palm. The burning sensation ran down to the tips of Promise's fingers. She snatched her hand back and sucked air between her teeth.

Blood sprang to the surface of her skin. Porta grabbed hold of Promise's wrist and pulled it toward Chase, who lay between them. She turned the cut palm downward and directed it over the length of the body. Blood dribbled.

Porta began an incantation in a language Promise couldn't identify. Tears spilled onto her face. Sadness for this remarkable boy who loved her. For Michelle. This was all wrong.

"I was perfectly healthy until I came to your house," Promise said beneath the babbling. Her coughing continued. Intensified.

Porta disregarded it all.

Promise's blood dripped, and she chose not to watch where it landed. She kept her eyes on this desperate, pathetic woman, and she pitied her for thinking any of this abracadabra charade would work. She hated Porta for believing it, and she hated herself for ever hoping it might be true.

A terrible grief settled on her. She had no power to raise a gnat from the dead. No amount of her own willpower and discipline would keep herself alive. It was definitely not within her abilities to help Chase.

"You're just what he said you are," Promise muttered. She tugged her wrist out of Porta's grip.

Porta continued without her, still holding that knife, chanting and swaying. The woman's high cheekbones were flushed, and there was a sheen on her forehead. Half moons of sweat cupped the armpits of her blouse.

Chase was unchanged.

The reality of his death terrified Promise, like the clean sliding of a snake over the tops of her feet. This is how it would go: when Porta saw him still dead, she would send Promise to join him.

Even now, Promise didn't want to die. She

still wanted to be remembered — and not for crimes she had never committed or even planned. She still wanted the lungs Chase had promised her. She still wanted to live, for Michelle, for her parents, for everyone who had ever loved her.

A raucous pounding sounded above. And a doorbell, hit several times.

Porta continued as if visitors upstairs and a dead body in her basement were the norm.

Promise was as far away from those stairs to freedom as she could be, and both Chase and the witch were barriers. She took a stealthy step away from Porta.

Porta's arms fell to her side and her chant ended. She stared down at Chase. "It does seem that I was wrong about you," Porta said.

"Someone is here," Promise murmured.

"They'll go away."

"I never lied to you about who I was."

"That's true enough. You're no immortal, are you? In fact, what are you now? Not a singer. Not a model." Now Porta's eyes met Promise's, and Promise was aware of her unkempt, unshowered, unattractive state. "You're just a common girl, willing to do anything for attention, no matter what it takes."

Promise wasn't sure if that was true or not.

"It's no wonder my son liked you. Birds of a feather."

"Porta —"

"Do you know how much time I've *wasted* on you? You cheap trick! You foul omen! How did you do it? Who put you up to this grand production? What have they paid you for your trouble?" Her furious knife cut the air in front of Promise's throat.

Promise dodged, gasping.

The doorbell sounded again. The knocking came harder.

Porta threw the knife at Promise. The butt of the handle *thunked* on the glass window behind her and then dropped point-first into the upholstery of the bench. Promise lunged toward the stairs and heard a tearing. The blade had pinned a corner of the robe and held her back for half a second.

The short time was all Porta needed. She reached for Promise's neck and barreled into her, as strong as Promise was weak. The bench caught Promise at the back of the knees as she went down under Porta's weight. She heard her own skull crack against the thick glass of the ocean-view window. She sensed the witch release her and turn away.

She slid sideways behind the bench and felt the knife blade slice against her thigh before the floor stopped her fall. She smelled her own blood. She heard voices upstairs. Zack's voice. The carpet under her cheek was coarse.

Chase's body lay on the other side of the bench, his lifeless fingers stretched out toward her as if still trying to coax her away from this death. She reached for him and saw the severed *Ameretat* on the floor.

"I'm sorry," she whispered to Chase. "Please forgive me." The gray dots in her vision gathered to form a thick fog. Behind Chase's head, the idol stared blankly at Promise and hugged her broken, blood-stained bowl.

Before Promise's eyes closed of their own accord, she saw a shiny green shoot rise from the basin and slither out across the floor.

38

Finding one's center quickly in a crisis was a critical skill for a woman of Porta's means and reputation. Though Zack's voice aboveground had shocked her nearly as much as every other event of the day, she rose above the disaster as she had risen above every other disaster of her whole long, disastrous life.

None of her prior efforts had ever come to this. When it all settled down, she would need to examine where she'd gone wrong.

She turned her back on the sight of the dead bodies. Dead, almost dead — their status was of little importance to her. They were a mere distraction. What was important was that someone other than she would be to blame for all this. Her son seemed willing enough.

Her mind worked quickly. Her body followed suit.

She smoothed her hair. She tucked in her

silky blouse. She took deep, easy breaths and measured strides toward the fire pit. The pan she'd placed over the flames was smoking, overheated. It would have to cool down before she warmed the incense.

"Mother!" Zack's artificially sweetened voice traveled down the stairs. "Some people to see you!"

She left the skillet where it was. She let the fire burn. She turned the lever on the chimney vent and closed the flue. If the crack on the head didn't kill Promise, carbon monoxide fumes would. They should work quickly, in fact, on a small woman of such poor lung health. She hadn't coughed since striking the glass. A good sign.

Porta faltered only for the time it took to dismiss the troubling thought that a cliff fall, a car wreck, and a water-conducted electrocution had not achieved their most likely results on Promise.

To help the gas along, she opened the closet underneath the stairwell and shut off the air-purification filters that separated the oxygen from dust and allergens and other invisible gunk in the room.

"Mother!"

"Up in just a moment, dear."

Porta closed the closet, steadied herself on the balustrade, and ascended the stairs.

She entered the kitchen and closed the door behind her.

Zack was sweeping up glass into the dustpan and refusing to look at her. What was he up to? Two young men in uniform, barely older than her son, stood side by side near the kitchen table. She beamed.

"Officers! To what do I owe this pleasure?" She leaned forward eagerly, offering her hand. They returned the gesture and introduced themselves, but she was of no mind to pay attention to names. "I'm still moving in, you see, and haven't had many visitors. May I make you some tea?"

"No, thank you," said the one with the crooked nose.

"I imagine you're here about Zack," she said, going about the tea-making process anyway, looking carefree. "He's just back from a getaway to clear his head."

"Actually, I've been in town the whole time," Zack said.

"The feds will be glad to know where you are," the other one said. This one had a utility belt so loaded that it ought to have pulled his pants down. Definitely a rookie.

"They're looking for me? I answered all their questions at the hospital. Thought we were done."

Porta scooped some loose-leaf Ceylon tea

into a diffuser. She'd intervene only if it looked like Zack was about to talk himself into trouble.

"What?" Zack said when the silence accused him of being ignorant. "Here I am. I haven't skipped town."

"Just classes?" Rookie asked.

"The term's over."

"You haven't responded to investigators' efforts to contact you."

"Dead phone. No computer. Go to the campus post office once a week. Sorry." He dumped the glass shards into the trash can, then turned around and reached for the door to the basement. He pulled it open.

"Just where do you think you're going?" Porta spilled some of the tea leaves across the stained countertop.

"Putting these away." He held up the whisk broom and pan. "What'd you think I was doing?"

"They go in there," she said, pointing to the pantry.

Zack glowered at her and tossed the items in on the shelf. He pulled out a kitchen chair and started bouncing his foot against the leg of the table. Porta stepped away from the counter and shut the door to the basement.

"What happened to the window?" Rookie asked.

Porta glanced up. Zack laced his fingers across his stomach.

"A large bird," she said.

Zack smirked at her.

"A very large and frightened gull, in fact. He came in, he went out. It's a wonder he could even fly after that."

The guy with the misaligned nose said, "Mrs. Cerreto, we —"

"Ms. Cerreto," she said, putting on a kettle. "Never married."

"We won't take much of your time, but we need to ask you some questions about a client of your gallery, a Mrs. Brandy Bell."

"Oh yes, of course. That was so sad. I heard about it this morning. But I'm sure I know nothing about it."

Nose withdrew a piece of paper from his shirt pocket and unfolded it. "Is this the piece of art you sold to her?"

Porta fetched a pair of reading glasses off the kitchen island where she usually read the newspaper and looked down her nose at it. "That's a color copy of it, yes." She held out the paper toward Zack. "Isn't it, dear?"

Zack stopped tapping and sat up straight in the chair.

"My son took that photo. He's quite good

when he wants to be."

"Mrs. Bell's husband —"

"Mr. Bell. Oh, he must be taking this all very hard."

"He's made some strong accusations against you."

"Mr. Bell? Against me? Whatever for?"

"Is it true you have a private viewing room in your studio?" Nose asked.

"Yes. Would you like to see it?"

"And do you spend time with clients in that room?"

"Only long enough to make sure they are comfortable and to answer their questions."

"Tell us about when you showed this photo to Mrs. Bell."

"Oh, I can't say I recall the specifics too clearly. She was upset about something, but she didn't speak, you see, so I can't say what was on her mind. She indicated she wanted a closer look at the image. I arranged it for her." Porta shrugged and leaned against the counter, waiting for the water to boil.

Zack said, "Mother prefers an incense that clouds the memory a tad." He had not yet taken his eyes off Promise's photo.

"Listen to him, teasing his own mother about her age." Porta laughed.

"You mean there's incense in the room?" Rookie this time.

"And why not?" Porta wanted to know. "Appealing to the senses is a very old technique for making customers feel happy enough to buy something. Take a whiff next time you go to the grocery store or a restaurant or . . . or an auto dealer! It's practically a science — the eyes, the ears, the nose. All targets of American capitalism. If that makes me a little wicked, so be it."

"Tell us about this incense, what's in it."

"For goodness' sake! What can proprietary information like that have to do with poor Mrs. Bell?"

"You never know."

"When a judge tells me to give up my only secret for the world to know, I'll be happy to make the distributor a matter of public record. Otherwise, you'll have to come on into my gallery and check it out with your own handsome noses."

She flashed a winsome smile at both of them. Neither appeared to catch her barb.

"You never know," she mimicked. "Perhaps you'll leave artistically enriched." She picked up the cigarettes sitting on the counter. "Would either of you care for a smoke? Hand-rolled, special blend." She nodded at the busted window panes. "We have plenty of ventilation."

They didn't acknowledge her.

Nose: "When do you plan to reopen your shop?"

"Wednesday. I took a long weekend to rest up. End of summer and all that."

"So soon after your grand opening?"

Her smile stiffened. "It's more work than you think. I don't have any employees."

Rookie: "We understand you had an altercation with a local artist?"

"Artist? Oh, you mean the boy, the amateur? No. The idiot — pardon me. I've shown my age. I do believe I'm supposed to say, 'the young man with autism.' He was disruptive. I asked him to leave."

"In what way was he disruptive?"

"He was rude to my patrons. Autistics don't understand social politeness, you know."

"My nephew has autism," said Rookie. "He can be awkward, but never rude."

"How nice."

Nose: "He gave a drawing to Mrs. Bell."

"I wouldn't know about that."

"Mr. Bell tells us he did. Did it upset you?"

"If I don't know about it, how could it upset me? She bought work from me. It sounds callous to say that's all that matters, but it is."

"How well did you know Mrs. Bell?"

"She visited my gallery twice." The tediousness of the questioning began to grind on her.

Zack asked, "Why did she jump?" and brought a halt to the conversation.

The kettle whistled. Porta poured the water over the diffuser, glad for the diversion of Zack's emotions.

Nose finally said to Zack, "You mean Mrs. Bell?"

"Yeah."

The officers didn't answer.

"Did she leave a note?"

"I'm afraid we can't discuss an open investigation," Rookie said.

So, straight out of the academy!

"Because this picture with Promise, it was an accident. Even her surviving, I guess, was an accident." He shot an accusatory frown at his mother. "I always thought of this as a survival picture, not a death picture. Did Mrs. Bell think she'd survive?"

"How could they possibly know what she thought?" Porta said too loudly.

Zack slammed his open palm down on the table and shoved the picture away. When he stood, his chair hit the wainscoting behind him. "You know the problem with you? Well, there are so many I guess I can't narrow it down to just one. But you need to start caring more whether people live or die, for starters. Because the way I see it, not a single person on this stinking planet, starting with me, is going to notice when you're gone."

"I apologize for him," Porta said to the officers. "Apparently autism isn't the only disorder responsible for rudeness."

Zack said, "He was here, at this house, this morning. His name is Chase, Chase something, and he's a better artist than anyone she's got hanging in her gallery."

"That's true," Porta said.

Nose said, "True that he's better or true that he was here?"

"That he was here, of course! If he were better, which he's not, he'd have his own gallery for bothering people. I find his drawings quite childish."

Zack seemed too stunned by her honesty to offer up any more indicting information.

Porta waited for the official demand requiring her to fill the ensuing silence. She used those precious seconds to invent the story she would need to leave this house without cuffs around her wrists. If Zack intended to coauthor the tale, the outcome might swing wildly out of her favor.

Nose cleared his throat. "Why was he here?"

"He came by to see a mutual friend who was also here. Promise Dayton."

"What did you do to her?" Zack demanded.

"Gracious, Zack!" Then Porta said to Nose, "If offering a girl comfort is a crime, I'm afraid you'll have to arrest me. A very close friend of hers passed away this weekend."

"All her stuff is still here," Zack said, pointing upstairs. "I saw it."

"Yes. Your jealousy is unbecoming, son."

"It's not —"

"She and Chase went out. She pities him, see. She has a soft spot for lost causes." She leveled these remarks at Zack. "No idea when they'll return. Goodness, I think we've drifted quite far from the topic of Mrs. Bell."

Nose stood from the table and pocketed his notes. Rookie stuck his thumbs in the pockets of his uniform slacks.

"He was alone!" Zack insisted. He threw open the door to the basement. "He went down there alone! He hasn't come up. Was Promise down there too? Did you kill both of them?"

"Zachary. Please, you're embarrassing yourself." She set her teacup on the counter.

"You should look!" he shouted at the officers. "I know he's there. He's probably dead. If you killed her too . . ." He took two steps toward her, and she raised her arms to defend herself.

Rookie stepped between them. Zack threw up his hands and turned away.

Porta took a deep breath and covered her heart with her palm. "Thank you," she said. "You can imagine what stress he's been under lately. His head is cloudy, I'm afraid."

"You have got to be kidding me!" Zack protested.

Nose walked toward the door and said, "Do you mind if I have a look?"

"There's nothing to see," she said, feeling her heart work a little harder to move oxygenated blood to all the vital organs. This was not part of the plot she had in mind for her story. "But by all means." Her smile felt limp. She looked at Rookie and gestured to the door. "Feel free to join him. I think I can handle my son."

"I think I'll stay right here," he said. Nose started to descend. Zack started to follow. "And you can stay right here too."

Zack put his hands on his head and turned away, facing the broken window as if he badly needed the ocean air.

Porta's mind whirled, seeking a revised ending to this story that was more desirable than where it was headed. Her eyes bored a hole into the back of Zack's head. He didn't notice. Rookie shifted his weight. They waited.

And waited.

In what was probably a matter of a minute or less, though it seemed much, much longer, Nose re-emerged into the kitchen, slipping a small flashlight into a loop at his waist.

"That's the strangest basement I've ever been in," he said.

Zack spun.

"You realize you shouldn't burn —"

"It's vented," Porta said. "The air is filtered. It's all to code."

"It is? Well, it's all weird, but as far as I know it's nothing illegal, so I think we're done here. We might have more questions later, ma'am."

Porta clasped her quivering hands behind her back and bowed slightly at the waist. "Thank you, gentlemen. I hope I was at least somewhat helpful." She felt sweat on her brow and hoped they would attribute it to the summer temperatures. Her eyes were on Zack, evaluating his next move. "I trust you can see yourselves out."

39

Chelsea abandoned a meeting with a midlevel client and broke speed limits getting home after Wes, having left three urgent messages on her cell phone, had the receptionist interrupt her with news of a family emergency.

Chase was gone again, but this time Wes wasn't telling Chelsea everything would be okay. Instead, he told her there was something she needed to see. Now. He wouldn't tell her what it was. "I can't describe it, but it's important," was all he said.

She wished and wished she had stayed with Chase at breakfast and never left.

Wes met her in the driveway.

"Why did you wait so long to call me?" she accused.

"I thought I could find him."

She rushed into the house. "Where have you looked?"

"Downtown. The sweet shop, the library,

the clothing store."

"The gallery?"

"It's closed."

She dropped her purse onto the floor of the kitchen. "He was upset about Mrs. Bell. Could he have gone to Vista Park Bluffs? I never should have told him about that."

"Chels, you need to see his studio."

She realized then that Wes hadn't uttered a word of his usual optimism or confidence in Chase's abilities. She couldn't read his eyes.

Chelsea grabbed the banister to avoid a misstep as she raced upstairs.

In Chase's bedroom, the spinning blades of the ceiling fan cut through the heat. She turned her back on this and entered the studio at the other end of the short hall. The doorway framed an artistic view of the wide desk in front of the window, the built-in shelving on either side, the rows and rows of neatly arranged containers, no two alike, on each shelf. Brushes and pencils and chalks and stumps protruded from the holders that didn't have lids.

Everything looked as it always did. She sensed Wes pause in the doorway and turned around. Then she noticed.

"Where are his drawings?" she asked.

The walls, which had been papered from

ceiling to baseboard with his black sheets and minutely detailed drawings, were bare. The tiny dots of hundreds and hundreds of thumbtack holes looked like creative texturing rather than punctures.

"Did someone take them? Take him? Why?"

"They're on his desk."

They were. Stacked several inches thick like a slab of obsidian. There was an index card placed on the top of this pile, held in place by a paperweight. Chelsea picked it up. Chase's precise lettering on the card read THE LONGINGS.

"Why would he do this? Where is his portfolio?"

"I think this might explain some of it." Wes showed Chelsea a spiral-bound sketchbook at the left side of the desk. The white card atop it said FOR MY SISTER.

Chelsea turned back the cover. A sheet of translucent paper covered each of the black sheets. She gently lifted the first one and revealed a portrait of her parents kissing each other. The tenderness of the image caught Chelsea off guard. She never knew that Chase thought about their parents — or anyone — in these terms. But Chase must have imagined this scenario, because there was no other explanation for the fact

411

that they were old, aged beyond even what they would be today, if they were here. Home. Together. Underneath the couple was the label GREAT BASIN BRISTLECONE, *Pinus longaeva* — ALTHEA TREE, *Hibiscus syriacus*.

"You looked through this?" she asked Wes.

"I did. I thought maybe he'd left a message about where he'd gone."

It was right that Wes had seen these pictures. If he hadn't already looked, she'd have asked him to go through them with her. He stayed by the door as she turned the pages.

"He's never drawn people," she said. "That I know of."

"I didn't know either. They're not bad. Not as good as the trees, but not bad."

There was a portrait of her looking so much like Chase, as alike as when they had been children. In white chalk under the image he had written WESTERN REDCEDAR, *Thuja plicata* — A LONGING FULFILLED IS A TREE OF LIFE.

She held the portrait up for Wes to see. "Do you know what this means?"

"Not the meaning you're looking for. But I did a lot of reading about trees with Chase. The common name for the *Thuja* genus is arborvitae. Trees of life. Evergreens."

"I'm a tree of life?" she asked.

"That would make Chase one too, wouldn't it?"

On the next page was Promise, the woman who'd captured Chase's mind and heart so swiftly that Chelsea had once felt jealous of her. Strangely, Chase's rendering of her here stripped away everything but affection for the girl. She sat barefoot on the great twisted roots of an enormous shade tree, her eyes closed and her head tilted back against the strong trunk. A headset like one would wear in a recording studio covered her ears, and Promise's fingers pressed against these on each side of her head. She appeared to be singing.

Beneath this picture was the caption DRAW THE LONGING, FOR TIME IS SHORT.

"So you think these pictures will help us find Chase?" she asked, turning to the next drawing.

"No," Wes said.

"Then why —" The fourth drawing was a wedding altar. In the background, an illuminated window shone on a lattice archway covered in roses. In the foreground, Chelsea in an elegant white dress faced Wes.

Chelsea lingered on the idea of this scene, oddly unembarrassed that Wes had seen this

413

before she had.

FILL THE HEART, FOR DAYS ARE FULL.

"So, Chase thinks we ought to stick to-gether," she said.

"Looks that way."

She wanted to look at him but couldn't.

"I think you put him up to this," she teased.

"The truth is, he's been kicking me in the tail about it for a long time."

"But you're a stubborn one."

"Oh, I'm not the stubborn one in this equation."

She went to the next page, the last one that wasn't blank. Here Chase had drawn the boy sculpture that stood in the front of the ART(i)FACTS gallery. He had taken the aerial perspective, so that the boy's up-turned face looked directly out of the page and was the focal point.

The beauty of this drawing was mysteri-ous and remarkable. For one, the face was clearly Chase's. It possessed his unassuming features and his open expression that invited people to trust him. It was mature and childlike at the same time.

And for another, unlike the sculpture, the eyes in this image were open. And they were looking directly at Chelsea.

I LOVE YOU, the caption said, accompa-

414

nied by the eye contact that Chelsea had been longing for her entire life, as real as if her brother himself were there in the paper.

She touched the white light that shaped his face, not caring that the medium on the paper would transfer to her fingertips.

"Why would he do this?" she murmured. "It's like he doesn't plan to come back." She felt Wes place his stabilizing hand at the small of her back so that she could lean into him just so, as if they'd been comforting each other this way for years.

"Why would he leave? He can't just leave. We have to find him."

"Let's get started."

40

Zack watched Porta tap a cigarette on the counter and then lift it to her lips. She lifted a lighter to the tip and took a long draw to get the glow started.

"Where's Promise?" Zack demanded.

"I told you, she took a walk with that idiot."

"When, exactly? What time did they leave?"

Porta extended the cigarette to him. He refused it. She insisted, waving it at him and nodding. *C'mon, c'mon.* He snatched it away just to get her to stop. "What time?"

"Can't say for sure. A half hour ago? Maybe twenty minutes."

"You liar. Her boots are upstairs in her room. She would have taken her wrap."

"On this fine day? I do believe she left in sandals. Summer love, you know."

Zack lunged at Porta, aiming the burning tip of the cigarette at her face. She dodged him, and his wrist hit the countertop, scattering a few ashes.

"You fool boy! Sit down!"

"Why would I do anything you tell me to?" he shouted back. But the humiliating answer to that question was a fine depressant for Zack — he twenty-something, his mother seventy-something, and she the more agile of the two, physically and intellectually.

That truth made him instantly, consciously dissatisfied with something new: his own failure to break free of her and choose his own way, a way that did not recognize her as queen. He had failed not because the choice was impossible, but because it was merely difficult.

The awareness calmed him. He willed himself to focus and, strangely enough, in the absence of drugs and fury, found himself able to think clearly.

"What did you do to that detective guy? Cast a spell on him that made him blind? Or maybe you already hid the bodies."

"It's high time we talked. I'll tell you everything."

Porta started talking, but he wasn't listening to her. She had never spoken truth to him and surely wasn't about to begin now. He was considering her sideways insistence that he not go into the basement. He was recalling the tremor in her hands that had made tiny waves in her teacup. And he was trying to place the scent of the glowing, aromatic cigarette between the first and second fingers of his left hand. It smelled familiar and unfriendly. It smelled like a plot.

Only an hour ago he would have surrendered to the lure of it. Now he fought it. For the love of Promise or Chase or whatever was in that basement that she didn't want him to see, he resisted the peace of an intoxicated mind.

His mother was igniting her own stick as though they were going to sit down and have a heart-to-heart, and her lips were moving and she wasn't looking at him and Zack found this all tragically, morbidly ridiculous. He wiggled the smoking stub between his fingers, letting the orange ashes rain to the floor, and he decided not to stomp them out. They'd leave tiny sooty holes.

". . . know how you feel about her," Porta was saying when he tuned back in.

No, you don't.

"But the truth is you're just a child yourself and can hardly trust your feelings at your age. You'll understand this when you're older."

"Older like you? As in, too old for wisdom to be worth anything because you think you've finally outgrown it?"

"Ignore me, then. It will be your loss." She blew a huff of smoke in his direction. The gesture was pathetic, coming from a woman her age, coming from any mother at all. What was she trying to do?

Zack remembered then that the odor of the cigarettes was the same as the incense she burned in her shop. He said, "So what you're saying is, I should trust *your* wisdom about my feelings?"

Porta's fair skin was paler than he remembered it being. She took another long draw on her own drug. "Exactly."

Ignore me, then. It will be your loss. "I think it's time I started thinking for myself. Correction: I think it's time I started thinking about someone besides myself." Zack threw his cigarette out the jagged hole in the glass window. He yanked open the door to the basement and took the stairs down two at a time.

The sound of the door slamming and being braced by something from the other side — the kitchen table, or maybe the kitchen chairs — reached him before he hit the last step. For the first time in his life, he didn't care about anything his mother might do.

Porta's breath came fast and made her light-headed. She couldn't stop the trembling in her arms and legs, the vibrations that shook the tea in her belly. These sensations had nothing to do with her concoction, her use-less concoction, which she quickly extin-guished in the kitchen sink as Zack threw himself into the pit.

It had never been so hard to bend him to her will.

She had to go; she had to move more swiftly than she ever had in her life. She slammed the door behind Zack and grabbed the kitchen chair that was within arm's reach. The police officers had been gone less than five minutes. The one had seen her basement and been unconcerned, and she devoted no more than two seconds to wondering which of the gods had intervened on her behalf, and how. The deity would settle accounts with her on that point soon enough. There were no free gifts. What mat-tered more in these precious seconds was how swiftly she could preserve herself.

Porta wedged the top of the ladder-back chair under the doorknob. It didn't have to be strong, just stubborn enough to fight whatever weakness the carbon monoxide let linger.

She looked at the clock hanging over the stove. It usually took her fifteen minutes to drive from here to her gallery. If she hurried, she could make it in ten. No, not the gallery — she needed to be seen by someone who knew her. She needed to be able to prove where she had been, and at what time.

The nice old man who ran the Irish pub next door to her shop would serve her well. He'd be happy to sell her a conversation and a receipt with a time stamp on it. She'd linger until the alcohol took the edge off her shakes. She might even thank him with a little flirtatious banter.

And afterward she'd rush home and free the door of its chair and she'd call the police, begging them to return to the scene of a shocking, unthinkable tragedy: a young man and woman, murdered, and their killer dead by his own hand, having subjected himself to carbon monoxide fumes.

Oh, Officer, if only I'd stayed behind! But Zack and I argued, and I had to get out. He was upset, he was so jealous of that boy — it was the drugs. He has a history, you know. But I never believed he was capable of murder. When they came back from their walk, he must have . . . Oh, it's too terrible to think about! That he'd take his own life comes as no surprise, perhaps, but these innocent people? Oh, oh, I think I'm going to pass out!

Porta jiggled the chair to make sure it was steady. She rushed now as she never rushed, grabbing her keys off the hook by the door to the garage and leaving her house without bothering to lock any of the doors.

41

Zack had never set foot in his mother's home prior to that morning, and this descent into the basement was also his first. The smell greeted him. It wasn't an unusual odor as basements went: damp soil mixed with heavy air gave it the personality of a greenhouse. One of the mahogany boards under his feet squeaked and announced his presence even before Porta slammed the door on him. He reached the bottom.

Amazingly large windows that overlooked the Pacific Ocean were the last thing he expected to see in a room like this, but he noticed them only because the glare that hit his eyes was temporarily blinding. The center attraction of this strange space was not the jaw-dropping panorama, but the carpet of ivy that blanketed the floor. The ivy was dense with heart-shaped green leaves, and when Zack stepped off the stairs into it, seeing no clear space for his feet, tangled vines made his walk uneven.

Twisted tendrils rose up each of the three columns that gave the room structural support. They had also climbed each of the walls. Mounds of leaves near the windows covered what he assumed was furniture.

"Promise?"

The plant rustled as if his voice were a breeze. A movement turned his head away from the windows, and he saw the vine creeping toward the only exposed space in the room: a self-contained fire pit under a hood and, against the wall, a cabinet topped by a countertop.

The ivy shifted and swelled, moving the way ocean tide rises on the beach. A living shoot reached out and attached itself to the leg of the fire pit, encircling the post three times. He watched the plant close in. It advanced by inches, then paused. The space stilled, and he was the only breathing creature once more.

He had hoped not to be.

"Promise, are you down here?"

The vine's visible growth set him on edge. He took a cautious step. Pictures from classical mythology and contemporary spiritualists hung around the room, cheap pictures that valued flashy fantasy elements above true artistic skill. Mass-produced glitz. He hated them.

On the far wall, nearest to the large window, was an image of a woman standing with her back to the room. She held the earth in her hands and lifted it toward the sun. The composition was geometric, created by clean computer-generated lines and solid colors that made no use of dimension or shadow. And so the paintlike spatter across the skirt of her robes seemed out of place. Zack moved toward it over the spongy vine.

A leaf reached up under the hem of his slim jeans and brushed his ankle. He flinched, lifted his foot, and swatted at the sensation.

The spatter on the woman's dress was not part of the picture, he saw when he stood close enough. It lay on the glass and then trailed onto the wall.

Beneath this morbid spray, the red bill of a baseball cap protruded from the vines. Zack untangled it and saw on the white netting near the clasp a stain that matched the color of the wall spatter. The hat's crown was limp from wear, the bill pliable and round in his fist.

"Chase!" he shouted, gripping the cap and turning in an aimless circle, looking for signs. "Chase, where are you? Promise?"

Zack dropped to his knees and cracked his kneecap on something solid. The pain that shot down his shins was inconsequential. He'd fallen on a large shard of broken emerald rock. The piece was dirty, sticky with soil and tacky blood. Zack hoped it wasn't blood, but what else could it be? The whole mess was entangled with knotty white roots.

He dropped Chase's hat and started digging through the plant, collecting watery green scrapings under his short fingernails.

"Chase! Promise! Say something! Tell me where you are!"

A few of the leaves snapped off their vine as Zack tried to dig his way through them. Rustling, like a wave of whispered protest against the assault, spread out through the mass of foliage and rattled up the walls, up the columns in the middle of the room. The whole plant seethed as it had when he first entered.

A vine snaked out and wrapped itself around Zack's left wrist and would not let go. Though the leaves were fragile enough, the tendrils were powerful. He tried to shake it off. It held fast and encircled his arm again, squeezing. His fingertips began to tingle.

The stem oozed a white liquid at the joints

where he'd broken leaves off, and the substance burned his skin. Zack dug harder at the mass with his free hand. It was urgent that he find Chase and Promise, though he couldn't imagine how anyone could breathe under the suffocating tangle. His mother was a beast, a monster. A killer. Why had she done this senseless thing?

He continued to cry out their names. He balanced himself on his left knee and kicked at the jungle with his right foot. Leaves crumpled, but the vine would not give way.

When it became impossible for Zack to see his left hand, because it had been overtaken like a bug swallowed in a Venus flytrap, he began to panic. The sea of leaves was roiling now, and noisy. The growth began to wind up his arm. The weight of it pulled down on him and buckled his elbow.

Waving leaves tapped the glass window. The mass crawled farther up the walls and also took to the stairs. It occurred to Zack that Porta had blocked the door upstairs in order to prevent the cancerous plant from overtaking her entire house.

With a great shout, Zack lunged away from the hold on his arm and fell sideways toward the window. The motion carried him into a firm mound that gave way when he hit it. The object might have been a seat or small table, covered and hidden. He groped at the solid mass as if it could provide him with the leverage he needed, even though it was as unstable as he was. Instead of freeing himself, his motion merely dragged the entanglement with him. A fresh leaf unfurled from a newly sprouted vine, which wrapped itself around his rib cage, then moved up toward his shoulder.

Zack strained and kicked, clawed and thrashed. The mound, which turned out to be a narrow bench, flipped forward onto its side and revealed Promise, who had been tucked away beneath it.

"Promise!"

She lay with her back to the glass window where it met the floor. Her body was wrapped in an old robe that was hiked up at her thigh, which was bloody near the knee.

"Promise! Get up!"

The plant held him back from her, but he reached out with his sneaker and prodded her in the belly. "Please, Promise. Listen to me!" He could see her chest rise and fall.

The movement of her lungs, paired with the creeping vine that rose along his torso and slipped its fingers around his throat, brought a strange memory to his mind: a botany experiment he'd done during his sophomore year, in which he and a partner had to calculate how many plants of a certain size, bearing a certain number of leaves, under certain circumstances, could produce enough oxygen to keep a certain person alive for one hour. The answer, with all its variables and general averages taken into account, was about four hundred.

Zack wondered — irrationally, he acknowledged — how many leafy plants would be equal to this basement jungle, and whether it would be enough for him to live on when the vine started to squeeze and choke.

The rough carpet fibers underneath Promise's cheek reminded her of the sand she had landed in after falling from the Vista Park Bluffs. The rug and sand, she noticed when she opened her eyes, were the same grainy brown color. Even more strange was that she could also feel the same rumbling vibrations of the ocean, and the cool moisture of the scented air on her exposed skin, and the strange, strange sensation of being able to breathe without coughing.

She tested whether this ability to exchange carbon dioxide for oxygen was reality or memory by taking a very deep breath. It was sweet and full.

The air that came out of her when she finished caused a movement in front of her face. When she focused, she saw a glistening green leaf, shaped like a heart, quivering before her like a shy valentine.

"Chase?" she asked before remembering why.

His name brought truth to her mind, and she jerked up off the floor, feeling a sting on the skin of her thigh and a shooting pain up her left arm. It had been pinned by the bench, which had somehow tipped over onto her wrist. She wriggled her fingers free of the trap and felt the cut Porta had sliced into her palm. She'd been reaching for Chase's hand. The bench barricaded her efforts to find him again, but she had new hope. If she could rise from her own ashes with this kind of strength, there was a chance for him too.

Grabbing the lip of the fallen seat, she pulled herself up.

He was gone. Gone? Or buried? The leaf that had tickled her nose was the mere fringe of a living shroud that now covered the floor. Rather than growing over her, it appeared to have crawled over the bench she'd fallen under, like ivy over a trellis. It took her several seconds to make sense of the rustling plant, and even then her confusion would not clear out. That little green shoot that had risen out of *Ameretat*'s broken bowl had grown into *this* blanket, this new carpet that consumed the entire basement. Porta's sacred soil had bloomed! Here was evidence of an immortal life. But had it been borne of a dead man's blood?

Chase couldn't be dead. She hurdled the bench and bent at the waist. She grabbed at leaves and started yanking, looking for the man who loved her so innocently and irrationally. The plant bled a milky substance as its pieces came off in her hands. *Don't be dead. Please, don't be dead . . .*

Promise tore the thing apart, stronger than she believed she could ever be, her lungs full of hope and rich, rich oxygen.

Her fingertips brushed against skin.

"Chase!"

She cleared out the density, which was more like tugging madly on a bundle of tangled Christmas lights. A mouth appeared, a cheek, a nose. And short black hair, slick and close to the head.

"Zack?"

She uncovered his neck. The fingers of one hand were entwined with a ropy green noose at his throat, where he'd scratched himself trying to pull death away from his windpipe. A bluish line bordered his parted lips.

She freed his fingers, intending to slip hers into the gap between his skin and the vine, but it constricted on him faster than she could react and persisted in its squeeze. Tearing at these sinewy stems did no good. They were woody and thick and wouldn't be cut except by something sharp.

Promise jumped up, scanning the room for any possible tool. Tickling leaves caressed her calves where her weight made a depression in the organic floor. At the back of the room, near the stairs, she saw a bright fire burning in a portable pit, and cabinets supporting a narrow countertop. She ran toward them, hoping to find something useful.

The rhythm of her feet seemed to awaken the plant. The leaves shivered and shifted like papers scattered by wind. She felt the ground surge and lost her balance, then regained it. The vines had scaled the fire pit, and flames were reflected in their shimmering leaves. They danced like a strange green blaze and pressed in toward the heat. Above and behind the makeshift kitchen, she saw them ascending the stairs.

A single leaf came too close to the flame and shriveled into a black lump that gave off a small column of grim smoke.

On the countertop, a rope of braided onions lay next to a small butcher block and a bottle of water, and Promise remembered the knife Porta had thrown into the bench. She ran back to where the furniture lay on its side, high stepping over the uneven floor.

Promise thought then that Porta had seen the plant sprout, had understood that Chase was the one who had made it do so, and convinced him to run off to do her bidding, leaving Promise and Zack to die.

I love you, she heard Chase say, and the idea that he had abandoned her became more impossible than anything she was presently witnessing. But there was only one other rational explanation for where he was — under this forest, lifeless — and she rejected that too.

The plant had begun to close in over Zack's face once more, and Promise's desperation grew when she realized the knife had fallen loose of the seat cushion.

"Where are you?"

She reached out and took a fistful of Zack's shirt in her cut hand, not wanting to lose sight of him. With her other hand she probed blindly for the missing knife, risking another slice across her skin. She feared Porta might have taken it with her. Promise stretched her body to its limit, reaching out as far as she could without losing hold of Zack.

On the edge of her vision she saw smoke thickening around the fire pit and noticed that the low hood was failing to suck it up into the vents.

A new voice at the back of her mind asked her why she cared what happened to this man, after all he'd put her through and how little he seemed to care about how his actions affected her and others. The voice surprised her, because it was not her own voice, but Porta's. Promise's first response was a mental question of her own: *Why would you care so little for your own son?*

Of course, there was no satisfactory answer to this, and the silence in Promise's mind gave rise very quickly to an even more challenging question: why had Chase loved her the way he did, having hardly known her, and in the complete absence of her own reciprocal affection?

Her knuckles knocked against a bony handle buried in the leaves. She withdrew a long-bladed knife from the tangled mass and noticed that this smooth movement was enough to sever a few of the leafy stems. She hoped freeing Zack would be as effortless.

Smoke was collecting on the ceiling and in the stairwell. The plant continued to crowd in around the fire pit, ignorant of what was happening to it in the scorching heat. Vines had barricaded the cabinets now and crowded the steps.

She bent over Zack's body, fearing how long he'd been in this state. There was no way for her to know. Why had he become entangled in the first place, and why had she not?

Vines fell free of him as the blade sliced through. The point nicked his ear when her unsteady hand tried to guide the knife through the tightest rope that pinched his throat. But that was the worst she did to him. The stem snapped in two, oozing milky protest, then Zack was free. And not only his throat. The plant slipped away like a foiled killer, receding from his body, unwinding itself from his torso, arms, and legs.

Please don't be dead. Please?

She leaned her ear over Zack's lips. He wasn't breathing. She pressed her cheek against his ribs. The faint sound of a heartbeat knocked on her ear, begging her for help.

Yes, yes, I will help. I will love you the way Chase loved me, without any more reason than that I choose to.

She fumbled around with his forehead and his chin, making an awkward attempt to remember the guidelines for giving a person mouth-to-mouth. A flash of self-preservation pushed through her: *You don't know what you're doing. You'll kill him trying to save him. You're putting yourself at risk. You should just get out. Save yourself.*

She thought of Chase, murdered while trying to save her. She imagined Michelle, dying without her best friend by her side. Could any of that have been prevented?

It was impossible to say, but Promise did know one thing: she hadn't tried to prevent any of it. Now that would change. For as long as she could breathe, she would brace herself against all death, and not only hers. She would do it by calling on the power of love.

She cupped the back of Zack's neck with one hand and lifted gently, then pinched his nose and lowered her mouth over his.

Promise breathed.

42

For the first time since her father had gone, Chelsea relied on someone besides herself. She had never needed anyone as badly as she needed Wes today.

Wes found a clear, close photo of Chase that had been taken while he was drawing on the back porch of their home. With photo in one hand and Chelsea by the other, he directed a methodical search for her brother, starting at the computer in their father's den. He scanned the photo and in five minutes had it posted on every social media site of which he and Chelsea were members. He sent it with a prayer request to his church's pastor and prayer chain. He attached it to an e-mail requesting public eyes stay on the lookout for Chase, then sent this to his contacts list and to Chelsea's. He forwarded it to the university's pressroom, along with information that Chase might have been seen with Promise Dayton.

Then he printed several enlargements of the photo on bright white paper for handing out and posting where they could.

Chelsea did whatever he told her to do.

They went to the police station first and filed a missing persons report, hoping that Chase's special needs might give his status a slightly higher priority than the average competent adult, who might go missing at will. Contrary to his usual habit, Wes articulated Chase's challenges and social difficulties so articulately that Chelsea's fears for his safety increased. This filing took no less than two hours and required a close accounting of Chase's unusual activities of late.

When they finished this exhausting process, Chelsea sat in the passenger seat of Wes's car and tipped her head back against the headrest, eyes closed.

"He's probably gone looking for Promise," she said.

"If he hadn't left all those drawings in such nice order behind, I might say the same thing." Wes put the key in the ignition.

"Can we find her?"

"We can try," Wes said, calling up the web on his cell phone while the car idled. "She's had enough media attention — I should be able to find someone who knows where she lives, if the information isn't public already."

"Why her?" Chelsea asked.

"What do you mean, why her? She's a crazy-good singer, and she's always present at events that go really, really wrong. She's the paparazzi's dream."

"I mean why does Chase think he's in love with her? How'd he pick her?"

"He said the pine tree told him about her."

"And that clarifies everything."

Wes chuckled. "In his mind it does."

"Chase was really preoccupied with this idea of her dying, of not wanting her to." Chelsea held his drawings, which he had labeled "the longings," and she paged through each one while they talked.

"I read somewhere that she's got a terminal disease. Something genetic."

Chelsea pressed some of her brother's artwork against her chest and glanced at Wes.

"Found it," he said, and put the cell phone on his dashboard. He dropped the gears into reverse. They pulled out of the police station.

"It sounds so harsh for me to say it, but we've all got to die of something someday."

"Everyone except those of us who have the hope of heaven, Chels."

"Well, yeah, but even then most of us will die a physical death."

"Maybe that's not the death Chase was ever concerned about."

"What?"

"Maybe all along, with all these drawings, with the thing about Mrs. Bell and Promise and these 'longings,' he has been trying to show people something else. Time is short, days are full."

"He told me the longings are the truth about a person."

Wes chewed on this for a second. "You mean what they want out of life?"

"Or maybe what God wants for them. Maybe even what God can give to them."

Wes reached over and squeezed her hand.

Chelsea said, "Do you think Chase understands all of that? About eternal life and hope and God's promise to us through Jesus? I can't believe we've never talked about it."

"Oh, I believe he probably understands it better than most of us."

Chelsea paged through a few more of his drawings. "When we find him, I want to ask him about that."

Three miles to the east of the university was a quiet apartment complex that matched the address Wes had found for

Promise. They parked and got out of the car. The midafternoon heat struck Chelsea full force. She carried Chase's drawings with her, fearful of leaving them in the hot car.

Wes led the way to her apartment number. The units throughout the complex were lined with tall blooming pink oleander higher than Chelsea's head.

A slender woman, whose silky hair and bright eyes matched Promise's, answered the door but left the screen between them closed.

"Is Promise Dayton in?" Wes asked.

"If you have questions for Promise, you'll have to direct them to her lawyer. Would you like his phone number?"

"Please, I'm Chelsea Ellis. We're looking for my brother, Chase. We thought Promise might know where he is."

"She's out of town."

"Is there some way we can call her?" Wes asked. "Or maybe you could call her for us? I'm guessing you're her mother?"

"It's been a difficult week, and she doesn't keep tabs on the location of every person she knows."

"Is there any chance you've seen him?" Wes said, holding up one of the flyers that bore Chase's photo and Chelsea's phone number.

The woman shook her head and moved to close the door. Chelsea reacted by grabbing the flyer from Wes and opening the screen. "May I leave his picture with you, please? In case he comes by? He has autism and might need our help. I really need to find him. He looks like me and he loves to draw."

It was the stack of black drawing paper and fine-lined white trees that changed Mrs. Dayton's firm refusal into curiosity. "Your brother drew that?" She placed her hand on the screen to brace it open.

"Yes. These are just a few. Do you want to see them?"

"No, it's just — I think he must have drawn a picture for Promise."

"He did. I was with them when he gave it to her."

"It's a remarkable drawing. You might think I'm strange to say this, but I find it very . . . perceptive. Very kind."

"Chase is both of those," Wes said.

Mrs. Dayton hesitated for a moment before saying, "Would you like to come in?"

Chelsea looked at Wes, feeling the urgency to keep moving. "Thank you, but we ought to keep looking."

"Because here's the thing," Promise's mother said, pushing the screen door to its widest opening. "I wonder if Chase — or you — might be able to help me figure out where Promise is."

Wes didn't have a GPS, but he had a map, which Chelsea consulted as he drove. Number 2310 Norris Lane was only a few miles from Promise's apartment. Promise's mother, Hope Dayton, had folded herself into the backseat.

Promise had gone away three days ago, and though she called her mother daily to assure her that she was okay, Hope was increasingly worried for her. The tone of voice, the brevity of the calls, the reluctance to give information about her health or whereabouts all amounted to uncharacteristic behavior. Promise had attended a friend's funeral Saturday, and someone there had seen her leave with a woman no one seemed to recognize. Stylish and blond, professional looking, elegantly aged.

"Porta," Chelsea and Wes had said at the same time.

Chelsea recounted the story of how they met Promise, how she had come knocking on their door thinking she was at Porta's home. Promise's confusion then gave them direction now. It took them only a few minutes to drive to the coastal neighborhood and locate the home.

"She obviously invests her money in other things," Hope said, climbing out of the car and getting a better look at the fading house.

Wes leaped over the brick steps and pounded on the front door. When no one answered, Chelsea left the porch. Hope stayed and pressed her face against the uncovered windows.

"It doesn't even look like anyone lives here," Hope said. Chelsea walked down the gravel path that wrapped the south side of the house and led into the backyard, where all the shrubs leaned to one side, windblown in the same direction.

A guesthouse, which was more deteriorated than the main building, shed paint flakes with each breeze. The door was open. Chelsea approached it, blond hair stripped from her ponytail and snapping her cheeks.

"Hello? Ms. Cerreto? Is Promise with you?"

A curtain inside flicked its corner as the outside air moved through the small room. Chelsea walked in and smelled the mustiness of neglect underneath the salt in the air. A rumpled old comforter with a nautical pattern topped a bare mattress. An open jar of peanut butter and a bag of cereal sat on the counter in the kitchenette, and the desk under the ocean-view window was littered with papers that greeted her the way Chase's once did, when they were pinned to the walls of his studio. Only now it was an ocean breeze that caused the pages to wave their welcome.

The white pages — lined notebook paper, scratch pad leaves, recycled junk mail, and so on — were dense with the doodles and drawings of a dull graphite pencil, apparently the only drawing utensil the artist had. For the most part they were aimless, abstract things with dark shadows at the heart of each idea. She pushed these around with the pads of her fingers, understanding somewhere in her subconscious that she was looking for a connection to Chase.

She found it.

At the center of the desk, under a single layer of loose sheets, was a drawing of a tree, a stooped weeping willow whose grief-laden branches bent all the way to the earth. Behind the drooping screen, Chelsea could see the form of a woman sitting against the trunk.

Chelsea lifted the page. The lines were coarser than Chase's, like an early sketch of a final piece, and the traditional black-on-white media emphasized shadow over light. But each stroke was full of disappointment that called on Chelsea's compassion. There was a *Z* like a sideways lightning bolt for a signature in the lower right corner.

"There's no one here," Wes said. He was leaning against the door frame. "At least, no one answering any of the doors."

"We should call the police." Chelsea decided to take the drawing with her.

"And tell them what?"

Chelsea had no idea. No proof Chase or Promise was here or had even been here. No broken laws. No reasonable hunches that could possibly get them to do any breaking into this sad house.

Outside, Promise's mother was circling the structure, looking through the bare windows, examining the broken panes that peered into an empty kitchen.

"Let's try the gallery," Chelsea said.

The trio left.

43

The bright yellow ART(i)FACTS awning was streaked with the dirty rivers of weekend rain that had washed off the dusty facades that rose over the storefronts. There was no evidence of the GRAND OPENING sign now, which was fitting. The shop was still closed in spite of the hours posted on the frosted-glass door.

But an hour remained before the end of the business day, and so Chelsea, Hope, and Wes split up to ask after Chase and Promise in the neighboring shops. They agreed to meet back at the pub at six o'clock.

Wes and Hope took off across the street. Chelsea lingered before the sculpture her father had forged when she was a pre-schooler. Her longing for it made sense to her now. It was her longing for her father's return, though she lived as if she'd never see him again in her lifetime.

What if he came back suddenly?

Chelsea laughed aloud. It was such a happy possibility, and it had never occurred to her. Chase would be —

She snapped herself out of the distraction and resumed her search for her brother, freshly anxious. The summertime sun wouldn't set for a while, but she sensed this disappearance was different from his previous one, maybe because Hope's anxieties for her daughter compounded it.

Chelsea canvassed eleven stores in the hour she had and wasn't surprised that no one had seen Chase. What did startle her was the number of people who knew who he was and had kind words to say about him. But no, they hadn't seen him at all for . . . days.

When she returned to the pub next to Porta's gallery, Wes and Hope were already there. Her heart was as heavy as their expressions.

Porta was on her fourth glass of gin and tonic when she glanced out the window of the sweet little pub where the dear old fisherman was happy to serve her and tell her *fish* stories, of course, and serve her again and — *oh!*

She saw that idiot boy risen from the dead of her basement, standing outside the window on the sidewalk. Her breath caught in her throat.

This was terrible, terrible. And how had it happened? She spun on her stool so her back was to the window. She had not considered this possibility at all. And what possibility was that, exactly? There was no way he could have survived that blow to the head. Well, at least no way that would explain him back on his feet so soon, and here, of all places.

She peeked over her shoulder and took another look. Well, that explained it. She exhaled slowly. There now. She thanked the gods that it wasn't him after all but his sister. A reasonable mistake, considering. That was a fright. Porta threw back the remainder of her drink.

His *sister?* And what relief was there in that distinction? The girl was nearly as terrible a presence. She'd be looking for her brother, surely. There were sheets of paper in her hand. Flyers. And friends along to help. They'd come in here and start asking around.

Porta opened her handbag and found her wallet inside. It took immense concentration to unzip the billfold, but she did, and withdrew a fifty-dollar bill. She was pretty certain it was a fifty. Calling upon her gin-

449

soaked poise, she placed the bill on the bar at a snail's pace, then patted it to make sure it hadn't fallen to the floor.

"There you are, love," she said, making the remark for both the money and the fisherman-bartender-owner. He — or someone — was there behind the counter. She smiled at no one in particular. Without closing the zipper on the billfold, she returned it to her handbag, and then allowed the stool to swivel away from the counter. She held on as the room rocked, then balanced while her shoes found the floor.

"Call you a cab?" someone asked.

"No, dear, I'm walking," she thought she said.

"Like a sailor," someone else remarked. She patted the voice on the head. Or perhaps it was the shoulder.

Porta used the rear door, because certainly the old owner's invitation of some weeks ago to pass through his pub as needed had no expiration date. Her forward-moving weight was enough to push it open — thank the gods there was no knob to turn and no stairs to manage! — and she stumbled into the access alley.

Her shop was to the le — to the right. Under that security light over there. She shuffled toward it, stabilized herself by leaning her right shoulder against the cinderblock exterior, then repeated the process of sifting through her handbag, this time for keys.

She would wait out the hour here. For that matter, she could sleep here if needed. If that blond twin found reason to get detectives back out to her house, they could unearth the tragedy themselves.

Except for that chair bracing the basement door shut. *Blast!* She'd forgotten about the chair! There was nothing she could do for it now. Too plastered to drive. Too risky to have wandered away from her alibi anyway, even though Zack and Promise should be dead by now.

In the name of all that was holy. Three deaths? Well, none of it was her fault.

Porta stumbled into her own gallery. She shut the door and locked it. She stood in front of her security keypad until the numbers solidified in their glowing green soup and she could remember the proper sequence. Not that it would be a bad thing to set it off and have a false alarm.

She chuckled at that but managed to do everything correctly.

There was no need for lights. The sun hadn't even set yet, and the skylights over the long, high-ceilinged room were almost too much. Porta groped her way to the decorative desk sitting in the front room and plopped onto the chair. This chair was really too small and uncomfortable. Tomorrow she'd order something more accommodating.

Porta picked up the phone and dialed the number of the home she had shared with her New York sisters. Anything to continue managing the record of where she was and at what time. A wave of nausea passed over her. She'd poured that gin into her stomach far too quickly for a woman of her size.

"Yeah?"

"Lemme talk to that witch Althea."

"Excuse me?"

"Not on your life! Where's Althea?"

"Lady, you've got the wrong number."

"Then Tonya will do. Or Candace. Any of the smug cats."

No one replied to that.

Porta pulled the receiver away from her ear and examined it, then shook it once in her fist and placed it back on her ear. Nothing.

"Rude."

She hung up and dialed again. This time her call dropped into a voice-mail box. She left a message for Althea and hung up again. Really, she needed to be more clearheaded if she wanted to be a reckoning force, or whatever it was called.

A little meditation, a little incense, a little courteous consultation with the dead out of respect for the dead: that should center her mind, get her back on her feet. It was the least she could do to ask for safe passage for her son. And even for Promise. The fates were in charge of their destinies, after all. Porta had nothing to do with it. But she knew how to place such requests.

Whatever happened to the autistic one was of no concern to her.

Porta began the motions of preparing for ritual, which were fortunately so familiar to her that she needn't be conscious to complete them. She gathered the appropriate scents and some matches from the storeroom. She staggered to her viewing room and entered, then closed the door. She warmed the rocks and scattered the incense over them and lit the candles in the four corners of the room. She cast her circle with the flip of a switch, and the projector in the ceiling threw the perfect and beautiful round lines across the floor of the room. She cut the door and entered and closed the door and sank — oh so sweetly relaxed now — to her knees in the center of the glowing blue rings.

She began her chant, her invitation to the underworld.

And somewhere in the middle, as her body begged for sleep, she remembered that it was her birthday.

44

Zack breathed. Air rushed into his body with the noise of wind through a tunnel and lifted his spine off the ground. His hands snapped out in search of something to anchor him and found Promise, and clutched her to him like the life preserver that she was. Zack flung his arms around her.

She remained this way, kneeling and bent over his chest, until the rhythm of their breathing matched each other's. His breath on her neck, and the rising and falling of his ribs, were a great comfort.

"We need to go up," she finally whispered. "The smoke's getting thick."

"Where's Chase?" he said.

Promise didn't answer. She tugged him up to a sitting position. The smoke from the leafy plant, which continued to smolder but not ignite near the fire pit, had collected on the ceiling and was dropping by the minute.

Wispy gray fingers curled around a painting of a woman surrounded by snakes in a fog.

Zack rolled away from Promise onto his knees. Promise crouched and faced the stairs. The vines had transformed them into a dense bank of leaves.

"You go up," Zack said. "Let me see if I can put out the fire and vent this place."

"Just come with me. Please?"

"We need to find Chase. Open the door. It will help."

Promise obeyed, taking the stairs on all fours to prevent herself from slipping down over the pervasive plant. Again, her movement over the top of it caused it to shift and swell. It crawled up the closed door ahead of her and wrapped a tendril around the doorknob.

She reached out for it and unwound the stem. It dropped back into the thick growth on the stair. The knob turned, but the door wouldn't open.

Beneath her, she heard the sound of a fan and hoped Zack had found the one in the hood over the pit. There was the sizzle of water poured over the fire and then a fresh burst of smoke rose to the door. She leaned her shoulder into it and shoved, and her foot slipped out from under her.

"It's stuck," she called, uprighting herself.

The smoke tickled her throat and made her cough. She covered her face with the collar of the robe and rattled the knob, freshly afraid of not being able to breathe again.

The noise of the fan increased, and the fresh smoke was pulled back into the basement as if by a vacuum. Zack appeared at the base of the stairs and bounded up to her side. He braced his body behind hers and wrapped both his arms around her shoulders, gripping the knob over her hands.

"On three," he said. "One, two . . ."

The heft of both their bodies, slim but working in unison, was enough to push through. They fell onto the kitchen floor. Looking up at the kitchen ceiling, Promise saw smoke flow out the door and across the room, seeking the outlet to fresh air provided by the broken windows.

"We should be dead," she said without moving. Her skin touched Zack's arm. She didn't want to pull away.

"By my mother."

"Porta closed all the vents."

"That's a lot of green down there, though. A lot more oxygen than CO."

"Is that how it works?"

Zack didn't answer, maybe because he wasn't sure if she was talking about science, or survival in general, or Porta's death bent in particular. Promise herself wasn't sure what she'd meant to ask.

"She killed Chase," Promise said.

Zack processed this. "I saw his hat," he eventually said. "Did she take his body?"

"I don't know."

"What's with that plant?"

Promise took a deep breath of clean air. Zack would probably not believe her. "I think it came from Chase. From his blood. In the soil. She hit him." As if any of that made sense.

He didn't laugh at her but said, "The darn thing tried to kill me."

Zack pushed himself up. The leaves of the plant were out the door now, creeping along the tiles of the dirty kitchen floor by millimeters. Zack stared at it for long seconds. He reached out and touched one of the leaves. It slipped across his palm in a gentle caress.

"What?" Promise said.

"You'll think I'm crazy," he said. "That's a given for most people, and considering the only stuff you know about me . . ."

Promise knew what he meant but didn't want him to stop talking to her. "Why would I think you're crazy?"

"I think Chase was trying to tell me something."

"You know Chase?"

Zack looked at her. "It was more like he knows me. Knew me."

"What did he tell you?"

"Well, he said plenty, but I meant the plant. If it . . . grew because of Chase."

"I thought you were going to say I was nuts."

Zack said, "Do you think there's any chance Chase is still alive?"

"No."

"We should try to find him." Zack gripped the stairway railing and leaned back into the basement, moving lightly on his feet as if worried about crushing the plant.

"I agree." Promise stood up and realized what she was — and wasn't — wearing. "I need to change. It'll only take a second."

Zack went down. Promise ran up, energized. In seconds, she threw off the robe and pulled on the black pants and blouse she'd worn to Michelle's funeral, then flew back down the stairs barefoot.

The crawling leaves were out in the hallway now and had begun filling the sparse dining room.

At the mouth of the basement, Promise heard a crash.

"Zack?"

"It's not me," he called up. "The pictures

459

are falling."

Promise followed his lead, trying to pick through the vine gently, using the banister to keep her weight from crushing the stems. But it too was entwined. At the bottom she saw, by the light of the panoramic window, holes in the wall at three places where hangers had been yanked out. Beneath them, vine-strangled pictures were tipped onto their corners, their frames broken at the joints from the impact.

A crack from the ceiling pulled her eyes upward. The vines that had scaled the three columns had also traveled across the ceiling and grabbed hold of the suspended projector that Porta used for her holographic circles.

One side of the projector fell out of the drywall, and a shower of fine white dust rained onto the leaves below.

Zack was bent at the waist, wading through the knee-deep growth and pushing aside the tangle.

"It's too thick," he said, holding up a red-and-white wad of something. "But I found his cap."

The sight of it filled Promise with sadness. "Use the knife."

"What knife?"

"The one I used on you." Promise thought

she knew where it might have fallen.

"If you used a knife on me I might have to reconsider thanking you."

Promise found the blade shortly and handed it out to Zack. He hesitated to take it.

"This thing doesn't like me. But since it's already worked for you . . ." He indicated with his hands that she should have at it. "The sculpture is right here."

Promise had no way of knowing how long she and Zack worked together to clear the area and find Chase. The thickest smoke gradually left them through the vents and the open stair, and the sun began to drop into the ocean, throwing bright orange shards of glare onto their heavyhearted efforts.

The plant did not protest against their hacking. The milk from its amputated limbs dribbled into the carpet, but the vines cleared away from the area, focusing their energies on growing up and out of the basement.

Promise was the first to see Chase's shoe, because she was bent over it, and Zack was behind her, taking the cuttings from her as she handed them off. She saw his socks, the skin where his pants had hiked up when he fell. She laid a hand on his fair-skinned ankle, cool to the touch. Zack swore.

"I was hoping not to find you," she said. "I was hoping that Porta was right about something for once."

Zack's hands were on his head as if to prevent it from flying off his shoulders. He'd crammed Chase's hat into one of his back pockets. "She's never been right about a thing in her life," he said.

"Then how do you explain this plant?"

45

The pub's sidewalk seating area was still closed as the result of Zack's crash. Cautionary tape roped off the area where the decorative railing had collapsed. The owner had replaced the broken window immediately, but the stamped concrete under the glass would be harder to repair. Great chunks had fallen out of the siding.

Wes and Hope took their pictures of Chase and Promise into the pub. Chelsea stayed outside, waiting for the summer air to cool as the sun fell. She was too distraught to eat, though she suggested the others get something for themselves before they came back out. Where would they go from here? Home to sit and wait for the police to call? Not on her life. They hadn't tried the university yet, though Hope said she had spent all of Sunday poking around there. Chelsea decided she would give it a run of her own when the others returned.

Two cars passed by, then the street was quiet again, except for the slow-night chatter of the pub and a disturbed muttering that caught Chelsea's ears. She thought it was the sound of an argument, but when she looked, she could spot only one pedestrian walking alone up the sidewalk. Though he was facing her and making brisk, determined strides, she couldn't make out his complaint.

She did make out his face, though. "Mr. Bell?"

The man whose wife had jumped off a cliff the day before seemed alone in the world, and perhaps he was. He marched by Chelsea, spitting out his unintelligible words as if they were curses. He carried a bottle in his right hand, something alcoholic, she thought, though his stride was even and straight.

She pivoted on the sidewalk as he passed her, then considered whether to follow him. He didn't appear to be in his right mind.

"Mr. Bell? Are you okay? May I help you?"

He stopped directly in front of ART(i)FACTS. She took a step toward him. He withdrew a gun from his left pants pocket and raised it toward the gallery and fired directly into the glass door. Chelsea gasped and recoiled. She covered her head with her hands and crouched. Shattered glass rained onto the sidewalk, and a few pieces glided across the concrete to her feet.

Mr. Bell's screams seemed to be louder than the gunshot. "This place is a death trap!" Onlookers poured out of the pub. Chelsea raised her head and scrabbled back into the crowd. She felt Wes's grip on her arm and let him pull her out of harm's way. From somewhere Mr. Bell produced a lighter, which he held up to a cloth strip that Chelsea only now noticed protruding from the glass bottle. It ignited.

"Burn in hell!" he cried out, and burst into sobs. "Burn in hell!"

He hurled the fiery cocktail into the gallery through the shattered door.

Promise sat at Porta's kitchen table and turned Chase's stained hat around in her hands while she waited for the police to arrive. Zack sat next to her. She wept for a while, disbelieving what Porta had done to Chase but feeling the blame for it. The sunlight over the ocean faded from orange to pink to purple. She smelled like smoke and soil and had chlorophyll under her fingernails.

Promise noticed Zack watching her and pretending not to. She placed the hat on the table and cleaned her cheeks with the heels of her palms.

"We stink," she said.

"Do you know what a strangler fig looks like?" Zack asked.

"What's that got to do with our stench?"

He shrugged.

"I don't even know what a strangler fig is," she said. "Sounds like some food people choke on."

"I don't think so, but I need to look it up."

"Why do you want to know?"

"It was something Chase said. Before all this."

Promise made eye contact with Zack and understood. His arms rested on the table, and he gripped a cup of water with both hands.

"Did he draw you a picture?"

Zack shook his head. "I sort of told him I didn't want one."

"That's too bad."

"It seems that way now."

Promise coughed a few times and closed her blouse at her throat in a fist. "I've been thinking about that picture of my lung, and I'm thinking that it wasn't about me not being sick. It was about learning to breathe. I think he completely knew what he was doing. I don't know how, but I believe it.

466

Don't you?"

"Actually, I'm not sure what you're talking about."

Promise turned her body to face his. "That feeling of bringing you back from the dead — it was a bigger thrill than anything I've ever experienced. I want to do it again. Not to you. I mean, I hope you're never in that situation."

He looked mildly embarrassed. She ignored this.

"Think about it," she said. "Can there be any greater accomplishment than saving a life? And maybe it doesn't look like what we think it looks like — keeping the heart beating, keeping the brain alive. I'm talking about the intangible stuff. The reasons why a person gets up in the morning. Because she wants to sing for the people she loves. Or go to Paris with a friend. Or take care of someone."

"I guess I don't know very much about any of that."

"Well, I highly recommend learning."

Zack smiled at her. She remembered the first time she'd made him smile, at the top of Vista Park Bluffs, and was unexpectedly comforted to see it again. He said, "I never was the brightest bulb in the shop."

"Oh, don't be silly. You're brilliant."

"By what standards?"

"By mine. So you should pay attention."

He laughed. "I guess it hadn't occurred to me that you'd care one way or the other."

"Of course it occurred to you. If it hadn't, you wouldn't have asked me about the figgy thing."

"Shame on me."

"You want me to care."

He shifted his attention to the glass of water. "Maybe."

This stupid pretense, this persistent need to act like he didn't need or want anything out of this life, made Promise angry. It also filled her with fresh grief.

"I'm sorry for what I did to you," she said. "For lying, and for turning my back on you."

Zack swallowed. "It's nothing. It's not like you haven't made up for it."

Promise bit her tongue.

He leaned across the table and pulled a paper napkin out of a holder, then folded and dipped it into the cup of water. He offered it to her. She took it with a question in her eyes.

"You've got . . ." He pointed at her cheek. "On your face."

A long pause passed between them. She wiped Chase's blood off her skin.

"I saw your book," Promise finally said. "I saw the pictures you drew of me."

Zack cleared his throat and scratched his head.

"I liked those drawings," she said. "Well, most of them. You've got a gift. You have an obligation to do something with it. And since you can't seem to let this topic go, I'll admit it: I do care about what happens to you."

The purple of the sky darkened to blue. Zack sighed, a heavy breath that could have meant anything. His demeanor clouded.

"We haven't decided how to explain this to the cops," he said.

"There's nothing to decide. All we can tell is the truth."

"It's crazy truth."

"Let them sort it out."

Zack scooted out from the table and stood, crushing the tangled green growth under his shoes. The plant had showed no further interest in Zack and had gone off to explore the rest of the house. Promise wondered if they'd soon have to step outside. She imagined the vine entangling the structure like an alien invader, crushing it to dust.

"We need to go," he said. "Now."

"What? We have to —"

"I have to find my mother. Go get your car keys."

Promise placed the wadded napkin on the table and stood up. "Zack, think about what you're saying. Leaving now will look worse than you think it does."

"Maybe, but I can't wait around." He snatched Chase's cap off the table. "I know how this works. They'll take us in for questioning if they don't arrest us right from the start. We'll be in for hours, maybe even days. Do you know what country my mother will be in by then?"

Promise was looking at the bloody hat, only half listening. She was thinking of Chelsea. Zack's intensity didn't soften.

"You can stay if you want," he said, "but I wish you wouldn't. Porta's the one who needs to face this — don't do it for her."

"We're all responsible."

"Not all of us. Not for this. Chase is dead, Promise."

Promise closed her eyes to shut out the sight of heartache multiplying like infinite reflections in face-to-face mirrors. "Did you know he had a sister?" she asked.

Zack didn't seem to care. "Are you coming or not?"

News of Porta's death was delivered to Zack

through his nose: the odor of smoke, the stink of that mind-altering incense, and a particular stench few humans can endure. In the passenger seat of Promise's car, he stroked the bill of Chase's ball cap as if it were a worry stone while the scents came through the open windows. Emergency crews had blocked the downtown street so that Promise couldn't park in front of the gallery; she took a space in front of an ice cream shop a block away. Zack's mind knew what all of it meant before his heart did.

He exited the Roadster and left the door open before she cut the engine. He ran around the corner and down the street as far as firefighters would allow, and the sight of the blazing building confirmed his intuition. Orange embers sparked against the dark blue sky the way Promise's shawl once snapped against that cloudy background. Ashes fell on his shoulders like snow in summer.

The sense of loss that stabbed him then was alien and unwelcome. This was justice. Wasn't it?

Chase's wadded hat was damp in Zack's grip. He clutched it and placed both hands on his head while he watched the essence of his mother rise into the night. He sensed Promise arrive beside him. A few seconds

471

later she wrapped her arms around his waist. It was his first memory of having someone to hold on to in a crisis.

Firefighters gave instructions and information to each other. The murmurs of spectators formed a droning hum in the background. Glass cracked, and after a moment of falling, one of the gallery skylights shattered on the ground. A second followed quickly. Water from the high-pressure hoses arced into the vacant space.

Zack watched a spark avoid the streaming water and shoot away from the structure. The glowing object could have been anything, really. The carbonized remains of art or carpet or wood or flesh. He wondered. It fell as if floating down a spiral staircase behind the firefighters' trucks, directly across the street from the engulfed art gallery. The ember landed on someone's shoulder. Chase's shoulder.

Zack blinked. It wasn't Chase but a woman who looked almost exactly like him. She stood in the light of a shop window, her eyes on Zack. On second glance he noted the makeup around her eyes and the more rounded cheekbones and the longer hair. But otherwise — Chase.

Her gaze went from Zack's face to the top of his head.

She started walking toward him, her stride short for such a tall woman, and tired in a way that he knew personally.

Promise separated from Zack and whispered, "That's her."

He wondered who she meant. And then all the perspectives on this unwelcome scene came together in his mind in a single, dark image.

Zack took his hands off the top of his head and held the woman's gaze as she reached him. She looked so much like her brother that Zack momentarily felt happy, free of the kind of nightmare that accompanied his worst high. Maybe all of this was nothing more than a terrible dream.

In the next second he wanted only to be high again.

"Chelsea," Promise whispered as a greeting.

The woman looked at her and granted a weak smile and then returned her eyes to the red hat.

A man with a soft belly and kind eyes followed Chelsea across the street. He dragged his hand down his beard before reaching out to rest his hand on her shoulder. Another woman was with him, her arms outstretched toward Promise.

"Thank God," the woman said. "What

happened?"

Promise welcomed her embrace.

Zack extended the ball cap to Chelsea. She took the wad as it was, without smoothing it open or examining it, and pressed it to her heart. With her free hand, she covered her eyes. The contorted shape of her mouth was like a silent wail.

"I'm so sorry," Zack said. And for the first time in his life, he truly was.

46

One Year Later

Promise was coughing again when she turned off of Norris Lane and onto the dirt driveway that led to Porta's house. She had sold the Roadster and bought this more practical blue pickup in the spring, then spent the leftover money on potting soil, plant food, plastic pots, gloves, clippers and trowels, and six-inch baskets. Two dozen of the woven containers in bright yellow, purple, turquoise, and red bounced on the seat next to her as the truck went down the rutted drive. An ocean breeze carried the sounds of crashing waves and crying gulls through her open windows.

The driveway curved around a stand of Pacific yew, and the ivy-covered house came into sight. It wasn't quite accurate to think of the home as *covered,* though the hardy vine that had taken root in the basement climbed every wall, gutter, and fixture. In truth, the structure was *overtaken* by Chase's vine. Not a single roofing tile or vent was visible. Window panes had cracked, then finally burst as growth escaped the house, and the doorways were impenetrable.

It was impossible to say why the plant had not gone any farther than the porch, the stoops, the hedges under windows. The flat leaves, dark green on top and a lighter green on the bottom, shimmered as the wind passed over them. Promise drove around to the ocean side and parked in front of the guesthouse.

Last fall, when police had conducted their investigation of Chase's murder, the mysterious plant caused detectives and forensic scientists considerable frustration. Promise had heard many unresolved arguments during the hours she and Zack spent giving their accounts of what happened — arguments about whether to tear the vine out and risk contaminating and even losing evidence, or whether to prune back as needed and risk overlooking some critical detail hidden under the leaves.

Efforts to cut the growth back only resulted in new problems. At every place the vine was clipped, fresh roots sprouted and took hold of the nearest anchor, be that carpeting, support beams, or holes in the

476

drywall where picture hangers had fallen out. By the time it was decided that the ivy should be uprooted, the task that faced them was something like trying to weed a golf course without any tools. The police — having recovered Chase's body, the broken *Ameretat,* the knife, and all the DNA and fingerprint samples they could find — gave up and abandoned the scene.

Eventually, after several months, Promise and Zack were cleared of all charges related to Chase's death. Mr. Bell's manslaughter sentence was reduced from ten years to seven because of the remorse he showed when he learned that the art dealer was inside her closed gallery that night. Zack spent a few weeks in jail for the DWI episode that damaged the pub at the Shore. Promise picked up a bacterial infection that kept her in the hospital through January.

In February, the university rescinded its expulsion of the pair. Zack had no intention of returning. Promise was still undecided.

For now, with fall classes a week away and the latest musical fully cast without her, she was content to spend her days doing creative work of an entirely different nature.

She got out of the truck and unloaded the baskets, taking them into the guesthouse. The little room had become a kind of gardening shed for her. She had turned the desk into a worktable and lined the windowsills and kitchen with potted plant clippings she claimed as her own. She thought of the place as a solarium, a bright spot in the world where her lungs and her spirit always felt lighter.

Her coughing stopped almost immediately upon entering the space. She began to hum a folksong about a bread maker from Paris.

Promise sang while she worked. She took a dozen new clippings from a shady corner at the front of the garage and spread them across the bed in the guesthouse. These sprouted roots in twenty minutes, fifteen if she was singing, and while she waited for them to do this she hand-mixed a new batch of potting soil, minerals, and plant food. At first she had expected the clippings to grow in anything — this was only logical, considering the behavior of the source — and so she had tried growing them in cups of water, sand, and cheap potting mixes. Strangely, these plants died, and the failure triggered a driving obsession in her to figure out what was needed to keep them alive.

She worked at it, reading books about gardening and separating plants and growing clippings and nourishing different species, until she had landed on a formula that worked. As for the scientific reasons behind the plants' life or death, Promise left the discovery of those to botanists from the university, who had taken interest in the ivy. They came and went from the property at will, because Zack didn't see the harm of it. As far as Promise knew, they were still working on classifying the samples. Their interest in the vine sparked enough curiosity in her, however, to make her think she might change her major.

Within an hour Promise had planted the latest clippings and set their pots inside the colorful baskets. She arranged these in a few short-sided cardboard boxes and then carried the cargo out to the truck bed. Using a few bricks, she braced the boxes up against the cab so they wouldn't slide around as she drove. She cleaned up the guesthouse and closed the door behind her.

Before leaving, Promise approached the house and ran her palm lightly over the thriving leaves. The whole house seemed to sense her, and every leaf shifted. She pressed her face into the growth that covered the area where the kitchen window once had been. She took a deep, cough-free breath. The oxygen this plant produced was more pure than what came out of her oxygen concentrator. At least that was her opinion of it.

She lingered for just a few minutes, appreciating the clean air and the scents of the sea.

Then she climbed into the truck and made the short drive to the Shore. Her route took her past Chelsea's home on Morris Street, around the corner where Marlene's Sweet Shop dished up dripping waffle cones for summer tourists, and to a metered parking slot in front of the Chase Life Gallery. Promise carefully backed into the space.

Next door, a middle-aged woman was smoking at a café table in front of the pub.

Chase Life was the name of the sculptured boy that had stood in Porta Cerreto's window for only a few weeks last year. The child that smiled at the sun was now covered in soot that Chelsea refused to clean off. It was the only piece of art that wasn't consumed by the fire. When it was hauled out of the charred remains of the gallery, the names of the sculpture and the artist were discovered etched into the base.

Chase Life, G. B. Ellis '83

Zack had immediately given the sculpture to Chelsea. Promise guessed that something about the pain of never having been mothered was what bonded those two like siblings. Later, upon learning that Porta's titles to the house and the gallery were legally his, Zack formed a plan, which he also presented to Chelsea.

The gallery was rebuilt over the winter and opened under its new name in the spring, which was when Zack left.

Promise got out of the truck and walked to the back while keeping a discreet eye on the smoker in front of the pub. The woman needed a beating heart, Promise decided. She lowered the tailgate and dragged a box toward her, then picked out a purple-basketed plant and carried it to the table, setting it in the shade of the umbrella. Promise smiled.

The woman exhaled smoke. "What's that?"

"A gift."

"S'not my birthday."

"All the more reason you should have one."

The woman grunted and took another drag on her cigarette.

"We give them away in there if you decide you want another one," Promise said, pointing at the gallery.

The lady cast an eye to the back of the open truck. "I like yellow," she announced.

"You do? Then you need a yellow basket too." Promise fetched it for her and returned, setting it next to the purple one. The woman balanced her cigarette in the teeth of an ashtray and leaned forward for a closer look at the plants. She lifted a leaf and glance at the underside.

"What are they?"

"I call them beating hearts."

"Never heard of 'em."

"They're special."

"Need any special care?"

"Water, light, good food. Mine like it when I sing to them."

This made the woman grin, exposing a set of stained teeth. "There's almost nothing in life that a good song can't heal."

That was all the thanks Promise needed. "I love you," she said before she returned to the truck and started carrying her boxes into the gallery. The surprised looks she got when she said that never failed to delight her.

Wes met her at the door and held it open for her, then went out to help.

"Hey, Chels!" Promise called out.

"Hi!" Chelsea replied from the back. "Be out in a sec. You bring more hearts?"

"That I did."

"Great. We're almost out."

Promise set the box on the floor near the front display window and started arranging the happy baskets around the feet of the sculpture. The plants she'd brought today should just fill the gaps. Plenty of people came by just to take home a free beating heart. Once through the door, though, they usually stayed to spend time with the art.

Promise had never visited the gallery while it was Porta's, but Chelsea had explained the changes. She had not rebuilt the viewing room where Zack's mother died but let the gallery remain open and simple with tall white walls, natural light, and a row of wrought-iron park benches down the center of the room. The carpet was a bold spring green. A selection of Chase's drawings hung in a single row on three of the walls, fourteen on each side and five across the back.

The grove of white trees created a striking effect. Each one had been matted with black board of the same shade as the drawing paper, then surrounded by slender silver frames. Nothing showy, nothing to compete with the art itself. The new skylights overhead dropped sunlight through the protective glass and made the trees seem alive.

Working together, Chelsea, Wes, and Promise had done their best to identify each of the trees Chase had drawn. The scientific and common names were printed on small placards, along with a summary of the tree's distinctive traits, and then were mounted next to each image.

Each time a piece was sold, Chelsea replaced it with another from Chase's collection. Proceeds paid for a full-time employee, utilities, and the cost of framing. The rest went to the Foundation for Autism Spectrum Disorder Awareness.

"Excuse me." A businessman wearing wire-rimmed glasses tapped Promise on the shoulder just as Wes came back in with two more boxes of plants. "I don't see a price on this piece. Can you tell me what it is?"

Promise stood. He was pointing at an easel placed near the row of park benches. The drawing on it was larger than the others and had been triple-matted in silver, black, and white.

"I'm afraid that one's not for sale," Chelsea said kindly as she emerged from the back with a framed drawing of a cottonwood.

Chelsea was leaner than ever, having been running out her grief for her brother. Since the gallery opened, however, color had returned to her cheeks, and brightness to her eyes. A large diamond ring on her left hand that was perfectly suited to her graceful fingers caught the outdoor light as she hung Chase's work.

The man looked at Chelsea and the portrait on the easel and then back at Chelsea, silently noting the similarities. Wes nudged Promise with one of the turquoise baskets he held. They exchanged amused expressions as Chelsea explained the story — the version for public telling, at least — behind Chase's self-portrait and the sculpture in the window.

"You hear from Zack this week?" Wes asked Promise as they put the last of the beating hearts in the display window.

"He sent an e-mail. It looks like he's going to graduate in a month or so," she said, stacking the boxes inside of each other to return them to the truck.

"What good news! So does that mean he'll be heading back up this way?"

"I don't think so. At least not now. Sounds like he wants to stay on and help."

Wes chuckled. "That's what Santa Barbara will do to a person. People don't leave that city unless they have to."

"Is that why he picked the Santa Barbara facility? He never did explain that to me."

Wes shrugged.

"In any case, I expected Zack to want out of rehab as fast as possible. But he says they

485

need volunteers."

"Ah."

"I told him I think he should go for it, if he can meet their criteria."

Wes offered Promise a knowing smile. "Your opinion means a lot to him."

Promise blushed and coughed once. "Well, it's a good way for him to stay clean."

"I thought Chelsea and I could drop by and see how he's doing."

"Drop by? When?"

"About two weeks."

Promise shook her head, disbelieving. "You will *not* spend your honeymoon with Zack!"

Wes chuckled. "No. But we'll be in the area. We could spend an hour with him."

"Ooo. You're taking Chels to wine country!"

Wes wagged a finger under her nose. "I'm not sayin'," he said as he walked off. He gave Chelsea a quick peck on the cheek as he passed her. The man with the wire-rimmed glasses prepared to go.

"Take a beating heart with you?" Promise asked him, holding out a plant in a red container as he stepped toward the door. Men seemed to like the red ones.

He stopped and fished for words, placing one hand on his jacket where his wallet must have been. "Uh, I'm afraid I didn't buy anything."

"No need, they're free."

"Hmm. Okay." He glanced around awkwardly before accepting it. "Uh, thanks."

"They like lots of light and water, and a song now and then."

His eyebrows arched over his glasses. She grinned at him and gestured to the self-portrait Chase had made for his sister. "He started the original plant. These are all clippings."

"That so? And you just give them away?"

"You can have all of them if you want."

The man looked alarmed, as if he hardly knew what to do with something this green. "That's . . . generous."

"Chase was too."

He held the plant with both hands and looked at it.

Promise said, "You should come back sometime. Whenever you need a place to just sit and think, have some quiet."

"I picked up on the park theme," he said, glancing around.

"Except you can come here when it rains!" She laughed. "We're putting up new pieces all the time. Chase drew all his pictures with someone in mind, you know."

"No, I didn't."

"He might have drawn something for you."

"That seems unlikely."

Promise held the nested boxes close to her and rested her chin on top of them. "There was a time when I would've said something like that too."

Curiosity replaced the veiled politeness in his eyes, and when she saw it, Promise knew he wouldn't be able to stay away.

"Well, thanks," he said, nodding toward his new plant.

"Sure thing," she said. "I love you."

He glanced around awkwardly, then seemed to decide it was better to pretend he hadn't heard.

Promise followed him out the door, laughing.

With everlasting gratitude to

Ami McConnell, L. B. Norton, and
Traci DePree
for your kindness and editorial prowess

Lynn McMahan
for her artful eye and help in teaching
me
about the qualities of various white
media

the courteous staff of Meininger Art
Supply in Colorado Springs
for helping me to grasp the subtle
differences in black papers
and for telling me about the
white-on-black drawings of Father Luke
Sheffer

Laura Rothenberg
whose memoir, *Breathing for a Living,*
helped to inform my understanding
of cystic fibrosis and the brave people
who live with it

Leah Apineru
because (among so many other things)
I wouldn't have a Facebook page
without you

Allen Arnold and the Thomas Nelson
team
for your long hours, unwavering faith,
and prayerful support

Dan Raines, Meredith Smith, and
everyone at Creative Trust, Inc.
for your wisdom and diligent
representation

READING GROUP GUIDE

1. Porta wants to live forever; Promise wants not to be forgotten when she dies. How is their yearning for immortality universal among humans? How do people you know express this desire for eternity in the ways that they live and in the choices that they make?

2. Promise believes that fame is the only path to being remembered by the world at large. Do you agree? Why do fame and celebrity have such a magnetic pull on the human heart?

3. What caused Porta's vision of the boy-sculpture speaking to her?

4. What was true about Porta's claim that art has power to speak into a life? What was false about it? How was Chase's art different from Porta's insofar as it held meaning for others?

5. If Promise were a friend who asked you why she didn't die at any of the times

when it seemed she should have, what would you say to her?

6. What attracted Zack to Promise? What was it about her that challenged his own despair? Which of her qualities and abilities might be her most valuable as a human being?

7. Why did Michelle's death trouble Promise more than any of the other catastrophic events going on at the time?

8. Chase's autism causes him to interact with people in ways that fall outside of social expectations. Why does his behavior cause people to feel uncomfortable? Does the difficulty lie with Chase or within themselves? Explain your answer.

9. How did Chase's understanding of people as trees allow him to connect with others? What do people and trees have in common?

10. Chelsea made it her life's focus to protect Chase. How did her sheltering help or hurt him? How did Chase's relationship with his sister inform Chase's love for and desire to protect Promise?

11. How would you live if you believed you were going to die at a young age? How would you live if you believed you were never going to die? What would be the

same as or different from the way you live now?

12. If you compared your life to a tree's, what kind of tree would you be? What kind of tree would you rather be, if you wish for something different?

ABOUT THE AUTHOR

Erin Healy is the best-selling author, with Ted Dekker, of the thrillers *Kiss* and *Burn*. She has received wide acclaim for her debut solo novel, *Never Let You Go*. She is also an award-winning fiction editor. She and her family live in Colorado. Visit ErinHealy.com